Killing Adonis

Books by J.M. Donellan

A Beginner's Guide to Dying in India
Killing Adonis

For Younger Readers
Zeb and the Great Ruckus

Poetry
Stendhal Syndrome

Play
We Are All Ghosts

Killing Adonis

J.M. Donellan

Poisoned Pen Press

First U.S. Edition 2016
Original Edition 2014, Pantera Press

10 9 8 7 6 5 4 3 2 1

Library of Congress Catalog Card Number: 2016937067

ISBN: 9781464207051 Hardcover
9781464207075 Trade Paperback

Poisoned Pen Press
6962 E. First Ave., Ste. 103
Scottsdale, AZ 85251
www.poisonedpenpress.com
info@poisonedpenpress.com

Printed in the United States of America

For my father, who is thankfully nothing at all like Harland Vincetti.

I

Medical History

"Shall we begin by taking it as a general principle that all disease, at some period or other of its course, is more or less a reparative process...?"

—**Florence Nightingale**,
Notes on Nursing: What it Is and What it Is Not

1

Cakewalking

"I hate this song."

"Freya, you didn't answer my question."

"I'll take a Moscow Mule. Cheers."

A disapproving frown fills Jane's face. "I didn't ask if you wanted another drink, Frey, I asked if you're serious about this."

"Yeah, I heard you. I was hoping I could change the subject. Look, I don't want to think of it so much as 'giving up on my lifelong dreams of working for the Red Cross in East Timor' as 'embracing my backup dream of sitting on the couch getting fat watching *Seinfeld* reruns.' East Timor will still be there in a year or two. Unless Indonesia forcefully reclaims it, I suppose."

"But this is what you've been working towards, what you *always* said you were going to do…four years' experience in a local hospital, then a job in East Timor. You bored us all to death talking about it. I get that you're upset about what happened to Valerie…."

Freya winces at the mention of Valerie's name, images of blood and steel ricocheting through her head. "No. You don't get it at all. If I had a religion to lose then, I would be losing it right now. What happened to Val was…Christ, you know what? We've been over this. If I start talking about it again I'm just going to end up the weird girl crying in the bar that everyone looks at. Let's talk about something else. You want another drink?"

"Vodka and Coke, easy on the vodka."

"Got it." Freya moves through the crowd of bleary-eyed early evening revellers. The air is a sweltering haze of foul-smelling smoke and ear-wrenchingly bad American electro-noise. It sounds like a drunken tattoo artist singing karaoke over the glitchy bleeping of an ancient Commodore 64 computer.

On nights like this the clouds of colour swimming in front of her eyes are usually more a source of entertainment than annoyance, but right now their buzzing and bouncing greatly vexes her. She ignores the "little Kandinskys" dancing in her vision and walks inside.

She passes through the doors of Ric's for, what, the ten-millionth time? How many hazy drunken nights has she begun, regretted, and then repeated here? Too many to count. She checks her reflection in the glass and is as satisfied as she ever allows herself to be. A curtain of crimson hair frames her elegant cheekbones and kryptonite green eyes. She would like to be a little thinner, she supposes. Her tight red dress, paired with matching red gloves, displays her curves that are teetering between "femininely seductive" and "a little more to love." But if she lost any more weight she could hardly criticise the waif-like creatures on TV and, more to the point, filling this bar, with half as much vitriol. And she enjoys doing that.

She stands at the bar waiting for the Barbie doll ahead of her to finish her mating dance with the bartender. When the girlish tittering and batting of eyelids goes on for too long she says, "Hey, Twinkle Toes, when you're done staring down at that fake blonde's fake breasts you want to rustle me up a couple of drinks? I'll take a Moscow Mule, heavy on the Moscow, and a vodka and Coke, heavy on the part that isn't Coke."

"Hey, sweetheart, I'll serve you these but, after that, you'd better slow down."

"Sorry Nosebleed, I have a strict policy of not taking advice from anyone who has brand-name tattoos on his neck."

"Nosebleed? Shit! Is my…?"

"Not yet. It's a preemptive nickname. Call me 'sweetheart' one more time and it'll suddenly be highly applicable."

"Jesus, I was just being friendly!"

"You and Merriam-Webster have very different interpretations of 'friendly.' Now hurry up with that booze. I've got a future I need to avoid thinking about."

The bartender complies with a grimace. Freya grins at him and walks back outside, holding the two glasses as proudly as a hunter bearing fresh kill.

Jane's brow is still furrowed with the same endearing yet irritating concern. She takes the drink from Freya's hand, nods appreciatively, sips it, then says, "Christ! Freya, are you sure you asked them to go easy on the vodka? This is like making out with Dostoyevsky!"

"Yeah, pretty sure," Freya lies. She's a good liar. It's a skill she prides herself on. The clamour of the bar rushes in to fill the silence between them. Finally Freya says, "Listen, I know I'm getting a little worked up about this. I don't mean to be a bitch. I just need a year in a cakewalk job before I get back to saving the world one penicillin injection at a time.

"After what happened to Valerie, I need some time out. Or off. Or maybe in. I won't spend the next ten years as a guilt-ridden workaholic until I get knocked up by some surgeon who decides two weeks before the baby's due that he's staying with his wife. I need one lap around the sun. To paint, eat, drink, live, love, drive to the beach. Then I'll get back to turning into the person I've spent the last quarter-century trying to become."

"But it's crazy to give it all up. All through university, you worked twice as hard as any of us. Even if Karen had slightly better grades…"

"Karen had slightly better breasts, too, and a tendency to display them to any tutor with questionable morals. I'm happy to take second place with my integrity fully intact."

Jane sighs, leans back into her chair, and takes another swig from her allegedly half-strength vodka and Coke. "Okay. Fine. Are you really serious about wanting a cakewalk job?"

"I just want to go cakewalking for a year, I swear."

Jane nods begrudgingly. Freya can see the disappointment in her friend's eyes, but she has more than enough guilt to wrestle with on her own, let alone deal with someone else's. "Jane? You've got that face on. That face you get when you're trying not to say something you really want to say, like when you found out that the girl Mark left you for was admitted to the emergency room after the collagen in her lips exploded…."

"Alright, alright, alright. I do have something and, from the sound of it, you'd be paid really well to do almost nothing, plus the job's right here in Brisbane."

"Are you kidding me? Why the hell have you been holding out on me?"

"Well, the whole thing's a little…unusual. But if you really want to put your work in East Timor on hold for a year, well, I know how goddamned stubborn you are."

"Like a mule, Jane; an adorable mule."

"Alright, but don't say I didn't warn you. I have this little 'help wanted' card that a weird rich lady gave me at that fancy benefit at the Tivoli last week."

Jane reaches into her handbag and removes a pristine white card that's more like a wedding invitation than a job advertisement. Freya inspects the front.

WANTED: NURSE
(a proper girl, not a silly male)
PRETTY (but not too pretty)
CLEVER (but not too clever)

"Hmm. Not big on tact, these people, are they? Certainly sounds weird enough to be interesting. Now, can we leave the serious talk 'til tomorrow when we're chronically hungover, and start getting properly drunk?"

Three, or maybe four, or maybe sixteen hours later—it's hard to tell after inhaling heroic quantities of booze—Freya finds herself at a bar she swore on her mother's grave to never enter again. She mumbles an apology to her dearly departed and downs the last of her drink.

"Callum, do you think I'm a fuck-up?"

Callum sips at his whisky before answering. "Freya, I think that even da Vinci would be asking that if he was as drunk as you are now, although he might phrase it differently."

"Everyone's doing...like...amazing things...and I'm not. I want to find out about the world before I try to save it. And maybe date someone close to normal before I start collecting caesarean scars, a mortgage, a husband who resents me for letting myself go too quickly and a little house on the prairie."

"Jesus, has Jane been drilling that stuff into you again? Why'd she go home so early, anyway?"

"She has to do some disgustingly wholesome activity tomorrow morning, like bake cupcakes for the homeless whilst running a marathon to raise awareness for canine epilepsy or some crap. That girl is always so da–*Oh my God, I love this song!* No... wait...fuck. I love that David Bowie song they sampled to make this piece of shit. Now everything's going all purple. I *hate* when everything goes purple. You know what I mean?"

He smiles and shakes his head. "Rarely, if ever. But, yes, I understand. I'm hardly the poster boy for the Suburban Australian Dream."

"Oh yeah, I forgot. Hey, everybody, look at Callum...he's a boy who likes boys. Isn't that so different and *interesting*?"

"Frey, if I didn't love you to death I would beat you to death with this bar stool."

"I wish you were the first person to tell me that. Tonight. And Jane's not so bad—I shouldn't be so harsh. She just makes the rest of us look like jerks because she's such an overachiever. She found a job offer for me. Says it's easy and the pay is good, but it sounds a little weird."

"You gonna check it out?"

"Sure, why the hell not? I've got the card in my—" Freya's sentence aborts in midair as she begins madly hammering Callum's arm with her fist.

"For the love of God, Freya, what the hell is your problem?"

"Look!" she whispers in reverential awe, pointing at the street outside. "It's her!"

"What the hell are you whispering for? Her who? Oh, *her*! Yes, she is something, isn't she?"

They watch as the "her" skilfully navigates obstacles presented by the drunken horde as though she were in a platform video game, dodging multicoloured projectile vomit, flailing limbs, lascivious leers, and glasses smashed haphazardly on the pavement. She glides through each of these minor perils with the unwavering grace of a Russian princess. Her eyes are focused straight ahead, each step is poised and dainty. She is dressed, as always, in an outfit so grandiloquent that it very nearly defies the laws of physics.

A feather boa curls around her neck like a flamboyant serpent, her dress clings like a second skin, and her bright red heels clack heavily on the concrete like a war drum. She ignores the heckles thrown her way—not so much with silent defiance as the imperious manner that shows responding is completely beneath her.

"She is *so* amazing!" Freya sighs in admiration.

"Really, you don't think she's a little strange?"

"Obviously, but that's the whole point. She is what she is and she doesn't care what anyone else thinks. She's so *enigmagnetic*!"

As though she can hear Freya and Callum across the crowded street, she turns for one brief moment and glances their way.

Marilyn Monroe locks eyes with them and treats them to a dazzling, confident smile, then disappears into the throng.

Freya smiles at the space where Marilyn once stood, before staring drunkenly into Callum's handsome brown eyes and murmuring, "If you weren't my best friend and annoyingly gay, I would definitely take you home with me."

"Thanks, that's the best offer I've had all week. One last round?"

"Please, madam, you are talking very loudly! I must concentrate my driving."

"Yeahyeahyeah, very, you know…studious of you or whatever. I guess they raise 'em good in Tajikistan."

"As I said before, I am a proud son of Turkmenistan."

"Right! I knew…I knew it was one of the 'stans. Pakistan, Uzbekistan, Kurdistan, Cantunderstand. Ha! Lil joke. You like that one? No? Nothing? No dice? Doin' the ol' stare straight ahead and pretend you can't hear me, huh? You know what, I'd probably do that too if I was driving around some drunk idiot who didn't know how to tell the difference between countries. Fair call. Hey, you know once when I was on holiday in Fiji I met this American guy who wouldn't stop staring at my chest and he was all like 'I love the choc-o-late from your country.' And I was like, 'Are you talking about *Austria*?' I mean, Christ, how can you be so ignor—Wait, this is my house! Okay, lemme…I gotta find my…Oh fuck…"

"What is problem?"

Freya rummages through her handbag. "I think…I think I lost my purse in the Beat…or maybe the Bowery."

"Madam, I must have my pay."

"No but, see, s'okay cos I keep a twennie in the letterbox for this 'xact reason."

Freya tumbles awkwardly out of the cab with an impressive lack of grace. Her bare feet collide with the cold cement of the footpath, painfully alerting her to the fact that she has also lost her shoes. She snatches the twenty-dollar bill she keeps hidden in an envelope beneath a rock behind the front fence and hands it to the taxi driver.

"Peace out, brother," she slurs, holding up two fingers in what she imagines is a magnanimous display of cross-cultural solidarity, but more closely resembles the gesture of a pop star posing for the paparazzi on her way into rehab. The driver considers demanding the extra dollar-twenty-five she owes him, but thinks better of it and speeds off into the early morning, where a microwave dinner and his long-suffering wife await him.

Freya struggles with the lock on the door and bursts inside with a series of crashes. She stumbles up the stairs to her apartment, opens the door, and hurls her handbag against the wall, where its contents spill out like the organs of a goat beneath a voodoo knife. In the rubble of makeup, aspirin, and fast-food vouchers is an extravagant white-and-silver card that she vaguely recalls Jane giving her, somewhere between their fourth and fourteenth Moscow Mule.

The card lies there, incongruent with its squalid surrounds. If the card had a voice, it would no doubt be a royal accent lamenting the agony it was enduring among this trash and riffraff. Freya giggles at the thought of a talking business card, then picks it up and whispers, "Sssssh, sssssssssh." She squints to discern the words hiding within the grandiose flowing font. She realises that she has not yet read both sides of the card. Through the thick clouds of her drunken stupor she can barely read the contact information accompanying the message:

APPLICANTS WITH AN EXCESSIVELY
CURIOUS AND INQUISITIVE NATURE
ARE DISTINCTLY NOT WELCOME.

LIGHT DUTIES. LARGE PAY.

NO QUESTIONS ASKED OR ANSWERED.

Freya lacks the mental energy to be sufficiently confused by the strange cluster of words printed in embossed silver on the card. She carries it over to her desk, opens her e-mail, attaches her CV, and clicks send. Precisely two seconds later she is struck by the horrific realisation that there is no "undo" function on her e-mail and her CV is now recklessly hurtling through cyberspace. She is about to perform some sort of panicked dance that will involve manic arm-thrashing and an eclectic collection of yelping noises, when the extraordinary quantity of alcohol rushing through her bloodstream overpowers her and she passes out on the keyboard with a satisfyingly heavy clunk.

2

Everlastine

You wouldn't recognise his face if you saw it in a crowd. You wouldn't know his name if you saw it printed in a newspaper. You probably wouldn't even recognise the name of his company if you saw it on a stock listing. All of this is by design. Though his appearance would indicate the contrary, the portly, dishevelled man standing in the hallway with the putrid crimson beard molesting his face is among the richest men in the world. Wilson Davies trades through a labyrinth of shell companies and sub-sub-subcontractors, intentionally managing his operations so that the left hand does not know what the right hand is doing nor which filthy places it's been.

You'd know his products, though, guaranteed. Go and open your bathroom cupboard. There? See that? No, not the condoms you haven't touched in an embarrassingly long time. Next to those. The pills. The little white packages of magic and chemicals in neat cardboard boxes. He makes those just for you. You and every other sap on the planet seeking a quick fix. Sure, you might think you have a choice of sixteen different brands of painkillers at the supermarket, but in actual fact more than half of them are an identical formula displayed in different-coloured boxes with varying price tags. He owns the patents, he owns the production facilities, and he owns the distribution networks. Collectively, his myriad companies have an annual turnover that would cause the American national deficit to dash to the bathroom and then have a quick lie down on the sofa.

Wilson pops one of his favourite products into his mouth. It's his Maltese Falcon, his Jewel of the Nile, his Heart of the Ocean: Everlastine™. When his labs showed him the stats on the beta product, he nearly puked with excitement. All the potency of Viagra with the blissful side effects of massively increased tactile sensation and a barely-subtle-enough-to-be-legal euphoria. He'd produced it at a cost of two dollars and forty cents a pill, and it hit the shelves with an asking price of ten times that. He's always been good at finding ways to make money: withholding AIDS medication in Tanzania to drive up demand, contaminating water supplies in Northern India to create the need for antidiarrhoeals, but nothing came close to spinning money like Everlastine™. When it came to cash, the life-threatening needs of the Third World couldn't hope to compete with the income-generating sexual neuroses of the First.

Currently, Wilson is working on an extensive campaign to convince women of a newly discovered and yet surprisingly common "Stress-induced Female Sexual Dysfunction Syndrome." The appropriate placebo has already been developed, branded, and packaged. As soon as the "health reports" are filtered through the appropriate news networks, Wilson will sit back and watch the deluge of dollars fill his numerous offshore bank accounts.

He grins broadly as he slams open the door to Alicia's room. Her painfully contrived pout and "come hither" gaze clearly demonstrate how much he repulses her. As if he could even begin to care. He pays her well enough to do a decent job of faking it. She's wearing an elegant silk robe that slides easily down her perfect shoulders. He can feel the Everlastine™ kicking in; a warm familiar rush of strength and vigour storming his senses. He reaches eagerly for her, licking his lips like a Viking prince reaching for a plate of spit-roasted pig.

He feels the warm touch of her skin and then…

And then…

He watches his hand as it slumps limply to his side. A feeling of pins and needles mixed with a burning sensation buzzes through his body, and then there is nothing. Nothing at all. He watches in confused horror as his body slumps backwards off the bed and slams heavily onto the wooden floor, just shy of the plush, inch-thick rug. He watches as a sticky red pool of blood spreads out towards it. He tries to move his arms, wiggle his toes, move his eyebrows and yell. Nothing happens, and then nothing happens again and again and again. His thoughts barrell madly around in his brain, screaming at his nerve clusters and neurological pathways.

Above him he watches Alicia's wide blue eyes fill with fear and listens to her Hitchcockian scream fill the room. He would like to cover his ears. He would like to do a lot of things. From the periphery of his vision he can barely make out the madam, Sylvia, charging in with her heavily armed doorman, concerned that he has tried to hurt Alicia.

"Call the police," he hears her crisp voice command. A small storm of terrors and fears jostle for his attention, but fiercest and foremost of them all is:

Is this it? Am I stuck like this? Will I never move again?

Sylvia prods him with her stilettoed foot and sighs before saying, "Motherfucker, that rug is a one-of-a-kind from Kashmir. You owe me three hundred bucks for dry cleaning."

The tiny lake of blood touches his lips.

If he could taste it,

it would be

sickly

sweet.

3

Elijah

The phone's ringing shakes Freya from the embrace of sleep. She thrashes her hand around the desk trying to smash the sound into a thousand silent pieces. She jerks upright. Her head is pounding like a sweatshop the night before a rush deadline. Finally locating her phone, she stabs at the red button to decline the call but her fine-motor functions are horrendously impaired and her finger lands on the green. A cold, articulate female voice attacks her eardrums from the speaker.

"You have a pretty name. Not common, but not too unusual either. I thoroughly abhor the idea of trying to fumble my tongue around some ridiculous garble of consonants like Agneshka or something. You aren't vegan or kosher or anything preposterous like that, are you?"

"No, no I'm not…who is this?"

"You should know, we had a lot of applications, but they all wrote insufferably loquacious discourses about themselves and how they joined the medical profession to make the world a better place and so on and so forth. Honestly, young women these days seem to so consistently harbour the misconception that the whole world is interested in their dreary biographies. The job we are offering, a monkey could do. But we want a pretty, quiet monkey who has the good sense to not stick her nose where it doesn't belong. For which the monkey in question will be very generously compensated."

"You want a monkey?"

The caller sighs wearily. "Oh dear. You aren't stupid, are you? Stupid won't do at all. I have neither the patience nor the inclination to deal with stupid."

"I can categorically assure you I'm not stupid. I am, however, currently not sure who is accusing me of being so?"

"Your CV, mailed this morning. At 5:43, I see. I like a girl who gets up early and doesn't fuss around with niceties and chitchat. You are speaking with Evelyn Vincetti. You do still want the job, I assume? You haven't changed your mind in the six hours since you applied for it? Capriciousness is another habit that I will not suffer in an employee."

"The job! Yes! Of course, silver card, lots of mon—ah, marvellous opportunities."

"Quite. You will come to dinner. You will dress elegantly, but not ostentatiously. You will arrive promptly at seven p.m., not a moment before or after. Write this address down." The words come as a rapid-fire sequence of statements of fact rather than requests. Freya scribbles the address on the envelope of an unpaid bill as Evelyn speaks.

"Any questions?"

"No, I suppose not."

"Correct answer. I look forward to meeting you."

Freya opens her mouth in an attempt to formulate an appropriately formal expression of gratitude, but finds herself listening to the dull tone of a dead line.

"Shit. Shit. Shitshitshitshit." The hangover Freya is combating is of superhuman strength and, at 6:23 p.m., shows no signs of abating. She groans as she opens her wardrobe door in search of attire that is "elegant but not ostentatious."

She grabs at dresses one by one and hurls them to the floor, muttering appropriate rejections. "Too slutty, too small, red-wine stain, too eighties, no shoes to match, too boring, tiny tear I got running away from a security guard that I never got around to fixing... This one?"

She throws on the simple blue dress and a pair of white shoes, then darts her eyes back and forth between her box of gloves and her box of large bracelets before deciding on the latter. She removes a simple wooden piece Jane brought her back from Bali that fits snugly over the part of her wrist she needs to conceal. Outside, a car speeds past, blaring some bass-heavy eurotechno which, for a moment, floods her eyes with a kaleidoscopic sea of red and orange as the little Kandinskys dance in front of her face.

"Argh, shit shit shit! I don't need this, not now, not now..." She bangs at her temple, despite knowing it won't help. Biting her lip and breathing deeply to calm herself, she darts out the front door, then steps back inside when she realises she has forgotten her keys. Freya runs back up to her apartment, rescues them from the pile of handbag debris she spilled on the hallway floor earlier and clutches them between shaking hands. She steps back outside where the door of her off-white 1993 Toyota Camry greets her with a rusty squeak. She checks her reflection in the rearview mirror and turns the keys in the ignition. The clunking engine sounds like it's chuckling at her hangover.

"Jesus fucking on a motorcycle..." Freya whispers. She checks the address on the envelope, then the number on the letterbox, then checks again. The mammoth mansion sprawled across the riverfront looks like the kind of place God would have as his weekender. As Freya exits her Camry, she catches a glimpse of a gargantuan yacht moored out the back of the mansion. She guesses it's roughly twice the size of her entire apartment.

Motion-sensing lights fill the driveway as she approaches. She squints through the glare and struggles to keep her balance as she trudges through the gravel, each step punctuating the percussion in her brain. She breathes deeply, uses her phone to quickly check her hair and rings the doorbell.

She hears the ring somewhere inside and eventually the door is opened by an imposingly large and sombre grey-haired man in his fifties. His piercing brown eyes remind her of the look she imagines a lion bestows on an antelope when it doesn't feel particularly hungry. "You must be the girl," he states in a tone suggesting the observation is vaguely unsatisfactory. "Come in. You are on time. That's a good enough start."

Freya follows him into the lobby and discovers that the mansion's interior is even more remarkable than the outside. The main hall is a countryside of polished marble, paintings, vases, sculptures, and antique furniture that could give the Guggenheim a run for its money. Behind it lies a vast ballroom staircase that has been oddly augmented with a rubber ramp. Flanking the enormous staircase are corridors with red carpet runners that sit on top of the marble like long tongues in the mouth of a pale white china doll. Each of these corridors hosts a cavalcade of thick oak doors adorned with elaborate vine carvings. She is smart enough not to let an awed gasp escape her lips as she crosses the floor into the dining room.

A table with heavy mahogany legs carved into the feet of some great mythical beast and set with glistening silver and crystal runs almost the full length of the room. Two blond women seated at its far end stand to greet her. The first, who appears to be in her late twenties, has exactly the petite figure that Freya is fond of reproachfully critiquing. She welcomes Freya with the pearly white smile of a real estate agent. The other woman is middle-aged but has clearly employed every available means of alteration and augmentation to appear as though she was born after the invention of the compact disc. She greets Freya with a mirthless display of teeth as she takes her hand.

"Hi, I'm Freya, lovely to meet you," Freya uses her best firm-and-confident-because-I-want-this-job voice.

"I had hoped you'd be a little thinner," the older woman says, not so much to Freya as to herself. She casts her eyes up and down Freya as though examining a wall hanging at an auction. "Still, you are quite presentable. Bright eyes, that's a good quality. I'm Evelyn. Do you drink Merlot?"

Freya answers, "Yes," though it's her second preference to slamming the arrogant Evelyn to the floor like a Mexican wrestler.

"I'm Rosaline!" says the younger woman as she shakes Freya's hand with new-puppy zeal.

"Freya. Nice to meet you." Her disgust for Evelyn is overtaken by the confusion of her hand being worked up and down in an earthquake of ebullience.

"And you met my husband, Harland, of course," says Evelyn, waving her hand towards the man standing behind Freya.

"I did, yes."

"Wonderful. Well, we're nearly all ready to get started then. Maria!" she bellows. A small, rotund Latina woman appears from the kitchen.

"Yes, Mrs?"

"Fetch Jack, would you? We're ready to eat now."

"Mr Jack, he ask can I take dinner to him in his room. He busy working."

"If you can call it working. Very well, Maria, bring dinner out for the rest of us now."

"Yes, Mrs."

As Harland takes his seat at the head of the table, Freya feels he would make a convincing Mafia don or corrupt ambassador. He sits with his shoulders set straight against the high-backed chair and raises a glass of red wine to his lips with unhurried stoicism. Freya catches a glimpse of the bottle's label. The wine is older than she is.

Evelyn vanquishes the rest of her wine, brings her hands together in a firm clap and announces, "So! Freya. Now that you're here we can get down to business. I'll outline what's prohibited. If you have a problem with any of that, there's obviously no point wasting one another's time, is there? Should you agree to abstain from everything I list for you, we can get you started straightaway. Sound good? Excellent.

"First of all, no fraternising of any kind on these premises. Your friends, boyfriends, second cousins, book club, long-lost sisters, and Tupperware parties are not welcome here. You want to socialise, you do it elsewhere. There is to be no smoking in the house or anywhere on the grounds. No illegal drugs of any kind are to be brought onto the premises, and believe me, if there are we *will* know about it and it shall not end well for you."

Evelyn studies Freya's face for a moment, looking for signs of resistance. Freya does her best impression of a smiling, courteous employee.

"Next, and this is critically important...do not ask questions. Not about our business, not about our personal lives, not even about the weather. Should any of us wish to communicate with you we shall initiate that interaction and you may continue accordingly. You are to be our employee, not our friend. Our last nurse failed this horribly, with regrettable consequences....

"Everything that goes on here, Freya, stays within these walls. This is our sanctuary and we will not tolerate an employee spreading gossip and slander. Harland," says Evelyn, turning to her husband, "anything you wish to add?"

"Evelyn, you know how this works. I handle the business, earning the money and doing the things that actually matter. The tiny kingdom of this house is yours and yours alone to administer."

Evelyn narrows her eyes at him before turning back to Freya. "Do you anticipate any problems in adhering to our rules?"

Freya pushes aside the various venomous responses clamouring for release and answers simply, "None at all." Her gift for feigning congeniality is unparalleled. Years of restraining herself from strangling annoying hospital patients have taught her to conceal her anger, bottle it, and then release it like a pressure cannon at the appropriate juncture.

"Excellent. You will be paid two thousand dollars per week, in cash. This income is not to be reported to the tax department or anyone else in government. Harland will set up a phantom job for you in one of our businesses so that you will have some vocation to offer future employers. Now, if you'll excuse me, I have to run to the lavatory. Talk among yourselves." Evelyn's heels make a series of loud, commanding clicks across the marble floor as she exits.

"Don't mind her, she's kind of a bitch but at least she tells it to you straight," says Harland as Maria places a plate of lobster and salad before him. Freya resists the urge to lunge at hers with her bare hands, taking her cues from Harland as to how to disassemble it daintily.

"Yeah, she's a doll really!" Rosaline giggles. "Plus you and me are gonna be such good friends, talk about girl stuff, go shopping, all that jazz. Hey, you could even come to my Zumbalates class with me!"

Rosaline reminds Freya of a girl who joined her high school after ten years of home schooling. A decade locked inside her storage-container-sized apartment with only her mother and their six cats for company had made her disconcertingly perky. She makes a mental note to google "Zumbalates" in order to find out what it is without having to endure some twenty-minute dissertation. "Sure, that sounds great," she lies politely. Rosaline flashes her real estate agent smile as Freya captures the first bite of lobster and her body trembles with ferocious satisfaction. *For this kind of food and pay, I'd work for Mussolini.*

"That's an interesting bracelet you have there! Can I have a look?" Rosaline's hand darts out across the table to touch it, shifting it a fraction down Freya's arm before she snatches it away. She wonders if Harland glimpsed what was hiding underneath, but he merely regards her with a stony face.

"It was my grandmother's. Family heirloom and all that. I didn't mean to be so jumpy."

"Oh, honey, I totally understand. I shouldn't have been so presumptuous."

"How's the lobster?" Harland's tone indicates he doesn't care for a response.

"Best I've had all week!" chirps Freya, telling the truth for the first time this evening.

◇◇◇

Maria clears the culinary battlefield; remnants of lobster and soufflé are strewn amid the rubble of resplendent silver cutlery.

"Well, I trust you enjoyed your meal, Freya?" Evelyn asks, smiling with a faint glimmer of sincerity that appears foreign on the landscape of her face.

"I did! Thank you!"

Maria begins to clear the plates and asks, "You like, *senorita*?"

"*¡Si claro! Gracias, Maria. ¡Muy rico! Me gusta mucho.*"

Maria's eyes widen with excitement as Evelyn's narrow into a tunnel of accusation. "You speak Spanish?" they ask simultaneously.

"Oh…only…you know, *un poco*. I learnt some at high school, but I can't do much besides order food and tell someone that I think they have a very beautiful donkey…"

Maria laughs and touches Freya gently on the shoulder. Evelyn and Harland are eying her as if she'll produce a basement-assembled explosive.

"So, Freya! We haven't given you the tour yet, have we?" yelps Rosaline, breaking the silence.

"Quite so." Harland rises from the table. "You've been admirably abstaining from questions as per our instructions, but it's only fair that you know where it is you are working and what it is you are doing here, isn't it?"

Freya nods. She feels suspended in a gorgeous bubble of opulence and luxury, but she is nagged by the voice at the back of her mind insisting that she is about to be press-ganged into becoming some sort of drug mule or high-class prostitute. She doesn't want her little bubble to burst, but she can't very well stay seated at the table with half a glass of a 1985 Merlot in front of her, can she?

She drains her glass, savours the exquisite oak-with-a-hint-of-fruit flavour enveloping her tongue and follows her hosts across the vast marble floor and up the lavish sweeping staircase. They pass room after room: billiard room, bathroom, exercise room and an entire room filled with crockery. *What kind of family has an entire room devoted to crockery?* she asks herself. The house is the size of a boutique five-star hotel, and twice as ostentatious. She needs to suppress her inquisitive nature, but she cannot shake the fear that a meth lab resides somewhere within these walls.

"Your room will be here, just a few doors down from Elijah's. You will handle the majority of his care, but Rosaline, Harland, Maria, and myself will help with many of the basic tasks. Jack may also emerge from his cave to assist from time to time. I'll give you a roster, but understand that we are paying you a premium rate and will expect premium service. You may be called upon at odd hours to perform tasks that are outside of your usual job description."

Evelyn fixes her with a penetrating glare. Freya holds her gaze and starts planning how she's going to spend her first pay cheque in order to distract from her mounting apprehension.

"Besides our bedrooms, most of the rooms in this house are yours to enter as you please, provided you stay within the boundaries outlined earlier, of course. We'll give you a magnetic key, programmed to open only the rooms you are permitted to enter. Everything else will be inaccessible, to avoid confusion," Evelyn says in a tour-guide voice.

"Of course." Freya bites her normally razor-sharp tongue, which has been aching to deliver a hundred shades of sardonic scorn all evening. No comment, no matter how hilarious she may find it, is worth throwing away two thousand a week and all the lobster she can eat. She makes a mental note to record the evening's events and reenact them in full for Callum at the earliest opportunity.

"Our work keeps both myself and Evelyn busy at unusual hours, so we won't be around often, but Maria, Rosaline, or Jack, if you can find him, will be able to assist you should you need anything," Harland states as he stops outside an ornately carved door. He removes his magnetic key and swipes it against the lock. It opens with a quiet bleeping and the lights inside automatically flicker to life as he enters.

The windows, in an extravagant European style, stretch nearly to the vaulted ceiling, which hosts one of the most striking chandeliers Freya has ever seen. The room contains a magnificent collection of antiques, a library that appears both expensive and expansive, and a small kitchenette with a collection of appliances that hum and blink and pulse with more streamlined gadgetry than the average fighter jet. The rear wall appears to be some sort of shrine, covered in a vast and incomprehensible collage of photos, certificates, trophies, ribbons, and medallions. Through an open door in the far right wall she can glimpse an en-suite with a spa bath and marble-topped vanity.

As impressive as all of this is—and Freya estimates the value of the room's contents to exceed her projected lifetime income as a ward nurse—none of these adornments is the room's most striking feature. In the middle of the room, a sprawling web of cables snakes and crawls into one central point. They connect the monitors and machines and gadgets and gizmos to an immobile young man lit by the soft green aura of the mechanical devices encircling him. The forest of machines produces a quiet choir of beeps. Freya feels as though she has entered the church of some esoteric pagan deity. She opens her mouth to say something, then thinks better of it.

Beep.

Beep.

Beep.

"This is our son, Elijah. We'll leave you two to get acquainted," Harland says before the three of them exit the room and click the door shut on Freya and the young man.

The beeping of the machines translates in her vision as a stream of tiny, slender, white ribbons. She does not approach him straightaway but takes her time to inspect the library—early and first editions of Keats, Poe, Austen, Eliot, Pushkin—the wall of awards and accolades—under sixteens state swimming championships, Substantial Contribution to Amnesty International, certificate of outstanding merit and achievement from Médecins Sans Frontières—and the various twenty-second-century appliances—toaster with weather display, oven with holographic timer, espresso machine with voice activation.

It is only after she has carefully assimilated all this that she ambles over to Elijah. Freya glances over the monitors; she's seen similar equipment before, of course, but not of this calibre, not even at the best private facilities. These are either fresh off the factory line or custom made. Either way, expensive beyond the telling. He is in sleek satin pyjamas embroidered with the initials "E.V." across the top left corner of his chest. His skin is a surprisingly healthy hue, and his cheeks are freshly shaven, but it is clear from the apparatus connected to him that he has been comatose for some time. He's handsome, strikingly so. He has the strong, well-proportioned face that would look right at home on a Greek statue. Freya notes the extensive scarring on his right arm, and draws her finger lightly across the scar tissue.

The obvious questions detonate like a cluster bomb in her brain—*What happened to him? How long has he been like this? Who was he? What am I doing here? Will he ever wake up*?—but for the moment she suppresses them, to let them exist as hungry ghosts at the outskirts of her psyche. She reaches out and places her hand against his cheek. She feels strangely comforted by the warmth that greets her palm.

"Hi, Elijah," she whispers. "I guess you and me are going to be friends."

The door opens, startling her, and she snaps her hand away as guiltily as a child caught stealing biscuits.

"Wait outside," Harland commands crisply as he and Evelyn enter. She obeys and the door slams behind her. Her fingers dance over one another in an awkward series of arrivals and departures. A moment later the door opens.

"He approves," Evelyn states simply. She does not appear to be referring to her husband. "Have Maria give you the paperwork with the detailed instructions of your duties, and your keycard. You may move in and begin work on Wednesday. We look forward to seeing you then."

The door closes sharply, leaving Freya staring at the flowing vines carved into the oak. She turns away and studies each of the stairs as she descends them. In the living room, Maria is waiting with a folder with Freya's name scrawled on it. She places it in Freya's hands with a conspiratorial wink.

"Welcome to the family, *chica.*"

"Maria…"

"You gonna have plenty of questions for me, better you wait a little bit, get yourself settled in, okay?"

"Okay. *Gracias. Hasta luego*, Maria."

"*Hasta pronto, chica.*"

Freya sits silently in her car, staring at the manila folder. It seems appallingly mundane in comparison with the evening's events. Finally, she places it on the seat beside her and switches on the ignition. The radio is playing her favourite Bowie song, but it fills her eyes with a heavy swarm of gold and orange rivers, so she flicks it off and drives home in silence.

4

Pineapple Cutter

Freya had told her mother that fourteen was far too old for novelty birthday cakes. But the poor thing couldn't let go of her bible, the Women's Weekly Children's Birthday Cake Book. *And Freya couldn't bear to take away her mum's special joy as she stirred, baked, iced, assembled, and presented her annual vibrantly coloured confectionary monstrosity. This year, she had chosen the caterpillar.*

Butterflies infested Freya's stomach as her mother and father carried it around the corner, awaiting the inevitable disapproval of Stacey "my family has six cars" Morrison and the unbearable eye-rolling of the one and only love of her life, Daniel Harcourt. Although thirteen days later she would stumble in on Daniel fingering Stacey in the staff toilets at the local Donut King and never speak to him again. To her surprise, her friends squealed with excitement when they saw the vast sugary mass offered before them.

"Cool, Mrs M!"

"Yum, this looks amazing!"

"Wow! Your mum is the BEST!"

She watched as her mum lit up with pride like an incendiary grenade. "My pleasure, kids..." Freya shot her mother a warning glare at the use of the forbidden k-word, "I mean...everybody."

They sang the inevitable happy birthday song, which she had recently learnt was controlled by a corporation that charged ten thousand dollars per use in films and TV shows. She grinned, basking in the attention, but at the back of her mind she couldn't silence the thought that if her life was a movie then this moment would cost more than her dad had earned so far that year.

"Make a wish!" her mum beamed.

Freya closed her eyes and wished with the sum total of her mental fortitude for Daniel to love her forever—though, had she been able to see thirteen days into the future, she may have chosen more wisely. She blew out the candles in one great heave, then cut the first piece of cake.

"Oh, we need the cake server. Hang on!" Freya ran into the kitchen and started pulling drawers open. Someone turned up the stereo in the living room and as the music swarmed across the house, the rush of colour filled her vision: a kaleidoscope of silvers, greens and golds. The little Kandinsky effect was stronger than ever before. Freya felt as though she had dived into a pool filled with food colouring and slammed her head on the concrete edge on the way in.

Melanie and Stacey were arguing over who had popularised the phrase "talk to the hand" at their school when she reappeared, her wrists covered in crimson. She was staggering, as though transfixed by the blood cascading from her arm. She watched as the wet, warm, droplets of blood splashed onto her naked feet.

"Oh my God! Honey, are you okay?" her father called as he ran towards her. Behind the cloud of colours her mother's pallor stood out. Despite the warm crimson trail down her wrist, despite the fact that Stacey "I have a flat screen plasma in my room" Morrison would be gossiping about this in the locker rooms on Monday morning, all she really felt was guilt for taking away that particular once-a-year joy.

"It's okay, Mum, please don't be upset."

"Freya, baby...what happened?"

◇◇◇

"How much longer?" demands Freya, drumming her hands on the dashboard.

"Five minutes less than when you asked me five minutes ago."

"God, Cal, you sound like my dad."

"You know I can't make them hurry and, for the money they're paying, I don't even particularly feel like trying. Why don't you start telling me about your latest catastrophe so we—"

"No! I told you, I don't want to open the emotional floodgates and get all weepy and confused and then get interrupted by a phone—"

Madonna's "Vogue" blasting from Callum's phone cuts Freya short.

"Sorry Frey, just a sec." Callum whips the phone to his ear. "Yes? Uh-huh. Uh-huh. Great, we're right around the corner, I'll be there in a few minutes." He hangs up and turns to Freya. "We have to switch cars; it won't take long."

"Switch cars? Who are you working for tonight? The Mafia?" she asks.

"Not unless they start paying me like these guys do."

They drive to a nearby parking lot that has the delicate ambience of a crack den. Leaning casually up against a sleek black Lexus is a tall, slender man dressed in a severe black suit and tie. Freya and Callum climb out of the car and the suit throws his keys at them. In return, Callum tosses him the keys to his Mazda.

"Drive it to the restaurant and straight back here, okay? I don't want a single scratch on it. You've got two hours. Here's your info."

Phil passes Callum a manila envelope. *People really should start using more impressive stationery for such occasions*, thinks Freya.

"Please, Phil, I'm a professional," says Callum, rolling his eyes. They climb into the Lexus and sink into the plush leather seats as Callum opens the envelope. "Sooooo, according to this we'll be going to ARIA this evening."

"Ritzy!"

"Yes. But remember, this is an assignment. You have to play your part. Here, you can read the script out loud while I drive. We have to make an entrance; people need to notice us as we come in. We'll laugh together, like we're both incredibly funny and slightly drunk. Drunk enough to be having a good time, not drunk enough to start yelling about that time in twelfth grade when Kerry Atwell double-dared you to streak through the staffroom wearing a Richard Nixon mask and you gave Mr Jamieson a heart attack."

"It was an Abraham Lincoln mask and I gave Mr Jamieson a stroke, thank you very much. And besides, it's not like he didn't recover. More or less."

"Right. That's a terrible story, by the way. Why do you always insist on telling it on first dates?"

"Why do *you* always insist on wearing enough cologne to immobilise all wildlife within a ten-kilometre radius?"

Callum laughs. "See? This is why you're my favourite wing-man." He kicks the car into gear and pulls it quickly out of the parking lot.

While rehearsing the script, Freya's mind fills with the image of Elijah engulfed by his machine forest. She can hear the gentle, soothing beeps of the monitors and machines, lilting, like a robotic lullaby. There is something alluring about him. Something mesmerising. She can picture each facet of his face with perfect clarity. Her palm still buzzes with the warmth of his cheek.

She is shaken from her daydream by their arrival at the restaurant. Callum roars the engine loudly as he does a loop around the block before pulling into the parking lot. Freya has walked past the grand entrance many times but never made it inside; the menu prices have ensured her absence as certainly as razor wire or any Rottweiler ever could have. It feels good to be walking through its doors, but she can't help thinking of herself as a wolf in royal sheep's clothing for the second night in a row.

"Remember what I told you: grand entrance, lots of playful laughter. We should look like the cast of a Moët commercial. Three…two…and…"

The second that his hands push on the door Freya unleashes a peal of laughter. She is conscious of eyes locking onto them as they swish inside: jealous, licentious, admiring. She rests her hand gently on Callum's shoulder and bats her eyes at him. He throws back a charming grin, and the two of them appear to remember for the first time that the rest of the world exists.

The maître d', who has been surveying Freya's curves displayed stylishly in a shimmering sky-blue dress paired with elbow-length white gloves and white Givenchy heels, snaps his eyes back to face level and greets them with the practised grin of his vocation.

"Good evening, sir and madam. Do you have a booking?"

"Yes, I believe my assistant booked a table for two under Fairweather."

"Ah, yes. Please follow me."

The table is located in the centre of the room, surrounded by a cluster of the city's wealthiest, most prominent citizens. "This place looks like the line-up for a Fortune 500 listing," Freya whispers.

"Ssh! You have to look like you belong here, remember? Don't gawk like an orphan who's snuck into the palace ball. Play along or I won't be able to take you on these little missions anymore. You remember what I told you?"

"Be good, act posh, talk about the thing, blah blah blah. So, anyway, that card that Jane gave me—"

"Freya, we have to do the script first, then we can catch up on the soap opera of your life."

"Fiiiiiiine."

"Okay, project your voice. Here we go…"

He takes her hand in his and stares directly into her eyes as he almost shouts, "Darling, convincing me to get that new Lexus was the best thing you ever did. I can't believe I doubted you!"

"Oh, I know! I mean, the leather interior alone is to diiiiie for! I know that you said we have to stop keeping up with the Joneses, but after I took a spin in Lisa's new little model I knew I couldn't go another day without getting one for myself!"

"You should have seen the heads turn at the golf club when I pulled up. Karl and Francine practically had to scrape their jaws off the floor!"

"Well, I'm not surprised, that crappy old Jag they've been getting around in is nearly six years old. Pretty soon they'll have to drive it with their feet, like the Flintstones!"

They burst into laughter and she slaps his shoulder. She glances quickly around the room with practised subtlety and can see Armani, Giordani, Giovanni, and Versace-clad aristocrats pretending they're not hanging on her every word.

She wipes her mouth daintily as she whispers, "Okay, enough with the Barbie and Ken act, can we get back to sorting out the cyclone-scale mess that is my life, please?"

He nods before saying, "Sure, that's enough for now, but remember: personal life, low voice. And I'll have to throw in a few more comments during the evening." He calls the waiter over and they order the most expensive items on the menu, in raised voices. The waiter commends them on their excellent choices and scurries to the kitchen.

"Jesus, Cal, I can't believe these stupid companies pay you to go into places like this and yell about their crappy overpriced products."

"Lab geeks have proved that pretty young people like us are influential. Be thankful, it's paying for the ridiculously pricey meal that you're about to eat. You didn't complain when I took you on that wine tour flashing our Cartier watches around, did you?"

"Yeah, but we had to give those back."

"They were three thousand apiece, Frey, and you got to enjoy the four hundred dollars' worth of wine you drank, and spilt, so quit your moaning. Now tell me, what's this week's catastrophe?"

Freya leans in close and says, "You remember how Jane had that weird job offer for me?"

"Yes, you said it sounded strange? What's the deal?"

"Looking after this comatose guy, changing drips, shaving, bathing, rolling him so he doesn't get bedsores, basic stuff. I could do it in my sleep. But the pay is ridiculous, plus it's under the table so I don't have to pay tax *and* I get to live in a gigantic mansion."

"What about your lease?"

"Jane's going to move into the apartment. She said she's sick of her stoner housemates playing *Call of Duty* until three in the morning and wants her own place."

"So, what's the catch?"

"Well, the family I'm working for, that I'll be living with... they're a little eccentric. That's what you're supposed to call rich people, right? Words like 'nuts' and 'bonkers' are reserved for the plebs, rich people are always 'eccentric.' And they are very, *very* rich. Their place is the kind of joint that Kubla Khan would have lived in if he'd had a little more cash to throw around."

Callum's face contorts in confusion. "Cooblah who?"

"Kubla Khan? The historical subject of Coleridge's most famous poem?"

He shrugs and shakes his head.

"How did you manage to get a perfect 7.0 GPA in Media Studies without ever reading a book? Books are media."

"Books come from an era when people lost their teeth in their thirties, scientists thought the Earth was flat, and doctors treated mental illnesses by drilling holes in people's skulls. I'm interested in media with more contemporary relevance."

"Right, and a future where undergrads dissect the inner meanings of the tweets of Hollywood celebs is going to be such an improvement."

"Listen, I don't make fun of what you do. Nor the fact that you are so caught up in the past that you don't pay enough attention to the present."

"I'm a healer, I help ease pain and suffering."

"*Oh, you're so right, honey, the power steering is magnificent!*" he exclaims loudly, before dropping back into a conversational tone. "Remind me again, how many testicles did you shave during your prac?"

"Point taken."

The waiter arrives and fills their glasses with a 1983 Cabernet Sauvignon that Callum has chosen based purely on its ludicrous price tag. The waiter smiles with a cold, professional lack of mirth and then continues on with a nod.

"So, this 'eccentric' family? Anyone I would have heard of?" he asks, raising his glass to his lips.

"The Vincettis?" Freya says.

He leans in close and whispers, "Frey, are you fucking insane?"

"Why?"

"Freya, you just chastised me for not reading novels. Have you never read the *Financial Review*, or the business section of any newspaper?"

"Cal, you know how much I make. Me reading the business section would be like a homeless guy reading the property guide."

"The Vincettis! Jesus, they're in the papers so frequently they should have their own column. They make Rupert Murdoch look like a private-school boy with a moderate-sized trust fund."

"Cal, stop fucking around and tell me what you know about them."

"I know that you could have found a lot better people to work for. Like the Sopranos, for instance, or Charles Manson."

"Oh, come on, let's not be so hyperbolic. What have they actually done?"

Callum leans back and announces, "*I know! I heard Brad Pitt drives a Lexus too!*" He leans closer and says, "Might be easier to list what they haven't done, Frey."

"Quit fooling around, you jerk, and give me some dirt."

"*Honestly, I'll never drive another car again. I feel like I've been behind the wheel of go-carts all my life!*"

"Would you cut the product placement proselytising for five goddamn minutes?"

Callum drains his wine, then notices for the first time a blond woman in a potent red dress at the next table casting her eyes up and down his frame. He returns her smile and raises his glass to her. She winks and then throws a contrived smile in the direction of her dinner date as he returns from the bathroom.

"Cal? When you've finished eye-fucking that blonde, I could use a little help here."

"Sorry, part of the job. Okay, I'll tell you what. I've got to slip to the bar and make a little noise there for a few minutes. Why don't you go to the little girls' room and powder your nose or whatever, then come back and we'll talk about exactly what kind of trouble you're in."

Freya heads to the bathroom and locks herself in a cubicle. Something about the tarnished silver lock on the door reminds her of the hideous charm bracelet Valerie insisted on wearing every day of her criminally short existence. She remembers every facet and angle of the doctor's face in the emergency room. The stupid thick platform sneakers he was wearing, the irritating monotone in his voice as he pronounced, "She's dead."

Her wrist begins to burn and itch in that same place it always does when she gets stressed. She peels off her glove and scratches at the irritated skin. She lets the salty stream of tears travel down her face, cursing the fact that this will require extensive makeup repair work. She rips away a fistful of toilet paper, pulls out her compact mirror and dabs at the black rivers. A few minutes later she emerges and begins to do a few final touch-ups in the giant mirror. The granite benchtop is cool against her hand.

A teenage girl in high heels opens the bathroom door, teeters towards her and then staggers forward. Freya grabs quickly at her hand to steady her. The girl glances at Freya's wrists as she pulls her upright. Her gaze hovers on them for a few moments before she looks up at Freya and says, "Thanks, I'm such a klutz in these stupid heels. My mum says they make me look like a lady, and then she won't even let me drive the Jag. She makes me wear 'em whenever we go to these stupid swanky restaurants filled with posh jerks. No offence."

Freya smiles and says, "None taken."

The girl examines her reflection in the mirror and fidgets with her hair awkwardly before turning back to Freya and asking, "So, are you like an ex-emo or something?"

"What? Shit!" Freya scrambles for her gloves and wrenches them over her scars.

"No! Hey! I'm sorry, lady. I didn't mean anything by it. My friend Megan, she cut herself a few times, too. She had to go see a shrink and everything. Her dad's kind of an arsehole. He ran off with some skank last summer, thank Christ. Stupid bitch was only a couple of years older than me and Megan."

Freya shakes her head and finishes putting on the last few touches of eyeliner. "It's not like that. I'm not a cutter. Or emo, or whatever. It's just...I had an accident. There was cake. Everything went red for a while. And now I hate pineapple cutters."

"What?"

"Never mind. Listen, I hope your friend Megan's okay. And don't wear high heels if you don't want to. Especially if you're drinking. Not that you should be drinking. Um...okay...well, it's been nice talking. Stay in school, don't do drugs, always recycle and...um...never fall in love with a vampire."

The girl laughs and says, "Got it. Thanks."

Freya reemerges into the restaurant and spies Callum leaning against the bar chatting to the blonde who had been eyeing him earlier. She strides over and grabs him by the arm, hissing, "Don't you think we should be getting back to our meal, *honey*?"

"Well, I'd best be going," Callum's admirer says as she treats Freya to a smile that is more a baring of teeth than an expression of warmth, before flashing her eyes at Callum. "So lovely to meet you."

"Seriously, how can these women not tell that you're gayer than a San Francisco Kylie Minogue fan convention?" Freya moans as they walk back to their table.

"I can't help it if I'm a great actor, Freya, and I told you that flirting is highly encouraged. People are much more susceptible to suggestion when they are enamoured."

"Actor? Puh-lease, you're an overpaid product pimp. You're the call-now-for-just-$9.95-with-bonus-kitchen-knives guy, but with better dress sense. Now can we please talk about the Vincettis? What are they supposedly infamous for?"

Callum refills their glasses as the waiter arrives with their food. He places a sliver of barramundi in his mouth and chews it thoughtfully. "The Vincettis have been accused of everything from falsifying drug reports to political bribery to harbouring war criminals to running sweatshops that mysteriously burn down the day before an audit. The Halcyon empire is right up there with the Palmers and the Murdochs in terms of wealth, but their influence reaches way back to the mid-nineteenth century. And although the bulk of Halcyon's business is in pharmaceuticals, they also make clothes and electronics and manage finance, media, and property.

"It's a well-known fact, by everyone besides you apparently, that back in the eighties—the golden era of corruption—the Vincettis practically ran this city. It was rumoured they owned half the illegal casinos, although no one could ever prove it, not even during the Fitzgerald anti-corruption inquiry. Some people say they're Mafia, or Freemasons, even Scientologists. A few kooks claim that they're Illuminati. A lot of it's bullshit, naturally, but there are so many conspiracy theories about that family that even if ninety-nine percent of them are completely bogus, they're still people you've got to watch out for."

Freya's face colours with a blend of concern and scepticism. "That's the same logic that UFO freaks use to justify taking out anti-abduction insurance policies. People love making up crazy theories about the rich and famous. It makes the rest of us feel marginally better about being poor schmucks who can't get into the VIP lounge at the airport. Have they ever been convicted of anything?"

Callum chews, swallows, and fixes Freya with a serious glare before continuing as though he's presenting a tutorial on white-collar crime to an undergraduate class. "Corporate criminals don't get convicted, Freya. They get accused, investigated, deferred trial, acquitted, settled out of court, or fined, but never convicted. No one goes to prison. You have to be part of an Enron-level fiasco to actually get sentenced, and in that case one of them, the CEO, Ken Lay, died before he went to prison. And George W. Bush still claimed the bastard as one of his closest personal friends.

"If you walked out of this restaurant right now and robbed a petrol station with a handgun they'd give you at least ten years, but that's blue-collar crime. If you set up a corporation that steals the life savings of three thousand little old ladies and use it to finance a sweatshop in Indonesia, you get a lengthy trial that you show up to in a suit once every couple of months before passing everything onto a scapegoat or, worst-case scenario, spending a few years in a minimum security facility that's more like a resort than a prison. Just because they've never had some guy with a wig and a gavel yell 'guilty' at them doesn't mean they aren't. Take that arsehole Wilson Davies who got poisoned the other night. He was linked to sixteen different companies under investigation, but they could never land anything on him because he always pushed everything onto some guy lower down the food chain."

Freya recalls seeing the photo in the newspaper of a half-naked man sprawled across the floor, limbs at unnatural angles, blood pooled around his face. "He's the guy found paralysed in a brothel?"

"Yep, someone poisoned his personal stash of Everlastine™, and now it looks like he'll never move again. The same thing happened to the human test subjects for the beta product in Cambodia a few years back."

"Seriously? I may not read the business section, but how did I not hear about that?"

"Little brown people who don't speak English don't warrant a lot of prime-time news exposure. That slot's usually jam-packed with celebrity love affairs, right?"

Freya nods in resigned agreement, then takes a moment to drain her glass, returning it to the table with a heavy thunk. "You think the Vincettis are really as bad as that Wilson guy… responsible for killing people?"

"Hard to say. You can operate a company that provides alibis for fucking around on your partner because that's technically legal, but you pull a stunt like insider trading and the suits will throw you to the dogs. Like I said, the Vincettis have never been convicted of anything, but they've been accused of a hell of a lot. Are you comfortable working for people like that?"

"I don't know. I'm not working for them, really. I'm looking after this guy who's incapable of doing so himself. It's not Elijah's fault if his parents are drug-dealing, sweatshop-owning corporate criminals, is it? He still needs someone to look after him. He's so…frail and vulnerable."

"Elijah?"

"The guy in the coma. You should see him, Cal, he looks so strong yet helpless at the same time. Like a living statue—so serene." There's a trace of wistfulness in her voice she hopes Callum hasn't noticed. If he has, he fails to comment.

"I've heard of him. He's supposed to be the family's outlier, the saint among the thieves. He donated a whole lot of money to Amnesty International a while back. The tabloids lapped that up. How'd he end up in a coma?"

"I wish I knew. They keep the whole thing pretty tightly under wraps, made me sign confidentiality forms and everything."

"Which you're obviously doing a marvellous job of adhering to."

"Puh-lease! Like I could keep my big mouth shut to my best friend about something as weird as this. Of course, it goes without saying that if you whisper a word of it to anyone I will stab you right in your pretty face."

"Naturally. Which reminds me: *I love feeling the wind on my face when I drive with the top down in my new Lexus!*"

◇◇◇

Freya opens the door and trips gracelessly as she steps inside. She places her heels next to the umbrella stand, then goes into the kitchen and fills a glass with vodka, soda, and ice. She swirls it gently in her hand before drinking. She walks down the hall, each creak and footstep loud against the night silence.

She enters her cupboard-sized studio and slips on one of her paint-splattered T-shirts. She sips from the vodka with her left hand and takes a paintbrush in her right. Careful not to smear the stereo with paint as she presses play, she waits until the chaotically coloured sounds of Messiaen's *Turangalîla* fill her ears and bring the familiar harlequin clouds swimming before her eyes. She is curiously comforted painting while listening to the music of a man who, like Kandinsky, had the same condition as her.

She transfers the polychromatic waterfalls cascading in front of her pupils onto the canvas with slow, measured strokes. The wash of white is gradually transformed into a vibrant, stained-glass sea. When she is satisfied that her hand is too tired to wield the brush any longer, she strips down and throws her clothes in the hallway and steps into the shower.

Freya watches the colour run off her skin and swirl down the drain, then dries off and pulls on her pyjamas. She takes a slender, well-worn volume from her bookshelf and collapses on the bed. Her fingers run up and down its battered spine. There on the cover is the face whose contours she has committed to memory, every curve and wrinkle, every fault and facet. She remembers the first time she read the title: *Notes on Nursing: What it Is and What it Is Not. By Florence Nightingale.*

It had grabbed her by the throat and shoved her nose between its pages. She had checked it out from the library fourteen times before her father finally bought a copy of her very own.

Freya opens to a random page: *"Every nurse should be capable of being 'confidential'...she must be no gossip, no vain talker: she must, I need not say, be strictly sober and honest...* "Freya closes the book and stares around the room at her paintings, all cacophonic messes of light and colour.

"Thanks for nothing, Florence." She turns to the front of the book and reads the note her younger self inscribed so many years ago. As her eyes scan those clumsily scrawled words for the hundredth time, a smile creeps across her face:

> Dear growned up Freya, this is you wen you were little, only eight and three qurters (witch is more than half but less than a hole) old. I

am writing to you to re-mind you that being
a nurse and making people betterer is the most
imporantest thing in the world. Pleas remember
to grow up to be a great nurse and not decide to
becom sumthing boring liek a bank lady or a
car selling person becos that would make me cry.
You shold go somewhere where there are lots of
poor peepul who really need nurses and help them
like maybe Africa or Papua New Guinea Pig or
some other place what I havunt learned about yet
because I havnt learnt all the cunt-trees but is
still really poor and has lots of sick people. Pleas
read this book lots of times just liek me and
remember to be liek Florents Nightingail.

Freya closes the book and stares around the room at her paintings, all cacophonic messes of light and colour.

Sorry little one, looks like you'll have to wait a little while longer.

She grabs her teddy bear, Mr Christopher Rumples Worthington CXI, from her bedside table and places him in her suitcase.

II

Initial Symptoms

"People lose their health in a dark house,
and if they get ill they cannot get well again in it.
More will be said about this farther on."

—**Florence Nightingale**,
Notes on Nursing: What it Is and What it Is Not

5

Jack

Beep. Beep. Beep.

Beep.

Beep.

Beep.

Tiny ribbons of soft shimmering gold pulse in front of Freya's eyes then fade into oblivion as new ones are birthed a heartbeat later. It's like watching the life cycle of some empyreal firefly. She sits still and silent as she watches them dance and fade, thinking about the first time she saw ribbons like this. She remembers the smell of hospital-grade disinfectant and the placid look on her father's face as he lay in the bed, its steel frames so cold against her tiny fingers. She remembers asking her dad about the golden ribbons, and listening to him giggle as he mumbled something between a limerick and a lecture in response. At the time she thought she hadn't been able to understand him because she wasn't grown up and clever enough. It was only years later that she realised he had been so jacked up on morphine he would have had trouble making sense of a Lego diagram.

Beep.

Beep.

Beep.

She looks down at Elijah's calm, immobile frame. Her hand hesitates for a moment before she takes the razor and draws it slowly across his face, felling the tiny forest of fledgling hairs emerging from his skin. She finds something simple and cleansing about the process. Watching the white foam being drawn away, leaving freshly shaven skin in its wake. She wonders if he can hear that sound from beneath the thick blanket of his coma, if he dreams about the machines that are his only constant companion. She draws the razor across his cheek once more.

Beep.

Beep.

Beep.

"Shit!" she curses as a tiny trickle of blood sullies the snow-white patches. "I must have shaved twenty goddamn testicles last year without a scratch and now this…" she mutters angrily to herself. She grabs a washcloth and presses it against his skin, watching as it, too, is sullied with crimson.

She wonders if he has felt the cut, if some level of his mind is commanding his body to flinch in response but to no avail, his nervous system little more than a vast web of inoperative telephone lines.

Beep.

Beep.

Beep.

Freya is puzzled by the wave of guilt she feels as she dabs a piece of tissue paper onto the still-bleeding wound. She finishes shaving the rest of his face, then removes the paper and is relieved to see the bleeding has stopped. She strokes his hair affectionately with her left hand, glimpsing the mass of scarred tissue beneath her bracelet as she does so.

"Sorry," she whispers.

"Freya."

She jolts and spins to face Harland.

"Harland! Ah...Mr Vincetti. You scared me." He neither apologises nor even seems to acknowledge her response. "It's okay, it's only a tiny shaving cut. Nothing unusual. I'm just not used to the contours of his face yet."

"You aren't going to go all *Sweeney Todd* on my boy, are you?"

Freya's jaw drops open as she stammers for a response, her brain flicking between vitriol and apology.

Luckily Harland saves her the trouble. "I was only joking. Humour has never been my forte."

I would never have guessed, Freya thinks as she gazes at his handsome yet severe face, which would be well suited to a funeral director or fascist politician.

Harland stands next to the bed and gently strokes the obscenely perfect hair of his sleeping son. "One day, he'll inherit the company. Everything my family has worked for since my great-great-great-grandfather, the first Elijah Vincetti, started with a tiny shop selling tonics and groceries to sheep farmers and prison guards over one hundred-sixty years ago, when this city was nothing but dirt roads and shanties.

"Evelyn and myself will be out until late this evening. Business and such, I won't bore you with details."

Images of Masonic meetings, voodoo rituals, witnesses being buried, and cops being bribed cartwheel and caterwaul through Freya's imagination.

"As she explained, you are free to make yourself comfortable. Maria will prepare your meals for you, or you can help yourself to the wine and food in the fridge. Rosaline is at her yoga for mums and babies class but will be back later. Jack is... around. You may see him if he elects to stumble out into the light sometime before the end of the current lunar cycle. One last thing..." Harland crosses the room in a few short strides, leans into her ear and says, "If you touch so much as one drop of my vintage Merlot in the cellar, I will kill you."

Beep.

Beep.

Beep.

"Kidding!" His face shifts into an unnatural leer and Freya slumps with relief. "I really should give up on the humour thing, shouldn't I? My apologies. Make yourself at home. We'll see you in the morning." He turns and walks out the door, slamming it behind him.

Freya is about to collapse from her emotional yo-yoing when the door springs open and Harland hollers, "*And no stealing!*" before slamming it again.

"Mary, mother of moonshine, I think I need a drink." Freya looks at the LCD clock display illuminated behind the black sheen of the bar fridge. "10:25 a.m. too early? Whaddaya think, Eli? You want something? Tom Jones? White Russian? G&T? No? Nothing? Fine, suit yourself." She mixes a Moscow Mule with her signature addition of Tabasco sauce and sips contemplatively.

"That's a nice blend. Cheers!"

Elijah remains still and silent. He looks like an unreasonably handsome wax doll.

Beep.

Beep.

Beep.

◇◇◇

Click. Another red security light, another forbidden room.

Click.

"Jesus, are they training a militia in here or something?" Freya grumbles as she moves to the next door.

It is 11:17 a.m. and so far her explorations of the house have unveiled everything from the mundane—half a dozen dusty rooms filled with old clocks and furniture—to the inexplicable: a room filled to the ceiling with nothing but boxes of Captain Choc's Chocolatey Chocoflakes, "*Now with* more *chocolate!*"

She has found rooms filled with clothes, shoes, vases, books, and magazines, whitegoods and appliances, linen, and golf clubs. And for every room that announces her permission to enter with a cheerful *blip!* there are another two that refuse her with a grim and obstinate *click*. Freya knows herself well enough to recognise that, sooner or later, she will need to find out what's behind those doors, even if it turns out to be merely an extensive collection of antique soap dispensers.

Click. Click. Click.

Three in a row, that's unusual.

Blip!

Freya flicks on the light and finds a hundred pairs of tiny eyes looking directly at her. She nearly yelps as the tiny human figures are illuminated; a small sea of toes, fingers, noses, and faces stares at her. She's always found dolls to be creepy, but the effect is amplified exponentially when they are in plague proportions. She closes the door quickly and moves on.

Click. Click.

Blip!

Freya eases the door open and is nearly forced to shade her eyes from the panorama of pink that greets her. From the pale pink rug to the rose pink ceilings, the room is covered in the stuff. It looks like Barbie's dream home. The room is crammed with enough oppressively girly toys and iconography to convene an emergency meeting of the local university feminist group. Barbies, babies, teddies, tiaras, dollies, doilies, and child-sized kitchen appliances adorn every available space in the massive bedroom, save for the far left corner, which is occupied by a cot and a mobile. Freya walks carefully over, as though in fear that a frilly landmine might explode at any moment and suffocate her with deathly kitsch.

A cloud of plastic butterflies suspended from the mobile hovers above the cot. Freya clicks the "on" switch and recoils as the room is filled with a ferocious explosion of sound and colour. "Hush Little Baby" tinkles through the tiny speaker as the mobile spins and throws its multicoloured lights against the wall. Her little Kandinskys collide with the swarm of pinks and blues and yellows projected by the mobile and she reels for a moment, disoriented and confused. She swats clumsily at the switch and doesn't make contact until the third swing. The lights and sound cease and she leans against the cot to catch her breath.

"Well, that was twelve kinds of unpleasant. I pity the child subjected to this little shop of horrors on a nightly basis," she murmurs, standing up straight and exiting the room as quickly as she is able. An almost palpable sense of relief overcomes her as she slams the door behind her, condemning the screaming oceans of pink and fuchsia to silence.

She takes a few deep breaths before moving on, wondering how much strange she can process within a single morning. The keycard hovers in her hand, willing her to fulfil its purpose. She places it gently against the lock of the next door.

Blip!

She slowly eases the door open and peers inside, then recoils with hysterical laughter. "You have got to be kidding me!" It's the polar opposite to the pink room. The yang to its yin. The sun to its moon. The North to its South Korea. It is swathed in nearly iridescent blue, filled with trucks and bears and plastic shovels and everything a child raised by the Disney Channel could ever want. Freya closes the door quickly, electing to come back and explore further when her synapses aren't already overloaded on fluorescent pink.

She returns to her investigations.

Blip! Deckchairs.

Blip! Skiing gear.

Click. Click.

Blip! Crockery.

Blip! Freya pushes the door open, preparing herself for another woefully mundane example of nauseating luxury.

"What the fuck?" she breathes as she steps into the room. She isn't sure whether to laugh or cry, whether this is a *Planet of the Apes* or a *Crying Game* moment of revelation. She picks up the tiny things, her fingers running over them as if to verify the reality her eyes are so irrationally insisting on. Boxes and boxes and boxes of the bizarre little woollen things emblazoned with Halcyon's logo, a bold H inside a circle with multitudinous lines reaching out in every direction. It's one of those intentionally ambiguous corporate logos that might be implying the rays of the sun or growth in all directions or business networks or any of a dozen other concepts associated with empire and economy. Freya feels as though she's wandered headlong into a fairytale. She slips a few of the tiny mysteries into her pocket, despite Harland's earlier threats. Her conscience squeaks a tremulous warning, but her curiosity slams a fist sharply into its face and reminds it to stay locked up in the dark recesses of her psyche where it bloody well belongs.

If such curious cargo inhabits an unlocked room such as this, she thinks, then that makes the possibility of untold and illicit wonders hiding behind the multitude of forbidden doorways all the more likely and enticing. She nearly skips into the hallway, the keycard dancing in her fingers.

Click. Click.

Blip! More old furniture and statues. She *harrumphs* in irritation, her appetite now whet for bigger prey.

Click.

Blip! "Oh, for Chrissake!" she groans. "Who in the hell needs three billiard rooms?"

Click. Click.

Blip! Ooohh! Jet skis! Probably can't get away with borrowing those until Evelyn warms up to me. Which, given the woman's cheery temperament, should be about the same time the melting ice caps consume California.

Click. Click. Aarp.

Aarp? Freya glances at the handle she has swiped the card across and is greeted by an imposing set of fortifications. The magnetic lock guarding this particular entry has a large full-colour screen that displays the words ACCESS DENIED in furious red letters.

Freya swipes the card again.

Aarp. ACCESS DENIED.

She stabs randomly at the keypad then hits the enter button.

Aarp. ACCESS DENIED.

“Well, I would’ve been an idiot to expect that to work.” She raps her knuckles against the door to check if it’s reinforced, then realises she has no idea what a reinforced door would sound like. She stares at it for a moment, willing it to open, near dizzy from imagining the secrets, horrors or treasures that may dwell on the other side. She touches her fingers lightly to the door, marvelling that a mere few millimetres of wood, or possibly reinforced steel, separate her from a cavalcade of wonders.

From somewhere inside, she hears a heavy *clunk*. It is the kind of clunk that comic book authors would depict in virile purple letters, typeset with jagged edges and punctuated by a lightning bolt for an exclamation mark, exploding in the air across her horrified cartoon face. Freya presses her ear to the door and waits for the sound to repeat itself.

Clunk! “Motherfucking son of a bitch, I swear to God I’m going to *kill* somebody if…” His irate whispers are barely audible through the possibly-but-not-definitely steel-reinforced door.

Freya knocks loudly and says, “Hello! Is someone in there?”

The clunking and whispers cease, replaced by a thick, oppressive silence.

“Hello?” It must be her conscience speaking, because her voice is frail and timid. The silence continues for so long that Freya begins to question if there was ever anything else. Perhaps the cartoon clunks and complaining voice are the products of her overactive imagination. The other option, logically, is that the house is haunted.

She turns away and begins to move on, when she hears the *clunk* again, louder this time. She realises it is in fact coming from the next room over. She notices a barely discernible pinkish tinge to the marble outside this door that peeks out from underneath the carpet runner. She is about to bend down and inspect it when she is abruptly interrupted by a typewriter being hurled past her nose before shattering in an alphabet explosion against the opposite wall. She watches the w, x, y, and z shoot through the air, caroming off ceiling and wall and floor. The typewriter lies broken and unapologetic at her feet. She prods it with her shoe.

"You have b in your hair." The voice is mumbling and compunctious. It's the kind of voice that should come with a ragged, bushy beard, so it confuses and perhaps even irritates Freya that the man leaning in the doorway is clean-shaven.

"I have a bee in my hair?" she responds, her hands flailing at her scalp.

"No! Relax! I said you have b in your hair. The letter b." He plucks it out and presses it into her fingers. "What's your name?"

She peers through the thick black frames of his glasses and notices the whites of his eyes have a peculiar blue tint. *The blues of his eyes?*

"Freya."

"Pity. It would have been a far more poetic moment if your name was Beatrice. Or Beatrix."

"Or Beyoncé?"

He nods and rubs his chin where his beard should be, as though he is pondering a Zen koan. "Sorry about nearly hitting you with the typewriter." Then he slams the door in her face, leaving her awkwardly staring at the clutter of consonants at her feet.

The door opens again and the regrettably unbearded face reemerges and says, "I'm Jack." It appears to be a complete statement, rather than an invitation for further niceties. He looks at the black silk gloves adorning her hands. "I like your gloves. No one wears gloves anymore."

"Thanks. It's kind of an Audrey Hepburn thing, you know?" The lie feels comfortable in her mouth. She has told it so many times she almost believes it herself.

Jack nods. He stares down at the shattered remains of his typewriter for a few moments, forgetting she is there. His eyes dart back to meet hers as he says, "I'm not used to company. Do you want to come in?" He motions towards the interior of his apartment-sized room, its contents so chaotic it would allow the population of an Ecuadorian village to play a protracted game of hide and seek.

"Sure," says Freya as she steps over a skateboard, several pairs of boots and a pile of *Crochet Monthly* magazines before she reaches a large three-seater couch, the primary purpose of which appears to be preventing boxes of comic books, novels, and shoes from residing on the floor.

"Like I said, not used to company. Here, ah, let me…" Jack removes the boxes, places them precipitously on top of various other boxes, and offers Freya a seat in the newly cleared space. He sits opposite her on his grandiose four-poster bed, one half of which is dedicated to the storage of gadgets and electronic paraphernalia.

Freya sits down and smiles at him. He returns the smile and opens his mouth as if he is about to say something, but then thinks better of it. An uncomfortable silence sidles in between them, wedged between the piles of clothes and boxes.

"So, you must be the new nurse?"

"I am, yes. Today's my first day, actually."

He nods firmly, clearly both aware of and pleased by this fact.

"Yes, that's good. It's nice to have you. Well, it's also a shame that Christine was fired, but I guess if she hadn't been then we would never have had you come along now, would we?"

"Can I ask what happened to Christine?" *Given cement shoes, thrown in the river, cut into tiny pieces and fed to piranhas, sold as a slave to a Mexican drug lord…*

"You can, but unfortunately I'm not sure that I can give you a clear answer. I think she had some sort of disagreement with Mum and it was all rather unpleasant and uncomfortable for a while there, and then the next morning she was gone. Evelyn can be slightly…temperamental."

In the same way that a force ten gale can be slightly disruptive, thinks Freya. "I'm sorry about your brother. He was…is an amazing person."

Jack grimaces and says, "So people keep saying. Elijah, the golden child. Elijah, the polymath. Collecting accolades like a masochist collects scrapes and bruises, cut down in the prime of his brilliant life."

Freya registers the subtle hint of scorn, files it for closer observation, and continues the conversation under the pretence of normalcy. "Were you close?"

"In as much as a dove can be close to a Concorde. But yes, we spent a lot of time together, before it happened."

"Um...can I...? I know Evelyn said I'm not supposed to ask..."

"You want to know how he ended up like Sleeping Beauty?"

"Yes."

Jack casts his eyes down and says, "You shouldn't ask about that. It's not something we talk about. Ever. That, and the contents of the Danger Room next door."

"Danger Room?"

"Yeah, you know, like in the X-Men? Where they ran holographic training scenarios? The room could be anything they wanted? Our Danger Room is the same. No one knows what's in it, so it's become a playground for fantasy and speculation. It is whatever you need it to be."

"No one knows what's in there? Not even you?"

"Especially not me." His face contorts into a frown. "You ask a lot of questions."

"I'm sorry, I know that's against the rules. I should go." She stands and moves to leave, knocking over a copy of *Fantastic Four* #381 (*FOUR...NO MORE!*) but Jack grabs her hand. His grip is firm like wet sand, strong enough to hold form but supple enough to disintegrate under the application of minimal force.

"Please, don't." There's a barely discernible tremor of desperation in his voice. "It's nice to have the company. It's been a while since I've had anyone visit."

"I would never have guessed," says Freya, noticing the collection of *Hustler* magazines slumped beneath his desk.

"Yes, the place is in such a mess. I keep trying to clean it. The problem is that cleaning gets my head very clear and focused, and as soon as my head is clear and focused I have an idea and then I have to write it down and once I've written it down I have to start working on it and once I've started working on it

I have to review it and once I've reviewed it I have to refine it… hence the state of disrepair."

"Doesn't Maria clean for you?"

He laughs and says, "She tried, for a while—a long while, actually, bless her. But then I told her to not worry about doing anything besides the odd bit of dusting when I noticed she had started crossing herself and hanging her head like she was walking to the gallows every time she opened my door. Plus, I don't like to be disturbed when I'm working."

"What is it exactly that you do…you know, when you aren't introducing typewriters to walls at a high velocity?"

He smiles and looks to the corner of the room and mumbles, "Oh, you know, bit of this, bit of that."

Freya's head whirls with images of book cooking, hacking, identity theft, money laundering. "Uh-huh," she replies. "You're quite enigmagnetic, you know that?"

"Pardon?"

"Enigmagnetic. Someone who is both enigmatic and magnetically interesting. It's a word my friend Callum and I made up."

Jack blushes to a warm red, which looks strange against the bluish hue of his eyes. "Ha. That's cute. I'll take that as a compliment. Anyway, my apologies. I get a bit funny talking about my work sometimes. Um…well, perhaps you might know *Chaos in the Kingdom of Cynthia Green*?"

"By Jason Velles? Are you kidding me? I fucking *love* that book!"

His face erupts into a luminous grin. "Well, I can honestly say I never get tired of hearing that."

Realisation dawns on Freya like a Tesla coil. "Really? Are you kidding me?"

"I know, I know…Same initials. Not very subtle as far as pseudonyms go."

"You wrote that? Are you serious? Why didn't you use your real name?"

"You'd be amazed how quickly manuscripts written by the son of infamously wealthy parents of dubious character get turned away. In any case, I wanted to create something new for myself. Something separate from my family name. From their empire." He pronounces the word "empire" as though it is a heinous vulgarity.

"I literally read that book six times. I was hooked right from the tagline. 'The multitudinous struggles of a young black paraplegic Muslim lesbian in the twenty-first-century corporate legal battlefield'. How did you even come up with that?"

He shrugs and responds, "Cleaning."

"I can't believe you wrote that book! I always pictured you as some rotund old Englishman with sepia teeth and an overbite."

"You have a peculiar way of complimenting a guy, you know that?"

"Are you working on anything now?"

He nods and shuffles uncomfortably. "Well, yes, I'm always working on something or other. I have a drawer filled with abortions. Ah…abandoned manuscripts. I call my books my children and hence the abandoned ones…well, you get the picture. I apologise. It's quite crude, I know. In any case, right now my main project is something I've been working on sporadically for a few years. It's called *The Sins of Adonis*. Tentatively."

"Can I hear some?"

He quivers as though he's suddenly realised he's forgotten his own birthday and then nods. He rummages in one of the drawers of his desk and throws a stapler, rubber-band ball, and old-fashioned fob watch onto the floor. He carefully removes a single white feather, stares at it for a few reverent moments and then places it carefully on his desk. He produces a pile of crumpled pages and reads:

> The first time I saw her I felt the jaws of lust grip me with a ferocity I had never known before. Of all the girls I have defiled, none had ever been so pure, so innocent, so unbesmirched as her. She looked as though she was composed of nursery rhymes and fables. As though she was wandering through life waiting for the rest of the world

> to become the technicolour musical that already was in her–

He stops and discards the sheet of paper to the floor. "God. I don't know where this stuff is coming from. Lately I can't write anything except…" He picks up the white feather and scratches at the desk with its point. "It's horrible, isn't it?"

"It's really not. It sounds very dark, but I'm intrigued."

"Please, I don't need you to be condescending," he says with the petulance of a three-year-old denied an ice cream.

She examines the peaks and valleys of his handsome but beard-needing face. She pictures him lying serene, connected to a vast web of beeping monitors and machines. "You look a lot like him, you know."

"Yes. I know," he replies, with a note of irritation. "Well, I should get back to not writing. You probably don't want to be here when the next typing appliance attempts to fly. That was the third typewriter I've smashed this year. I guess it's obvious why I don't use computers anymore."

"Sure. I need to go check your brother's beepers in any case."

"Beepers?"

"His machines and things. You know, because they beep."

"Yes. I get it. You're a little odd, you know."

Freya smiles and says, "Now that's the pot calling the kettle a common kitchen utensil for the heating of water, don't you think?"

He walks over to the door and opens it for her. It's only as he does so that she notices the scattered bruises populating his arm.

"I didn't mean it pejoratively. Odd is good. I'm quite fond of odd."

The door closes gently behind her.

6

Happymax

If there's one thing old money hates, it's new money. And if there's one thing new money hates, it's newer money. Kyle Engels is freshly minted and despised by anyone rich enough to know the asking price for a Maserati.

Six years ago, Kyle invested his life savings (thirteen thousand, four hundred and fifteen dollars, and thirty-five cents) in a randomly selected stock for a freshman dare in his college house. Luckily for Kyle, that stock was Halcyon Inc, which then went on to enjoy record-breaking growth over the next few years. He'd quit university a few months before graduating, having become so abundantly wealthy that something as abhorrently upper-middle class as a degree in communications was nothing if not laughable.

After twelve months of blowing the fiscal equivalent of West Africa's aid debt in the incessant pursuit of pleasure, he had the moderately good sense to reason that even the largest bank account is frustratingly finite, so he acquired a financial adviser. His adviser possessed sufficient good sense to realise that he could skim copious quantities of capital from Kyle without him being any the wiser, and used the money to set up a company producing toys. Crap toys. The cheap plastic kind in exhibition showbags that fall apart after two days of play, which, fortunately, is about the same time spoiled little rugrats lose interest in them and start yammering for the next flashy plastic thing that has caught their gaze. Happymax made the kind of toys that cause grandparents to moan about sturdy wooden trucks that had lasted for years "back in my day" and had been passed onto Jimmy so-and-so who had consequently unscrewed one of the little bolts and swallowed it thinking it to be a delicious metal lolly and had ended up in hospital but hadn't that doctor been a nice young man, Swedish wasn't he? Or Swiss? One of those funny European places that make chocolate in any case…

The point being that Happymax made toys that ended up on TV current affairs programs with presenters feigning grave concern as they read from the teleprompter about the monsters daring to profit from harming children. Happymax's toys frequently broke, occasionally splintered, sometimes came coated in toxic lead paint and, once in a while, blasted battery acid over the face of some toddler who may well have grown up to be a famous surgeon or painter or journalist or filmmaker or photographer but we'll never know now because they all ended up in the emergency ward with a non-functioning retina.

Kyle had blithely signed whatever waivers and contracts his morally unencumbered adviser had placed in front of him, usually with the pen shaking in his hand because of cocaine or ketamine use or whatever designer drug had been fashionable among the young and well-to-do that season. Although Kyle's role had been more third violin than conductor in the whole affair, he had tacitly funded enterprises that had maimed, mauled, and marred children across three continents.

All of this more or less explains why Kyle has come to find himself stirring out of the marshmallowy haze of an MDMA trip, tied up, with his face lying on a toy railway track and, furthermore, why the track is currently supporting a miniature steam train laden with a precariously balanced vial of battery acid chugging directly towards his bright blue eyes.

Excerpt from *The Sins of Adonis*

One of the central dilemmas of being rich, powerful and handsome is that finding challenges becomes increasingly difficult. The more money you have, the more people seem inclined to give you things for free. The more women you've slept with, the more they seem to sense your prowess and surrender themselves without letting you enjoy the thrill of the hunt.

I'd been told that Chloe's legs would be harder to part than the Red Sea, but in the end I had to do little more than compliment her hair and hand her a glass of champagne. I've exhausted an extensive selection of high-grade narcotics, ruined a few careers for the fun of it and crashed a few companies so I could sample the aroma of lives being incinerated. Having done all that, the dreary and inevitable question is: what next, what to get for the man who has everything?

Well, something he has to take, of course. I've tried other men's wives, and I can safely say that the ghastly bourgeois sexual appetites weren't half as fulfilling as watching their husbands' faces collapse when I revealed the habits I'd introduced them to under my tender tutelage. I've tried theft, beginning with prized heirlooms and personal possessions. Sending that anonymous email snap of Peter's prized 1914 Rolex watch in the hands of the Indonesian monkey that I'd tossed it to was a delicious experience. The impotent rage he fired back, even more so. I also particularly enjoyed sending Penny the footage of her beloved vintage Aston Martin rolling off a cliff into the embrace of an icy cold river several hundred metres below. The sound was glorious, though the joy was fleeting.

Honestly, the only field left to me to explore is violence. Of course, there's no way in hell that I'm letting any harm come to these chiselled features. I can't exactly involve myself with the local neighbourhood fight club. Rich people are even more superficial than the plebs. Just look at the helium-headed, basketball-chested blondes that most of the rich old coots in their twilight years clutch with their hoary old talons.

No, I can't be in the business of collecting scars and bruises. So my violence might have to be of the more underhanded variety. If I'm going to have to play the stealthy hunter, I might as well pick my targets carefully.

Mother always said shoot for the stars. I'd rather shoot at them.

7

Just Think of the Money and Free Booze

Freya is shoved from the arms of sleep by the sounds of slamming doors and ferocious arguing. She glances at the glowing green LCD display of her clock: 3:43 a.m., a time when she prefers to be either very drunk or very asleep, preferably both.

The arguing continues. Something is smashed. Another something topples over. A third something rolls and thuds against a wall. Freya stares at the ceiling, waiting to fall asleep again.

"If you are intending to sleep in with the specific intent of lowering my opinion of you then I must say you are doing an appallingly splendid job." Evelyn's voice snaps her savagely back into the waking world. "You should have been in Elijah's room at eight o'clock sharp."

Freya squints at the clock. It's 8:02 a.m.

"I believe I went to great lengths to emphasise the word *sharp*. We aren't running on island time here. Today is a big day, we've got a lot to do before tomorrow night, there's no time to waste. Hurry up and get dressed. I need you to run some errands."

Freya is so impressed by the fact that Evelyn is already clothed, composed, coated in several ounces of makeup, and spitting commands mere hours after her late-night/early-morning altercation that she fails to muster a response to her collection of commands and casual racism. Evelyn stands in the doorway waiting for Freya to obey her orders.

"Eveeeeeelyn?" Rosaline's squeal calls out from the central living room. "The caterer is here!"

Evelyn disappears in a tornado of vexation and perfume.

Freya stumbles out of bed and runs to close the door as she hears another pair of feet scurrying by. She leans her cold, naked skin against its frame and sighs heavily. "Just think of the money and the free booze," she reminds herself.

She dives into an uncharacteristically simple outfit of jeans and a black tank top, runs a comb through her hair and reaches for the door. It is only when her hand touches the cold steel of the door handle that she glances down at her left wrist and realises she has left it scandalously uncovered. She grabs a woven cloth armband that Jane bought her in Vietnam and ties it over her skin. Outside her door, everything is happening at the same time as everything else.

A team of chefs and kitchen hands scrambles between the kitchen and dining room with trays and trolleys, Evelyn barks directives at anyone within earshot, cleaners are vacuuming and dusting and sweeping, and Rosaline is flicking through colour swatches with a tall chestnut-haired man in a sleek grey suit. A woman with impossibly thick, black-rimmed glasses strides from wall to wall, adjusting picture frames and making notes. Her legs are a pair of tapering tall stories that begin in offensively overpriced high heels and culminate in an ending known only to a handful of rich white men with stock portfolios and country club memberships.

"Did I just wander into that singing candlestick scene from *Beauty and the Beast*?" Freya says quietly, endeavouring to avoid eye contact with any of the several dozen people scurrying around. Among the chaos and confusion, it takes her a moment to remember exactly where Elijah's room is.

She swipes her keycard, enters, and closes the door behind her.

"You're late."

For a split second she is stunned with disbelief at the fact that her patient is not only conversational but admonishing her, before she realises the comment has come from the far corner of the room. Harland is staring out the window, his hands clasped behind his back.

"Sorry. I'm still getting used to…everything."

Harland turns to face her. The tiny lines and shadows colonising his face betray his fatigue. "Well, I suppose we can take the fact that you have so recently relocated into consideration, but don't think for a moment that this kind of tardiness will be tolerated."

"Of course not. Again, I'm sorry."

"And don't try blaming the traffic on the Western Freeway, either."

"The…traffic?"

Harland exhales heavily and runs his fingers through his silver hair. "You know, when I crack jokes at board meetings the room roars with laughter. It may have something to do with the fact that every man and woman there owes their fortune to me, but still…It's his birthday tomorrow, you know?"

"I was wondering what all the worker bees were buzzing about."

"Indeed. So things are going to be hectic around here for the next day or two. He'll be twenty-seven."

"Good thing he's not a rock star then."

"Pardon me?"

"You know, the Twenty-seven Club. A lot of great rock stars died the year they turned twenty-seven: Jimi Hendrix, Janis Joplin, Jim Morrison…"

"Do you not think it's in rather poor taste to mention that fact in light of my son's current condition?"

"His condition? Is something wrong with Jack?"

Harland's brow furrows, transforming it into a Japanese minimalist painting of a series of wave patterns. "Jack? Why would…? Oh! No. Jack's birthday isn't until April, or June, or something…Tomorrow is *Elijah's* birthday. That's why everything must be absolutely perfect."

He moves over to the bed and lays his hand gently on his immobile son's shoulder. It is a gesture simultaneously awkward and sincere. "I'll need you to take his suit measurements."

"His suit measurements? For…a suit?"

"So, irony is a key focus in nursing degrees nowadays, is it?"

"No, but…"

"Neither of those are words of which I am particularly fond. Here." He throws her a roll of tailor's tape and moves towards the door. "Rosaline will also need you to help choose flowers and run around town with a few errands. She's not particularly good at making decisions, or anything else for that matter."

The door closes with a click.

Beep.

Beep.

Beep.

"Morning, Eli. Sorry I'm late."

She strokes his face gently, admiring its statuesque contours. She wonders what colour his eyes are, if they share his brother's strange blue tint. Freya unrolls the tailor's tape and whispers, "Some family you got here, handsome. Well, we'd better get you measured for your birthday suit then, huh?" The double entendre makes her laugh, blush and cough at the same time. It's only 8:07 a.m. and it's already been the strangest day of her life.

(So far.)

◇◇◇

Freya is staring out of the passenger window trying extremely hard not to think about pink and blue nursery rooms. The consequence is that she can think of nothing else. "And so what about you, doll, have you ever been in love?"

"Sorry, Rosaline. I was miles away. What did you say?"

"I was asking, have you ever been in love?"

Freya looks at Rosaline, whose happiness is so intense it almost has a palpable vibration. "I'm not good at the whole girly talk thing. My sex life can basically be summed up as a series of bitter disappointments, each more moronic and Bon Jovi-adoring than the last. Nothing even approaching the 'L' word I'm afraid."

"Don't worry, sweetie! One day you'll meet your perfect man, just like I did!"

"Well, daytime TV sure as hell seems to think so. So, who's your Mr Not Wrong then?"

The sound of the brakes screeching produces a sharp, angry red. It is this colour that Freya notices before she's aware the car is skidding to a violent halt. "*What?*"

"Did I say something?"

"Frey, do you honestly mean to tell me you don't know? Why the hell do you think I live at that house? Who do you think I am?"

"I guess…I guess I hadn't thought about that." The sound of the screeching car horn behind them manifests as a fog of blood orange in Freya's vision.

"Frey, Elijah is my fiancé. I'm the Vincettis' future daughter-in-law. Did you think I was the maid or something?"

"No! I mean, I moved in yesterday and…"

Rosaline bursts into a peal of laughter and playfully slaps Freya's shoulder, her mood switching with schizophrenic speed. "Freya, you are such a scream!"

Freya, dizzy with discomfort, elects to change the subject. "So, how did you two meet?"

"I'm so glad you asked! It's been a while since I've got to tell this story! I was on vacation in Austria and Elijah was living in a cabin composing the soundtrack for an English war film—"

"Elijah was a composer?"

"*Is*. He *is* a composer." A subtle hint of venom invades Rosaline's trill, but melts away like ice in an inferno as she continues.

"He's a brilliant composer, even though it's something he does in his free time. Anyway, he was between semesters at med school and he figured he'd use the downtime to get creative, and that a quiet ski chalet in the Austrian alps would be the perfect place for it."

"I've often had the same thought."

"Really? How fabulous!"

It is apparent that sarcasm does not thrive in the saccharine bubble of Rosaline's world.

"Anyway, I met him out on the slopes. You should have seen him! It was the first time he'd ever even seen a pair of skis, let alone tried to use them! Poor thing could barely stand! He looked so adorable, fumbling to get up out of the snow. I couldn't help myself, that gorgeous blond hair, that chiselled jaw. He was like a walking Greek statue, you know, David's *Michelangelo* or something?"

"You mean Michelangelo's *David*?" says Freya, electing not to add that Michelangelo was, in fact, Italian.

"Yeah, that's the one! Anyway, I helped him up and showed him a few tricks, we got along splendidly. He is such a charmer!"

"Did he get the hang of it in the end?"

When Rosaline laughs it sounds like a choir of Tickle-Me-Elmos. Eventually she recovers and pulls into the florist's driveway. As they step out of the car she looks at Freya and says, "Honey, he was a two-time silver medallist at the Winter Olympics."

"He *what*?"

"You should have seen him. So graceful, he was like poetry in motion. Although, don't tell him I told you this, but the fact he missed out on a gold, it really got to him. He's a humble soul, my Elijah, but competitive as hell when the mood is right!" Rosaline sighs and glances around conspiratorially before whispering, "Can I tell you a secret? Elijah and I have been trying to get pregnant for a little while now and I think it's going to finally happen soon!"

Freya looks into her bright blue eyes and wonders how someone so sweet ever became such a raving, certifiable nutcase. "Rosaline, do you mind if I ask you something...about Elijah?"

"Of course! Anything!"

"What happened to him?"

The cheer falls from Rosaline's face like a dropped towel, leaving her anger naked and exposed.

"Frey. I'm going to tell you this once. And once only. *We. Don't. Talk. About. That. EVER.* Got it?"

"Of course...I shouldn't have asked. It won't happen again. Scout's honour."

Rosaline's face lights up as though it had never been anything but drenched in bliss. "Swell! Let's go get fruit smoothies!"

When they return to the house, Evelyn is holding a bottle of champagne in one hand and a fistful of a terrified Portuguese chef's shirt in the other. "I don't *care* if they're out of season. Get them flown in from somewhere where they're *in* season. Honestly, we can't have a black-tie gala event without fresh strawberries! What the hell are we, immigrants?"

The chef mumbles an apology and escapes as soon as she relaxes her vice-like grip.

"Ladies! Did you bring the flowers? Are they spectacular?"

"Wait 'til you see what they've done for the centrepiece. Elijah is going to love it!" Rosaline announces.

Evelyn claps her hands together, satisfied. "I'm sure he will. Fantastic! Rosaline, be a dear and fetch Maria and put the flowers in one of the spare rooms, will you? Freya, could you come with me?"

Freya follows the rhythmic click-clack of Evelyn's heels across the marble floor. She approaches a table laden with champagne glasses and pours two, hands one to Freya and holds the other in her manicured hand before leading Freya upstairs to the balcony. It's not until Evelyn trips slightly on the staircase and awkwardly rights herself that Freya realises she is in fact quite drunk. Her speech has lost none of its characteristic causticity, though, betraying how accustomed she is to intoxication.

Well, we have that in common, at least.

They stare out at *The Sorcerer's Apprentice*-scale operation unfolding below: tables being set with white lace cloths, hedges being trimmed, decorators moving Italian furniture from one corner of the garden to the other and back again. Freya is glad that she has a drink in hand; the whole diorama is bewildering.

Evelyn drains her glass and places it on the balustrade. She reaches into her pocket, removes a silver box of cigarettes and a lighter. Takes one, lights it, and inhales.

"I thought that smoking on the grounds was forbidden?"

"When you make the rules, my dear, you also get to break them."

She offers the box to Freya.

"No thanks, I don't smoke anymore."

"Me neither, if anyone asks," Evelyn replies.

She drags and expels a grey cloud towards the blue sky above them. "I assume you heard…last night?"

"Heard what?"

Evelyn's lips curl upwards in what could, in polite circles, be termed a smile. "You're very sweet to be so discreet, dear, but please, we're both adults. Last night, Harland and me?"

"Yes. I did hear that."

Evelyn nods, gazes out over her little empire. "He can be an arse, that man. You should see him around those tiny-waisted, balloon-chested trollops that flitter about him. It does quite go to his head. He needs a good kick up the pants every now and then to remind him whom he comes home to. I do love him. I know I may not seem warm, but I'm not a monster. I love him, and my children. And Rosaline."

"I'm quite sure that you do, Evelyn."

"Especially Elijah. Especially him. My perfect, darling boy." The sudden warmth seems uncharacteristic. "It's hard to explain to someone who doesn't have children of their own, but Elijah… Elijah is like every dream and wish and hope I ever had made flesh and blood. Like my own little Pinocchio, but with a better nose. I so want the best for him. The very, very best." Evelyn pauses and drags intently on her cigarette. "Do you know why I hired you, Freya?"

They ran out of adequately qualified Mexicans at the illegal immigrant cheap labour fair? "I was hired under the impression that I was to be his nurse?"

"The *impression*?"

"Yes, Evelyn. If we are speaking frankly, I didn't spend three years at university to become an errand girl."

"Well, if we are speaking frankly, which clearly we are, you also didn't spend three years at university expecting to make the kind of money you're making or living in a house such as this, now did you?"

"I suppose not."

"I make no apologies for your misconceptions, Freya. However, a nurse's job is to care for her patients, is it not? And Elijah needs your care."

"He needs me to care for him by taking his suit measurements and picking up flowers?"

"I'm going to respond by simply reminding you that disobedience and unnecessary questions are two of my least favourite things, along with hippies and airports. But that's neither here nor there. You will do as you are told. We have a flexible arrangement in regards to your employment and your duties will be likewise malleable. You are free to leave, at any time, but you are not permitted to question my directives." Her words are sharp, measured and firm, but without any hint of anger. "I picked you for a reason, child."

"That being?"

"You're pretty enough, presentable. But you aren't Harland's type. He usually goes after blondes."

Evelyn picks up the champagne glass and holds it out in the air, watching the light reflecting in its facets. Her fingers open and the glass plummets to the ground. The sound of its shattering causes the storm of activity beneath them to stall for a moment. The worker bees look desperately at each other, stupefied into silence.

"Well? Don't stand there like a bunch of stunned fish! Somebody clean it up!"

She regains her composure with lightning speed, turns to Freya and says, "That will be all."

Excerpt from *The Sins of Adonis*

The first time I saw her I felt the jaws of lust grip me with a ferocity I had never known before. Of all the girls I have defiled, none had ever been so pure, so innocent, so unbesmirched as her. She looked as though she was composed of nursery rhymes and fables. As though she was wandering through life waiting for the rest of the world to become the technicolour musical that already was in her head.

I never loved her, I know that, but if I am being truthful I think it was the closest I ever came to love. And more than that, there was a part of me, however small, that believed I was turning into something abhorrent and she might be my last shot at redemption. As though by standing in the light of her halo for long enough I might somehow become cleansed.

The moment when those diamond blue eyes stared down at me was unbearably, searingly, incomparably magnificent. I couldn't wait to see those eyes shed tears, to look directly into them and feel the lies roll easily off my tongue and see them swallowed by this unimpeachable beauty.

"Oh dear! You poor thing! Are you okay?" She took my hand in hers and even through our gloves I could feel it.

Electric.

8

She's Waiting for Godot to Impregnate Her

"It's unnatural." Callum pokes his fork warily at the pancakes on his plate, as though they might contain traces of Soylent Green.

"It isn't."

"It is! It defies the preordained order of the universe!"

"You're such a drama queen. No pun intended."

"Whatever. You know I'm right."

"I know that you're a whiny spoilt brat who is far too precious about their pancakes."

"I am not precious about pancakes. I love pancakes. I want to have their babies, but it is simply *wrong* to eat a breakfast food at 3 a.m."

Freya sips her milkshake, wishing it was slightly more bourbon-laced, or at least some sort of magical beverage that would reduce rather than expand her waistline. She points at Callum with her fork and asks, "How many times have we had this argument?"

"Well, evidently not enough because you still manage to drag me to this godforsaken place twice a week."

"Callum, it's pancakes, in a church, at 3 a.m. What's not to love?"

"You mean apart from everything?"

"I don't let a clock determine when I eat what I want to eat. Pancakes are every bit as delicious at 3 a.m. as they are at 7 a.m. Cereal is just as time-saving and practical a food source at dinnertime as it is at breakfast."

"Anyone would think you'd been raised in a hippie commune."

"Anyone would be an arsehole."

She takes another forkful of pancake and berries and tries to ignore the terrible eighties power ballad dribbling out of the speakers as clouds of pinky-orange hover in front of her field of vision. She loves this place, this former house of worship converted into a pancake parlour soundtracked by terrible pop music for drunks and cheapskates. It's like a three-dimensional metaphor for all of the indulgences and shortcomings of the modern era. "You hear about Kyle Engels?" asks Callum.

"The Happymax guy they found tied to that kid's train set?"

"Mm-hmm. With his eyes burned with acid."

"Not exactly dinner conversation, Cal."

"Dinnertime left us several hours ago, but do you realise that makes two corporate assassinations in a week?"

Freya chews, swallows, shrugs. "They aren't actually dead."

"A minor technicality. They've both been maliciously attacked in the course of one week. A little unusual, don't you think?"

"It's a lot unusual."

"You know what else? I was reading in the *Financial Review* that the Davies Group was investigating a merger with Happymax."

Freya's eyes glaze over at the mention of the word *merger*. "Could we get to the part where I care?"

"Davies Group is…or rather, *was* run by Wilson Davies, who was poisoned a few days ago. What's more, if they'd successfully merged, then Davies was going to use its increased asset base to dramatically expand into the European markets, making them direct rivals with the two powerhouses there: Halcyon and Novoscorp."

"How do you know all this stuff?"

"'All this stuff' is the wheels and cogs that make the modern world tick, Freya. You chastise me for not knowing references to obscure literature and then you don't even bother to learn anything about corporate politics? These are the people who run the world and, unlike politicians, we can't vote them out of power every few years. So, in answer to your question: there are some real-world benefits to being a media junkie."

Two teenage boys in the opposite booth wail atonally along with the Pearl Jam song playing on the stereo. They are covered in a chaotic jumble of tribal tattoos, surf T-shirts, gold necklaces, tight pants, and haircuts that appear to have been executed by a drunk arborist with a fondness for asymmetry. Noticing her gaze, they begin to slither their hands through the air and flick their tongues, miming acts of furious fornication.

She flips them off with her right hand and uses her left to shovel blueberries into her mouth. "I think I like you better when you're yelling about cars in posh restaurants than when you're whispering conspiracy theories in pancake churches. Cal, this week has been way too weird for me to even begin thinking about other people's problems."

"I told you they were eccentric," Cal says in his well-practised, I-told-you-so tone.

"More like stark fucking mad."

"So, at the risk of repeating myself, why are you working for them? You should be in East Timor right now. Is this all because of what happened with Valerie?"

"You don't get it. I can't go yet. And yes, it is because of what happened with Valerie. Is that so wrong?"

Callum is eloquently silent as Freya continues, "Anyway, the daughter-in-law, Rosaline, is engaged to Elijah, right? She's got mood swings like a diva on dexies and she's obsessed with getting pregnant, *despite the fact her fiancé's in a coma*. She even goes to yoga for mums and babies classes, the whole bit. She has a pink *and* a blue nursery all set up and ready to go. They're both stuffed with clothes and Golden Books and teddy bears, the whole nine yards. It's like she's waiting for Godot to impregnate her."

"Waiting for who?"

"Godot. You know, in that Beckett play we did in Year Twelve. The guy they spend the whole play waiting for but who never shows up?"

Callum shrugs, then flinches as he is struck in the face by a blueberry. The teenage boys snigger. "I flunked drama."

"I can't explain all my metaphors in pop culture terminology, you know."

"Pity."

"Okay, so you know what else? They're throwing this party for Elijah, right, and I had to get him measured for his suit—"

"I thought you said he was in a coma?" A cluster of sugar packets lands on their table. Freya shoots the boys a warning glare, they respond with air violins and over-pronounced pouts.

"Right."

"So...why does he need a suit?"

"Get this; they're going to fucking wheel him out into the crowd like Lenin or one of those other snap-frozen dictators."

"Jesus!"

"I know, right? The weird thing is, I tried looking up information about the accident and there's almost nothing on the web. I mean, there's articles that mention it happened, but no details about if there were other cars or passengers involved or alcohol. They're all short, perfunctory six-line articles with no detail or explanation. I don't understand how one of the richest people in the country getting into a major accident got almost no news coverage. Plus there's nothing about him being in the Winter Olympics or composing soundtracks like Rosaline said."

"Do you think she's crazy enough to make that kind of thing up?"

"I think a girl who keeps a room filled with dolls and prepared His 'n' Hers nurseries is all kinds of crazy. But that isn't even the weirdest part. The place is huge, I couldn't guess how many rooms, and they're all protected by these magnetic locks. I have a keycard that lets me into maybe half of them, the rest stay locked. Fair enough, I suppose, but there's this *one* room—"

"Where they keep Elijah's evil twin?" Callum says in a mock theatrical tone.

One of the boys calls out, "Faggot!" Callum bites his lip.

"That's not fucking funny, Cal. It's locked with some kind of Fort Knox-style set-up. It's dead creepy."

"So, how long do you give yourself before you try to break in?"

"You really think I'd do that kind of thing?"

"Sure, who wouldn't? It's like a modern-day Pandora's box."

"How come in myths it's always women who cause all the woes of the world to come hurtling into existence? Eve, Pandora, Lilith, Helen of Troy? Can't you men take any goddamn responsibility for all the world's crap?"

"We've already had our periodic breakfast-foods-at-inappropriate-times argument, do we have to get into chauvinistic-attitudes-perpetuated-through-myth-culture quarrel tonight as well?"

"Fine. You gonna eat that last pancake?"

"I've got something for you to eat right here!" yells the taller of the two boys. The pair of them spray half-eaten pancake across the table as they roar with laughter.

"Hell, no. It's all yours, my culinary confused friend."

"Sweet." Freya shoves a forkful of Strawberry Fields Forever pancake between her teeth and watches the splotches of pink-orange shift into green as the opening chords of an old Aerosmith song begin. "So, you'll be there at seven?"

"What for?"

"The party. I need a faux date and you're easily the least unattractive man in this joint."

"I think I'm planning to have a headache tomorrow night."

"You can have your damn headache on Sunday! You can't leave me alone with those aristocrazies! Please say yes."

Callum rubs his forehead and sighs. "Fine. But there'd better be free booze."

"By the truckload, I promise."

"And you have to drive me home."

"Tomorrow?"

"Right now. I've had enough of this pseudo-breakfast travesty. What if someone sees me here?"

"No one else you know is unfashionable enough to set foot in this place."

"Well, that's true, nevertheless…"

They throw a handful of notes and coins on the table and stand up. The boys mime blowjobs at them. Callum sighs, looks at Freya and says, "Should we?" nodding in the direction of the boys.

"Yes. I think so." Freya walks purposefully towards their booth. She locks eyes with each of them in turn, then treats them to a sultry smile. She runs her index finger slowly down her chin, between her breasts, towards her waist. They stare in open-mouthed awe. Her hand reaches the bottom of her skirt and she begins to lift it delicately upwards. She pauses, looks at their dumbfounded expressions, and nods at Callum. He grabs their shirts with confident hands and rips them upwards, leaving their faces and arms buried. Freya snatches up the milkshakes on the table and, amidst a hurricane of teenage profanities, pours them into the laps of the two boys.

Freya takes Callum's hand and they galumph towards her car, laughing and whooping. She unlocks the doors and fumbles her key in the ignition. The sound of hands pounding the back of her Camry clangs over "Love Will Tear Us Apart" playing on the radio.

"You fucking fag! I'm gonna kill you!"

"You fucking *ranga* bitch!"

Her shaking hand finally fits the key into the lock as the boys' furious faces appear in the window next to her. Their hands slam against the glass. The tall one spits on the window. "Bitch! I'm going *to cut you up*!"

No longer laughing, Freya floors the accelerator and her Camry rumbles out into the street. "Shit. These punks really can't take a joke," she says, changing lanes too quickly and inviting the angry horn of a motorcyclist behind her. Her pulse is pounding. In the rearview mirror, Freya watches the boys maintain a surprising speed. "The little bastards can run, I'll give them that." The spit slides across her window.

"*Freya!*" Callum screams, pointing at the figure stepping out onto the road ahead. She brakes hard; the sound of screeching tyres wails through the air as the car fishtails and the world spins and shakes. With white-knuckled hands Freya wrenches the wheel hard into the skid. They twist, slide, and clip a light pole. The impact sends them flying violently forward and back again, the seatbelts stinging at their chests. The sound of shattering glass tremors through the air. The two of them sit frozen in the sudden stillness.

Freya looks up at the figure stepping onto the opposite side of the street and cannot help but smile as she whispers, "It's her."

Marilyn Monroe is clad in a sumptuous ensemble consisting of a pearl necklace, purple dress and heels, and her traditional ocean of makeup punctuated by her prominent beauty spot. She smiles and winks at them both, then disappears into the night singing "Diamonds Are a Girl's Best Friend."

9

His Infamous Clark Kent Impression

"Be your best self! You have to think, breathe, eat, and *live* success. Remember to visualise success at all opportunities: standing in line at the bank, waking up in the morning, *be your own success story!*"

The motivational recording enters the brain of Bradley Macintyre via his headphones as he waits for the train to Central Station and is jostled by a crowd of weary workers making their morning commute. He replays the words in his head as he hears them: *be your own success story be your own success story be your own—*

"Ow!" The broad-shouldered man in the blue suit does not apologise for knocking him sideways—whether this is because he is unaware of having done so or because he simply does not care is impossible to say. Bradley assumes it is the latter, because he has been an incurable cynic since an early age.

Today he has less reason to be cynical. Although he must endure the sardines-in-moving-tins commute, survival of this journey will reward him with his first day in his new job as personal assistant to James Tellerford, senior Halcyon board member. Bradley had rather hoped that the accusing glare of his girlfriend (a longtime member of PETA, Amnesty International, Red Cross, UNCHR, and Oxfam) would slowly fade as she got used to the fact that he would not be leaving Halcyon, despite what she claimed was a well-documented history of deplorable environmental and human rights abuses.

"Surely, if they were that bad, someone would go to prison?" was his impuissant reply. "I've got to work somewhere!"

"Yes, you've got to work somewhere, but that somewhere could also be anywhere else!"

Each time they have this argument Bradley is reminded that if she ever gave him the ultimatum of choosing between his job at Halcyon or her, he would choose the former. The decision is now calcified in his brain, prepared for that inevitable conflict. He has already steeled himself not to spit his answer out too quickly when that conversation eventually arrives, lest he make it obvious that he'd already considered this option in some detail.

Bradley takes his morning brew from his favourite coffee stand. Lakshmi—who has the winning smile of a home-shopping advert hostess and has often crept into his private erotic fantasies—hands him his half-strength latte and congratulates him on the new job. *She* knows what a big deal it is. Maybe he should break it off with Karen and date Lakshmi…

He strolls into the building and nearly spills the coffee all over himself when he is greeted by, "Fifteen minutes early! I knew you were the man for the job, Macintyre! 'What do you want to hire that snivelling twerp for?' the boys asked me. 'Get yourself a nice big-tittied blonde!' they said. But I told 'em! I told 'em you had potential! And you'd be—Hang on, phone's ringing, ah, just the bloody wife. Probably moaning about the kitchen fittings again. Did you know that cupboard hinges from France cost three hundred dollars each? What the fuck about frog hinges can justify three hundred dollars for a tiny piece of metal with a rudimentary utilitarian function? Are they carved from metal harvested from meteors by the olive oil-anointed hands of vestal fucking virgins? Still, it's got to be the best for my Tracy or I'll never hear the end of it. Eh, what's that? Oh, thought you were going to say something. Right, follow me, be quick about it. I'm throwing you in the deep end. Best way to learn. Ah, unless you're teaching a toddler to swim I suppose, in which case, well…Come to think of it that's rather a terrible analogy, isn't it? Never mind! It's on twenty-six, you wanna hit the button? Board meeting. All the big guns. Lamar, Davidson, Morecroft, that Asian bloke…what's his name? Wang? Wong? Wung? One of those anyway…and the Vincettis themselves. Your job is going to be to take notes on anything and everything and crunch those numbers in your head like I know you can. What's it they call you? Macintyre, the human calculus? Calculator? Ah, the human abacus! That's it! Knew it was one of those. Crunch those numbers, and if you see anything worth talking about, write it down and pass it to me, discreetly, mind, like I'm sure you did in high school. Notes about Jenny Redhead and what bra she's wearing, eh? Got up to a bit of that back in your day, didn't you? I bet, ha-ha! Alright, this way. And here we are! Where the magic happens. Sit down here. We're the first ones, which a lot of business types will tell you is poor strategy, but then again, a lot of business types are complete bloody rockmelons. Yes, rockmelons. You know, thick-skinned but watery on the inside? Right, we're going to sit here, two seats down from the Vincettis. Close, but not presumptuously so. It's a fine balance, my friend, a fine balance. Don't talk much, do you? Fine by me, that's for sure. Nothing wrong with being a little taciturn, far too many blowhards barrelling around these corridors already, no doubt about that. Okay, here they all come, and smile and wave—Oh, and if Harland starts doing his infamous Clark Kent impression, that's a bad sign, he…"

"What's his Clark K—"

"Eh? No time for chitchat. Shut your clam-hole and smile politely. I'm not paying you to chinwag."

The board members file into the room exchanging a monochrome procession of "hellos" and "how's the family?" as they take their seats. Harland and Evelyn are the last ones in; they are both shining with the blazing red corona of a couple fresh from an argument.

Harland speaks first. "Hello all, we're going to get straight into it and stick to racing through the highlights with a view to finishing by ten. Any objections? Didn't think so. First off, performance across all sectors was up 2.3 percent. Not a huge figure, granted, but given recent global financial conditions, certainly nothing to be ashamed of. Good work, ladies and gentlemen. Now, it's that time of the month, ah, ha...that is to say, hrm...I could have worded that better, couldn't I? It's time for the monthly review. Chris, why don't we start with you?"

"Sure thing, Harland. Well, for starters, we've had huge progress with the minimum wage negotiations in Indonesia. Our factories there are very profitable, but the proposed government increases would have forced us to pay the workers an extra 2.5 percent per year, which we obviously weren't happy about. Now, it did take some...Is this being recorded in the minutes? Can we have this off-record for a second? Thanks. We did have to invest some money paying off a few officials, but that short-term payment is going to save us a tremendous amount in labour costs over the next few years."

"Well done," says Harland. "No sense paying more money to have the same bloody job done, is there?"

Bradley, at this point, can hear the voice of his morally beleaguered lover whispering, "See! I told you so!" within the deepest, darkest regions of his psyche. He wills himself to ignore her and maintains a serious, thoughtful composure.

"Alright, Morecroft, you want to go next?"

"Sure, thanks Harland. Now, I'm rather pleased to announce that we've seen a slow but steady expansion across Southeast Asia. I've been particularly pleased with the synergisation of our production and transportation departments. Now, I don't want to open the kimono on the entirety of our projects there, but I'll try and disambiguate some of what we've been doing, particularly in regards to actualising net gain on deliverables." Morecroft is speaking with the giddy excitement masked as even-toned authority of a high-school debate team captain. He appears completely oblivious to Harland's eye-rolling and fake yawns. "Now, you'll have to forgive me for dogfooding here, but I'm going to use the…"

Tellerford passes Bradley a note, tapping it against his thigh. Bradley opens it to see the words: *Fuck. This is what I warned you about.*

He looks at Tellerford with bemusement. Tellerford nods at Harland, who has donned a comically large pair of glasses and is staring at Morecroft with a forcibly bored expression. Slowly, the other board members turn their attention from Morecroft to Harland and begin to nervously chuckle.

"Oh, please, tell me more. This is so interesting," says Harland in a loud monotone.

Morecroft turns from the projector screen to see Harland in his Clark Kent glasses and immediately deflates. "I'm…I'll just email you all the notes. I…ah, I have to go to the bathroom."

He scurries out of the boardroom and Harland laughs uproariously. Evelyn rolls her eyes at him and the faces of the other board members host expressions ranging from "Dear Lord, how did this man get to be head of a multinational?" to "Please pay attention to how much I am smiling at your pathetic attempt at humour and give me a raise."

"God, that was even more boring than the last time my wife dragged me to the opera!" says Harland.

"That joke might work, dear, if you'd ever actually attended the opera. Or if you were even remotely funny."

"Thanks, Evelyn. Always nice to know I've got you at my back. Poking knives into it, that is."

She groans and waves for him to continue.

"You know what? Let's cut to the chase. Big news is that the three-way merger with Happymax and the Davies Group is very fucking close to being inked. Obviously, the events befalling

Wilson Davies and Kyle Engels were cruel and tragic, and we will be making every effort to look after their families in every way possible. However, there's no shame in taking advantage of a business opportunity, and I'm sure both Engels and Davies would call 'fair game' if the tables were turned.

"Clearly this is going to open up all kinds of new revenue sources, supply chains, and diversification options. It will, in addition, allow us to manufacture some of our pharmaceuticals through Davies' labs, which should give us plausible deniability if we manage to manufacture something that doesn't fit guidelines but proves profitable. Basically, my lawyers have advised me that we might have an informal grace period of around six months where we can claim their labs were producing products that we weren't aware were substandard due to the communication problems inherent in acquiring a new corporation of that magnitude."

At this point, Bradley's conscience—in the guise of Karen's high-pitched squeak—has been rattling off a string of obscenities that Bradley can no longer ignore. "Are you saying…Are you saying you'll make drugs that don't meet approval…like, on purpose?" He's regretting the words even as they cascade out of his mouth.

Harland stops, removes a cigar from his pocket, smells it, and throws it at Bradley's face, where it hits him square on the nose and lands in his lap. "Consider that a parting gift. You're fired! If you breathe a word about any of this, we'll deny everything and sue you for defamation. And take everything you own. Now, be a good lad and kindly *fuck off*, would you?"

As Bradley leaves the boardroom, walks down the corridor, enters the elevator, crosses the foyer and exits the building for the last time, he plans his confession to Karen. "Karen, darling, you were right. Halcyon is an immoral, greedy, and fundamentally malevolent corporation that commits crimes against humanity and the planet. I guess, ultimately, I couldn't be with someone as wonderful and idealistic as you and work for Halcyon. It all came down to a choice between you and the company. And I chose you, my darling."

III

Diagnosis

"A short time ago a man walked into a back-kitchen in Queen Square, and cut the throat of a poor consumptive creature, sitting by the fire. The murderer did not deny the act, but simply said 'It's all right.' Of course he was mad."

Florence Nightingale,
Notes on Nursing: What it Is and What it Is Not

10

Birthday

The room is dark. There is music playing somewhere, but she sees no colours. This should be cause for confusion, and yet she feels only an eerie, blissful calm. He is smiling when she approaches, and she sees his eyes at last. She can't look away from them; they are twin blue moons floating in the galaxy of his face.

He is just as beautiful as she remembered, even in the darkness.

"Where are we?" she asks. Her voice echoes and reverberates around the walls.

"Somewhere you aren't allowed," he answers. His voice is different from what she imagined. Strong and confident, but also cracked and rough.

"I'm sorry I cut you."

"It's okay, it was an accident." He is statuesque, a perfect frame, with hypnotic eyes. The room is dark.

"Do you miss being awake?"

"Do you?"

"What?"

The room is dark.

Beep.

Beep.

Beep.

"That's strange. I can hear your beepers, even here."

"That's not my machines. It's your alarm."

"My wha—"

Freya jolts upright and slams her hand on the alarm. She staggers out of bed and into the shower.

It's Elijah's birthday.

◇◇◇

Freya hums "Happy Birthday" as she prepares Elijah's injection, thinking all the while that if this was a movie she could be required to pay thousands in licensing fees. This thought brings forth a rush of memories from her fourteenth birthday. She pushes them to the back of her mind and focuses on the task at hand.

"Well, birthday boy, I'm afraid all you're getting from me is a syringe filled with essential nutrients, clean sheets, and a fresh nappy. In the nursing biz they call it a 'purple faecal eater,' although you probably know that, being a doctor and all. Pity, if you'd been awake we could've shared a nice little in-joke there. Now hold on, this might sting a little."

She injects the nutrient supplements into his arm, then cleans the wound and tapes a bandaid over the top. "You know, you'd be a lot better off with a nasogastric feed. That mother of yours won't allow it for some reason, which I think is a little strange."

Freya lowers the railings of his bed and pushes him onto the stretcher. She always forgets how heavy dead weight is. She flinches as the word *dead* enters her mind. How strange it must be to permanently occupy the waiting room between this world and the next, to be simultaneously past and present tense. She strips his sheets and replaces them with fresh ones.

Beep.

Beep.

Beep.

Freya tucks the crisp Egyptian cotton sheets under the custom-made memory foam mattress. "I had a dream about you. Rosaline was right, you're quite charming."

She pushes him back onto the bed and begins to fold away the stretcher.

"You talk to him, too?"

Freya whips around and in doing so slams the stretcher down on her toes.

"*Fuck!*" she yells, and falls to the floor grabbing at her wounded foot.

"Oh! Miss!" Maria exclaims and runs to the bar fridge to grab ice. Freya removes her shoe and sock, places the ice cubes inside the latter and lays it on her foot. "I didn't mean to scare you."

"It's okay, it was an accident."

"Is broken?"

"No, definitely not. Hurts like hell though…aaaarghgghgh!" Freya bites her lip and scrunches her face as the wave of pain punches against her then slowly begins to subside.

"So sorry, Miss Freya."

"Please, you don't need to apologise. I guess I'm a bit jumpy. I didn't know anyone was listening."

Maria smiles and answers quietly, "*Chicita guapita*, in this house? There is always someone listening."

Freya takes the ice off for a moment, inspects the damage. It'll bruise, but it's nothing too serious. "Maria, how long have you been working here?"

"Ever since I come from Colombia, about four months ago. Right after Mr Elijah have his accident."

"Do you know how it happened?"

"I know we don't supposed to talk about it," she whispers. She runs over to the bedroom door, closes it, and creeps back to sit next to Freya. "I working here all this time, nobody say *nothing*. One time I ask to Mrs Rosaline, she very angry. Mrs Rosaline she *never* angry, so I confuse. Mrs Evelyn, later she come tell me I ask about it again, I will have regret." Maria looks at Freya and smiles. "You're pretty, you know that? In my country, men love women who look like you."

"They do, huh? What's a ticket to Colombia cost these days?"

Maria laughs and stands, begins dusting and polishing. "I tell you something else, I never seen nobody come in or out of that room you were trying to get into the other day."

"You saw that?"

"*Chicita,* you no listen? I tell you someone is always watching in this house. I see you talk to Mr Jack, too."

"Yes. He's nice. Very sweet. A little strange though, don't you think?"

"Everybody in this place a little strange, Miss Freya. You live here now, maybe you're a little strange, too?"

Freya laughs as she wiggles her toes and watches the pale blue bruise slowly darken in colour. "Do you think he'll ever wake up?"

"You are the nurse, Freya. You tell me. But I can tell you one thing, I don't believe half of what they say about him." She leans her lips close to Freya's ear and whispers, "*Mentiras.*"

Freya has to search her memory for the word she has not heard in several years. Its meaning arrives slowly, like a train pulling into a station. *Lies.*

Beep.

Beep.

Beep.

Maria continues cleaning as though nothing has happened, shifting one of the bookcases to allow her arm entry to the window behind it. As she begins wiping the glass Freya notices a small slip of paper fluttering down from the top of the bookcase to the floor below. On impulse, she snatches it and shoves it in her pocket. The pain in her foot is slow and steady now.

"You know, back in Bogotá, I used to run a bar?" Maria says. "*Corazon del Sol.* It was very famous in my city. You should have seen me back then, I had boys lining up around the corner!" She winks at Freya. "I miss those days. Even though Bogotá was a dangerous city back then. But still, I had some good times when I was a young girl! I bet I could have drunk you under the table back in my day. Maybe I still can!"

Freya grins and says, "I'll take that challenge."

"Ha! Okay, we see about that. Alright. I all finish in here. I see you later for the party, okay? You got a nice boy to come with you?"

"Yes. But just a friend."

"Well, I look forward to meeting him."

Freya basks in Maria's resplendent smile. It's nice to know that at least one inhabitant of this house isn't completely deranged. Maria collects her cleaning paraphernalia onto her trolley and begins walking towards the door. She stops in the doorway, turns back to Freya and says with a smile, "*Senorita*, you wanna find out what happened to him, about who he was, you gonna have to be patient. But no worry, there are plenty of other secrets in this house to keep you busy while you waiting." Maria winks at her and exits into the hallway.

Freya stands, collects her shoe and sock, and hobbles along the hall and down the stairs. The slow, throbbing pain in her foot wrestles with her curiosity. It's over quickly; after all, her curiosity always fights dirty. She swipes her keycard over a door and enters the room filled with the tiny woollen mysteries that had so perplexed her the day before, flicks the light switch and closes the door quickly behind her. She sits with her back against the wall. Outside she can hear the faint echoes of a string ensemble practising; she smiles as the cloud of greens and blues shimmers across her vision. She runs her fingers over the boxes.

"What the hell are these things? Jumpers for dolls? Why no sleeves, only holes?" Freya listens to the sounds of the music, hurried footsteps and barked commands filling the house and surrounding estate. This is a strange haven, but she is glad of the momentary quiet.

She slips her hand into her pocket and produces the stolen ("not stolen," she tells herself, "*borrowed*") note Maria had knocked to the floor.

Dearest Elijah,

One day, when your beautiful blue eyes open at last you will read this letter. Until then I am writing this mostly for myself, I guess. Which is fine, Dr Messingham said I need to do more for myself and stop focusing all my thoughts on you and the baby.

In any case, I need to tell you something. I haven't said this out loud yet, not to anyone. But then, who would I tell? Not Evelyn, that's for certain. You know I love her almost as much as my own mum, but I'm sure you wouldn't think me unfair to say she can be somewhat temperamental. Not Harland, wonderful man though he is. Lately he's hardly home and when he is he spends most of his time arguing with Evelyn. I don't mean to gossip darling, but I think...I think he may be sampling fruit from other trees, so to speak. Pardon me for being so crude!

And I don't see so much of my friends these days. Lily is busy with her two darling little boys, Amelia moved to Hong Kong because Scott got a job over there, Tracey's pregnant again and can't move around too much. I guess I'm the only one without children! But I know I mustn't be so fixated on that, even if my prime birthing period IS coming to a close and there are higher rates of autism in children born to mothers thirty and above, which is only three years away, not that I wouldn't love a baby with autism as much as any normal child...of course I don't mean to say that children with autism aren't normal! Oh, dear, I've gone and gotten all muddled and confused again. Back to the point.

The point, my darling, is that I finally found the courage to forgive you. I do. Really, truly and absolutely. It's been a long

time, and you put me through hell, there's no denying that. You were awful, in ways that I didn't know you could be. You did something that I didn't know a beautiful, perfect creature such as yourself was even capable of. Just thinking about it makes me feel flushed and nauseous and my mouth starts to taste hot and bitter...but it doesn't matter now. At last, I forgive you. When you wake up, we can be a family at last. I have the rooms all prepared for a little boy or a little girl, you'd love them! I have books and toys and all sorts of adorable little knick-knacks.

Hope you're having sweet dreams my dear.

Love always,

Rosaline

Freya folds the letter and places it in her pocket, making a mental note to put it back on the bookcase later. She gently rises to her feet, carefully checks no one is outside and steps into the hall. She limps back through the house and into her bedroom, where she changes into a pair of comfy old sneakers that will be kinder to her foot.

Freya lies on the bed, her legs and arms splayed. The sounds of music and preparation fill the house like a shaken jar of bees. She barely hears the knock at the door over all the activity. "Yeah?" she grunts. The door opens, revealing Jack, dressed in faded black jeans and an old black T-shirt, standing uneasily staring at the floor. He is unshaven, which pleases Freya. His stubble is like a preview of the beard that he really should have.

"I hope I'm not disturbing you?"

"No, it's fine."

"Do you...would you mind if we talked?"

"Of course not. What's up?"

"I have somewhere I want to show you. I'm guessing you haven't had a chance to explore the whole house yet?"

"I'd need a twelve-man team and a couple of months to pull that off, I think. This place is huge."

"Exactly, which is why you should let me show you the best spot around, save you the trouble."

"I like finding things on my own. Even though that usually means I end up taking a detour through the woods to get to the corner store. But sure, just this once."

"Great! Follow me." He grins and sets off down the hall with the stride of a child heading for Santa's lap. He leads her through the labyrinthine corridors until they find what appears to be the door to a broom closet. Jack opens it to expose a rusty ladder, incongruent with its lavish surroundings, then climbs up the first few steps and pushes open a trapdoor to reveal the bright blue sky.

"You aren't going to lure me up there and push me off, are you?"

"Please, if I wanted you dead I'd have paid someone to kill you already."

"That's far from comforting."

Freya climbs up the ladder, her injured foot slowing her progress. Jack offers his hand to help her up but she refuses, more on principle than anything else. "I'm fine, I have my own arms. So, you realise this is technically the best spot *on* the house, not in it, right?" she comments.

"If you want to be pedantic."

"I usually do."

Freya perches on the warm red tiles and looks out over the river. The view, she has to admit, is spectacular. A ferry chugs past on the water below, countless shades of green stare at her from the riverbank. Laughter echoes across the water, the air feels crisp and fresh. It's as close to perfect as a day is ever likely to get.

"Okay, I admit. This is nice."

"Sometimes I feel like I can see the whole world from up here."

"Well, being realistic there's probably only a fraction of a percent within visibility range."

"Again with the pedantic. I'm a writer, I have a tendency to hyperbolise. And to be honest, this *is* my whole world, more or less."

Freya eyes him with a faux-seductive glance and purrs, "So, do you come here often?"

Jack blushes and snorts a laugh. "Oh, Lord, it's been a while since I've heard a pickup line, or even a mocking facsimile of one. But yes, I come up here when I need to escape. So, more or less daily."

"I can think of worse places to be."

The sound of the ferry fades into the distance. The breeze blows out over the water. He looks at her with his curiously blue-tinted eyes. "He's twenty-seven today, you know."

"Yes. Harland told me."

"Should be quite a party."

"I'm guessing it'll be one of the top five best black-tie catered feasts with an Italian string ensemble I've been to all month." Jack smiles in response. She notes his body and demeanour have relaxed. Here on the roof overlooking this tiny portion of the world, he appears to be a man in his element. The jittery awkwardness has disappeared and he now resembles a contemplative king surveying his tiny kingdom.

"The little sleeping prince. Snoozing in wait to take the reins of the empire."

"Aren't you next in line? I thought you were the eldest?"

"Yes. I am. And I'll certainly get my portion. But the lion's share will go to Elijah, because of my, ah, situation. It's a long story."

"The good ones usually are, but I'll take that as my cue to bite my tongue. Harland tells me that your family started their business here over a hundred and fifty years ago?"

"Yes, 'founded by a poor Italian immigrant who arrived off the boat with nothing but the clothes on his back and the blisters on his feet who sold balms, lotions, and vegetables to the needy.' I assume that's the line you've been fed? It's a nice enough story, I suppose, but more than a little whitewashed. Elijah Vincetti the First opened up a general store with the funds he acquired from a young baker whom he robbed and subsequently murdered. He grew his kingdom by secretly dealing opiates and bootleg liquor along with milk and bread, until he had enough money to start bankrolling white-collar crime and financing political campaigns so he'd have all the key players in his back pocket."

"You don't seem particularly enamoured of your ancestry."

"Just because we share a gene pool doesn't mean we share a world view. My family is rather partial to 'remixing' the truth, so to speak. Especially when it comes to our darling Elijah." Jack pauses, cocks his head, bird-like and says, "I'm going to ask you something. It's a question you've probably been asked a lot before, and that people have wanted to ask but haven't plenty more times besides that."

"My wrist?" He nods. Freya sighs and says, "You know, the stupid ones always buy the Audrey Hepburn line."

"I'll take that as a compliment. But I have an insatiable curiosity."

"I thought people didn't like questions in this house?"

Jack smiles. "People love *asking* questions in this house, but they hate answering them."

There is a pause before Freya continues. "Okay. Well. I have this...condition. It's rare, and to be honest I don't really like talking about it. Maybe once we get to know each other a little better? And I would like to get to know you better."

He shrugs. "Well, I guess I can't complain about that. Alright, that's fair. If it makes you feel any better, I've got a somewhat strange and colourful medical history myself. But in the interests of getting to know each other better, can I ask exactly how you ended up here?"

"I'm supposed to be on a plane today. At ten-fifteen tonight. Economy, window preference. Chicken and pasta meal pre-ordered. I booked nine months in advance. Got one of those super cheap, non-refundable tickets. Ever since I was a teenager my plan was to graduate, get a few years' experience in nursing, go to East Timor and then save the world one injection at a time. It was a perfect plan."

"*But the best laid schemes of mice and men, go often askew*?"

"And of altruistic young women too, it would seem."

Another pause.

"So, obviously, I'm going to ask what happened."

"And, obviously, I'm going to have to tell you."

Freya tries to remember the last time she told this tale. Was it to Jane? Or Murray, the narcissistic surfer she'd wasted a few summer weeks on? She can't recall. She prepares the story in her head for a few moments before she begins to speak. It spills out of her.

11

Valerie

"Valerie's mum always said that she was lucky she wasn't born in the fifties, when a baby with cystic fibrosis would have been lucky to live six months. I always thought that was stupid. If you're going to start thinking like that, why not just wish that she was born in the year 2083, when they've developed a cure? Then she could probably get some sort of hoverboard or flying car or whatever to go along with it.

"In any case, professionally speaking, you aren't supposed to have favourite patients but, of course, everyone does. Valerie was mine. She knew full well she was going to consider herself lucky to ever see her forties, which meant that at seventeen she was technically approaching middle age.

"When I was a kid my dad got diagnosed with Hodgkin's lymphoma, he spent a lot of time in hospital. There was this one nurse there, Riley, who used to pal around with me and tell me jokes and stuff. I remember she had this amazing tattoo of Kandinsky's Three Sounds *on her arm. She was the first one to tell me about his work and get me interested in art. She was the kind of role model I wish*

more girls would have, instead of these vacuous, drugged-up celebrities that seem to plaster TV nowadays. I guess I wanted to be for Valerie what Riley had been for me.

"Like most CF patients, Val was in the hospital pretty often and I know it's egotistical, but she reminded me of myself in high school. She was young and sassy but still a little neurotic and unsure. Plus we both had a weird condition that made us into social outcasts. I worked with Valerie for nearly four years. That's longer than any relationship I've ever had with a boy, longer than I've ever lived in one house, longer than it took to get my degree. Val became like my little sister. I saw her grow boobs, get and then get rid of braces, saw her face erupt into a screaming red series of acne craters and then slowly heal again. All that shit teenagers have to endure, as if the hormones playing havoc with their brains and loins isn't enough for them to deal with. Every time she told me about some jerk who had dumped her to go out with one of the bimbos from the netball team I wanted to smash his car with a baseball bat. Every time she told me she got a 'B' for a class she could have sworn she was going to fail I wanted to buy her pizza and champagne to celebrate.

"Val had been doing pretty well for someone with her condition. She was getting to the end of Year Twelve and was all set to enroll in an architecture degree. She told me, 'I want to leave behind something solid and permanent when my body fucks up on me.' Don't even get me started on how long I spent bawling my goddamn eyes out when she told me that.

"So, at the end of last year, Val scored decent grades, but like a lot of teenage girls who spit on the graves of the founders of the feminist movement, she was more excited about the formal and after-party than her academic success, let alone her future. She'd picked out her dress months before, had the standard argument with her father over the exorbitant price, booked a limo, all that jazz.

"She'd even been asked out by the boy. What was he called? Tom? Terry? Doesn't matter. She was a high-school girl and she liked him, which meant, of course, he was the only living human on the planet with the requisite organs that she could even dream of touching. So, the week before the big night she's running her mouth off talking

about the dress and the boy and the party and this that and the other. Then she starts telling me about how she's ready, you know, to take the next step. I figure, fair enough, she's seventeen, and from the rose-tinted picture she's painted me, this Terry sounds like a stand-up guy. Can't be any worse than my first time, which was in the back of a Barina parked in the garage at Milton Bowl, by the way. They tore that place down years ago but I swear to God every time I go past there the back of my neck starts aching like it's got a door handle jamming into it.

"So, she's asking me advice on all the things—you know, technique, protection, all that. I didn't have the heart to tell her the truth, which was, 'Kid, he's seventeen, you'll be lucky if the whole event lasts longer than a Pepsi commercial.' I was very clear about the necessary precautions, though, professional responsibility and all that.

"Then a few days before the formal, she starts developing this heinous cough. Most people with CF get that; comes from the accumulation of mucus on the lungs. You have your up and down swings, but as a rule, things slowly go from bad to worse. The doctor, this guy named Kapsen, who was about a thousand years old and had all the wit and charm of a bucket of warm molasses, starts insisting that she's going to need to be kept under observation for at least a week.

"God, you should have seen her face. She looked like someone had told her that her grandma had been killed and eaten by her own cat. She started bawling her eyes out and she would…not…stop. Her mum was there consoling her, I was trying to tell her everything would be okay, meanwhile Kapsen the cold-hearted is droning on and on to her father as though Valerie isn't even there.

"I grab him by the shoulder and pull him into the corridor and growl, 'If you don't let that girl out, for that one night, *she is going to hate her life so much that she won't want to go on living.'*

"'Don't be ridiculous! She's a teenager, she's just being melodramatic. I will not put her health at risk for some debutante ball.'

"'Listen, aside from the fact that it hasn't been called that since before typewriters were cutting-edge, you know this is hardly a life-threatening situation. If you don't let her out to play dress-ups and

feel like a real, normal person for a few hours, you will break that girl's heart.'

"He glared at me and stormed off, but the next day instructions were given that Val be allowed out for the evening, so long as she was chaperoned by an adult from one event to the next, made sure to keep her mobile phone with her at all times and returned first thing the following morning. When I told Val, she hugged me so tight she nearly broke my neck.

"I set up her respirator as she spent the next forty minutes yammering on about how she was going to do her hair and makeup. Through the breathing mask she sounded like Darth Vader at a beauty salon. When Friday finally came round, the doctor told her that she seemed surprisingly healthy and how he was optimistic that things were going well.

"She looked amazing that night; you should have seen her. Although she insisted on wearing this ugly charm bracelet that I hadn't ever seen her take off. She gave me a big hug and I made her promise me that she would drink nothing except juice and soft drink or I would never speak to her again.

"She agreed and bounded out the door with her dad. He shot me a grin and said, 'She won't stop talking about you. I'm starting to get worried she's going to try and talk us into letting you adopt her.' They walked outside, pulled their little green Ford out onto the road and had barely driven twenty metres before they were hit by a black BMW and killed upon impact."

12

Simply Sasha

"Cut off his head," snarls Sasha as she swerves across lanes, a chorus of horns and hollering behind her. "I'm serious. This is me, the queen of motherfucking hearts, telling you I want his severed head served to me on a platter by the end of the week. If that tree-hugging, swine-loving piece of shit wants to play with the grown-ups then he'll have to suffer the consequences. The son of a bitch threw pig's blood at me, for fuck's sake! That was a one-of-a-kind Versace dress that cost more than your son's reconstructive surgery. Don't get snide with me, I pay you too much for you to ever talk back to me. I'm going to duck home and get changed into something slutty and expensive and then go to Elijah Vincetti's birthday and hopefully come home with someone rich and tasty. I want it solved by the end of the night."

Sasha Fairlane hangs up and throws the custom-made, old-growth African blackwood-encased, blue diamond-encrusted smartphone onto the seat next to her as she pulls into her drive-way. Her electric gates part like the legs of a high-class hooker and she drives through. Her house, which recently graced the pages of *Home & Design* magazine, is a monument to opulence. The French doors cost more than the average Parisian makes in a year, and the six-tier, full-lead crystal chandelier gracing the foyer gives the impression that diamonds are constantly raining from the ceiling.

She has earned her money through selling lies. Precious few who reach the dizzying heights of obscene wealth that she has attained have the luxury of dealing in truth and goodwill. Sasha's makeup and fashion line, Simply Sasha, has captured the hearts, eyes, and most importantly, wallets of women all over the globe. Her line of beauty products is desired above all others, and her marketing campaigns, which hard-sell beauty in strictly one-sized, slim-waisted, dead-eyed European model packages, have caused almost as much controversy as they have generated repulsively successful sales figures. When other beauty companies started to embrace the philosophies of "big is beautiful" and "bringing out the inner you," Sasha pushed in the opposite direction, plastering billboards, magazines, webpages, and TV shows with images of emaciated, photoshopped puppet poppets.

On an average day, she receives approximately seventy-five thousand letters, emails, cards, and tweets filled with gushing praise along the lines of "OMG I heart yr products soooooo much their the best and your so pretty! thx thx thx! xoxoxox." She also receives several thousand militant threats from anti-anorexia groups, concerned mothers, feminist campaigners, and animal rights activists. Until yesterday, she couldn't have cared less, but like the song says, "What a difference a day makes."

At 3:03 a.m. yesterday, a young freelance journalist and animal rights activist broke into one of Simply Sasha Inc.'s largest laboratories on the outskirts of Sydney. He filmed two minutes and twenty-three seconds of footage before security guard footsteps echoing down the hallways prompted his exit. He arrived home at 3:33 a.m., edited the footage with some explanatory text and a hastily recorded narration. His mouse clicked.

Click.
Click.
Click.

By 7:46 a.m., it was one of the most watched videos on YouTube. It was beyond viral; it was pandemic. News and radio stations pulled stories on foreign conflict and celebrity weddings and instead aired the horrific footage of pigs with chemical burns over every part of their bodies, sheep with frothing mouths and red-rimmed eyes, and monkeys with grotesquely distorted features. There were images of flesh and fur and blood and bone strewn like so much wrapping paper on a fifth birthday. By the time stores opened that morning, staff had cleared all Simply Sasha stock from their shelves for fear of rioters tearing apart their pristine displays.

School buses were packed with incensed tweenies furiously tweeting, texting, and occasionally even talking:

> OMG I dnt thk I could EVA use Simply Sasha Jr's anti-pre-premature wrinkle cream on my face again aftr hereing it was used on monkees & they're faces burnt of! WTF!

When the stock market opened and the armies of caffeine-sipping suits booted up their computers, one thing was clear: Simply Sasha's profits would be hurting worse than the aforementioned monkees' faces.

At this point, Sasha clearly has a lot on her mind. It is for this reason that a few precious seconds manage to trickle by before she notices the stench that invades her nostrils. She has no comparison, no point of reference for the disgusting odour because she is far too wealthy to have ever been within ten kilometres of an environment that could possibly produce smells of this potency.

Rubbish tips would be one. Or septic tanks. Abattoirs. But perhaps the most accurate description of the various revolting scents sending her recoiling at this precise moment would be the fumes of a killing field, littered with bodies strewn like autumn leaves, limbs either twisted at gruesome angles or scattered several metres from their former hosts. You could close your eyes, but the stench would still be there: overwhelming, overpowering, all-consuming. It is this putrid miasma that now floods Sasha Fairlane's six million-dollar mansion.

"Hong! What the *fuck* is this smell? Get this shit cleaned up right now or I will have you deported back to China so fast your moustache will hurt!"

Her maid, as it happens, is from Vietnam. The shadowing on her upper lip is the result of burns sustained in a cooking accident as a child. And her name, Huong, when pronounced correctly, actually means "perfume." Given the current circumstances, Huong might find this mispronunciation ironic, but for the fact that she is currently tied and gagged and trapped in the third-floor linen closet.

Sasha runs into the kitchen, assuming she will find Huong there. She does not see Huong. She sees blood, thick rivers of it. She sees guts, entrails, vast masses of torn and fractured flesh and fur.

And then she hears screeching. She turns and sees a pair of abominably deformed monkeys baring their teeth at her. Before her brain can even send the signal to her legs to start running they are on her; tearing, scratching, biting, clawing, screeching.

When photos of her mutilated face are posted on the Internet some hours later, user realgrrrl346 will comment:

> Well, at least her inner beauty matches her outer now.

13

A Gibbous Moon

Evelyn stands on the terrace, champagne glass clutched in gold- and diamond-adorned digits. She surveys the army of caterers and designers and photographers scurrying below. She is Cleopatra. She is Joan of Arc. She is Julius Caesar. This is her empire. The sun is sinking below the river, painting the sky pink with broad and confident strokes. Soon the guests will arrive. Everything must be perfect, like her son. Her masterpiece.

She turns and descends the staircase, sees Harland getting himself yet another drink from the dining room bar. "Harland, darling, let's save a few bottles for the guests, shall we?"

"We've got enough here to host the G8 summit five times over and you know it. Stop being a cow."

Evelyn bites her lip. She feels that familiar fury begin to burn, but now is not the time. Tonight must be perfect. "Harland, I would remind you of the importance of the occasion. Be civil for once in your life, you petulant, grey-haired dolt. This is about our boy. Our perfect boy."

Harland downs his drink with a speed that to others might be impressive but to Evelyn is merely vile, and says, "Yes. I'm glad we can agree on that at least. For all our strings of zeroes floating in space in bonds and bank accounts, I'd find the world a very dull and weary place without that boy. There's nothing in this life I'm half as proud of creating as Elijah."

"There, you see dear? You don't *have* to be a total cretin all the time, now do you?" Evelyn click-clacks across the floor to scream at the nearest caterer.

Harland pours another drink.

Freya surveys her collection of gloves before deciding on a stark white pair and then chooses a matching dress but with a classic thick black belt and oversized gold buckle. After selecting a red flower hairclip, she surveys the result in the mirror. She tries not to frown at the thighs she wants to believe are not too large but, minor flaws aside, she cuts a striking figure and she knows it.

"This oughta knock the socks off the lifestyles of the rich and crazy cast out there anyway," she mutters as she applies final touches of blush and lipstick, then goes downstairs to greet her date.

Beep.

Beep.

Beep.

"Oh, come on, Eli, that's what you always say. Today's your birthday, let's not be boring!" She has to admit that he does look devastatingly handsome in his tux. "I bet even unconscious you'd knock a few girls off their feet, hey, E? If ol' Rosaline wasn't likely to disembowel them with some sort of obscure home-shopping channel kitchen appliance immediately thereafter, of course."

Freya combs his hair and straightens his cuff links. "What the hell are you hiding in that sleepy little head of yours anyway?"

"Just the same cavalcade of lies and delusions as the rest of us."

Freya jolts and turns around to see Jack grinning in the doorway.

"Christ, you scared me!" Freya reminds herself that she really needs to start locking the door behind her. Jack is clad in his usual ripped jeans and black T-shirt, but tonight he's deigned to add a black jacket with rolled-up sleeves. He looks awkwardly handsome; black-framed glasses and a mosaic of bruises.

"Nice outfit."

He shrugs. "I don't need to dress up for these jerks. You know what kills me most about my parents' friends? They walk around acting like they own the world, and the sad thing is that's not far from the truth. These people own a lot of things, but they don't contribute anything new. They don't make, grow, create, or invent. They merge, acquire, downsize, and streamline."

"Doesn't Halcyon do exactly the same thing?"

"Not one to hold your tongue, are you? That's refreshing around here, I can tell you." Jack moves over to the bar and picks up two Peronis.

"I'm not ready to start drinking yet, still technically on duty, and all that."

"That's okay, these are both for me. As for Halcyon, if we're speaking candidly? The company my parents built must be one of the most unethical, aggressive, malevolent corporations on the planet. And the little sleeping prince here that they were grooming to take over would have only made things worse, if that's even possible. Until he went and fucked it all up, of course."

"You really feel that way?"

"You can't choose your parents, right? Otherwise I would have chosen Neil Gaiman and Jean Grey."

"Exactly what did Elijah do that was so bad? Was it the same thing that upset Rosaline—" Mentally, Freya adds a tally mark to the imaginary scoreboard where she keeps track of when her mouth has run ahead of her brain. Jack ignores the derailed sentence, walks past her and examines the wall of accolades and certificates. He puts the beers down on the windowsill and removes one of the two silver medals hanging from the wall.

"You know the medals from the last Winter Olympics contained recycled metal from old TVs, computers, and keyboards?

But that wasn't the most remarkable thing about them. For the first time in Olympic history the medals weren't flat, they were shaped into these undulating 3D patterns; they were supposed to evoke feelings of mountain ranges or waves on the ocean. The real genius of the design, though, was that if you looked at it from above, straight on, or, say, in a photograph, it would just look like a normal circular medal."

Freya looks at the elegant but very clearly flat silver medal in his hand. "But Elijah's medals are—"

"Very pretty, aren't they? Rosaline's very proud of her Elijah." He places the medal back on its hook, picks up his beers. "I know you have a lot of questions. You're going to find your answers in the Danger Room."

"Labelled in neat little boxes, I assume?"

"Can't say for sure. I've never seen inside there myself, but I know that's where you need to look. I'll even help you get in."

"Uh-huh. The question I'm obviously going to ask here is why are you telling me this?"

"The answer to which I'm obviously not going to tell you. At 11 p.m., the alarm system will be remotely reset and reconfigured to update the security software, so there will be no log recorded of entrances and exits. With a little sleight of hand, we'll be able to get in and no one will ever know."

"Why would I want to risk my job to break into my employer's private property?"

"I'm not exactly sure why, but I am sure that you will. Am I wrong?"

Curiosity has been scratching away at her for days. Gnawing. Chewing. Poking. Prodding. Not knowing what is inside that room is inconceivable. That, coupled with the urge to twist a hidden knife into Evelyn's back, is a temptation she has neither the willpower nor inclination to resist. Freya snatches one of the Peronis from Jack's hand and downs several quick gulps.

"Not about this, you aren't. Now help me wheel our little Adonis downstairs. We can't have our ball without its beau, can we?"

◇◇◇

The guests arrive promptly at seven. Hordes of Maseratis, Ferraris, Lamborghinis, and Mercedes vomit their cargo onto the Vincetti's driveway. Mountains of cleavage burst from the gowns of trophy wives and escorts, threatening to escape from their flimsy designer garments at any moment in a silicon storm.

Gifts that vary in size like cinema drinks—large, super large, ultra large, behemoth—are placed on the several tables orbiting the pool. The pile of gifts builds like a kaleidoscopic sacrifice to some sleeping pagan deity.

Freya has been instructed to act as the official greeter. She takes her place beside the drinks table to ensure optimal proximity to beverages. She manages to suppress the insistent voice that reminds her she didn't spend three years at university to be an over-glorified waitress with the counterargument that the aforementioned university years accumulated a financial debt that will be repaid much faster if said voice would kindly shut the fuck up.

She greets the guests with an admirable combination of restrained politeness and feigned interest that has been finely tempered over years of working with ungrateful, obstreperous patients who, in turn, often respond with a mixture of idle curiosity that brews and boils into pools of titillating gossip.

"I'm Freya, so lovely to meet you both."

"The pleasure is all mine, my dear. I'm Jim Crawfield, and this is my wife, Francesca, daughter of Frank Thorne, founder of the Sintomax Corporation."

These people talk like the twenty-first century Reader's Digest *edition of* Pride and Prejudice. *I just want to get into that damned room. Why can't you all drop dead like the stock prices of the various companies you control and leave the rest of us normal, mildly unattractive plebeians in peace?*

"–ineyard, you simply must come visit!"

"Of course! How kind of you to offer. I'd love to." Freya only manages to catch the end of the sterile, forced invitation as Jim leads his arm candy away. She hopes she has agreed to an empty promise of a weekend at a vineyard and not some high-class swingers' retreat.

"And you must be Freya?"

The Aphrodite in front of her wrenches Freya from her various neuroses. She is clad in an almost offensively simple sleek black dress coupled with an audacious necklace featuring a centrepiece diamond large enough to beat a man to death with. Black hair cascades down her shoulders, framing a face that has been chiselled to perfect alignment with the golden ratio through a combination of good genes and highly paid surgeons. Her figure is to die, lie, and kill for, and her eyes could bring a man to his knees, though whether it would be for him to offer her a marriage proposal or perform some other duty would depend entirely on the situation at hand.

"I must be. Lovely to meet you."

The woman raises one perfectly shaped eyebrow in query at the sight of Freya's gloves but takes her hand, though in a most ambiguous handshake. "I'm Yvette Rothwell. You're the new nurse, then?"

"Yes. I just started the other d—"

"Such a shame about the last girl, she was really quite sweet, you know? Not very clever, and far too curious for her own good, or anyone else's, but still…"

Freya bites her lip to avoid taking the unsubtly placed bait.

"Anyway, I assume you're getting along with the Vincettis, then? Aren't you such a lucky girl to be able to live in a place like this! I bet they spoil you!" Her tone is a practised blend of condescension and feigned congeniality.

"They've been very generous." *Aside from forcing me to put up with narcissistic, bourgeois…*

"So, are you with anyone tonight?"

"My partner, Callum, will be arriving soon. He's tied up with a business deal at the moment."

"I can't wait to meet him. What line of work is he in?"

"Carbon. He trades carbon. Right now, he's selling it to the Japanese. Conference call, to Tokyo, time difference and all that."

Yvette nods as her face twists into a simulacrum of a smile.

"Well, you will have to introduce me! Anyway, sweetie, I've just spotted Geoffrey, and I haven't seen him since gloves were still in fashion. Speak soon!"

Freya stabs a pair of retinal knives at Yvette's back as she saunters away, then downs her champagne and resists the urge to smash the crystal, electing instead to refill and depart from her post before she feels forced to kill someone.

She walks among the crowd of lawyers and bankers and CEOs and doctors and politicians and stockbrokers and real estate moguls and white-collar criminals. She notes the heads that turn as she passes and refuses to grind her teeth at the noses that rise in disapproval. Freya climbs the stairs to the second-floor balcony and watches the crowd shuffle and move about like so many pontifical ants. She feels distant and outside of herself, as though her life is a movie but she is the only one who has not yet read the script.

Footsteps approach behind her. She turns and sees Rosaline greeting her with a radiant, pearly-toothed grin. In spite of herself, Freya feels her tension release and she returns the smile. *She might be crazy enough to manufacture fake Olympic medals for her sleeping lover, but at least she's nice.*

"It's a lovely view up here, isn't it? I love when the moon is that shape. What's it called when it's big and round but not quite full?"

"Gibbous."

"That's it! Gibbous. It's so exciting, knowing that the big, beautiful full moon is coming. Watching it grow like a flower in time lapse. Don't you think it's gorgeous?"

Freya smiles. "Rosaline, can I ask you a question?"

"Of course!"

"How do you do it?"

"Do what?"

"How do you stay so fucking happy all the time?" Freya watches her flinch at the obscenity and would almost feel guilty if it weren't so ridiculous.

"Can I answer your question with a question?"

"You just did."

"What? Di—Oh, I see. Ha! Yes. That's funny. Well anyway, when you were a little girl, what did you want to be?"

"I wanted to be a nurse, like Florence Nightingale, and a painter, like Kandinsky. I planned to spend long summer days throwing the colours in my mind onto the canvas in front of me and my nights curing the sick and saving the world."

"Right, well, when I was a little girl I just…I always wanted to have a family, and be a mum. My childhood was…Well, I was very lucky. At first. Then things…umm…" Rosaline plays anxiously with the pearls around her neck and says, "I wasn't always called Rosaline, you know." Freya's eyebrows briefly ascend her forehead in response to this little revelation.

"When I was little, my dad's company made dolls. We were so happy, me and Mum and him. I guess you could say we were the model nuclear family! Well, for a little while, anyway…" The-artist-formerly-not-known-as-Rosaline's voice trails off quietly before she continues brightly, "Anyway, he let me name all the dolls which, as a little girl, was like having all my wishes come true! There was Angela Swansong and Laura St Clair and Anastasia Evergreen, but my all-time favourite turned out to be the most popular doll by far, Rosaline Redfeather. I named her after Rosaline in *Romeo and Juliet*, because Romeo praised her so highly, he was so completely in love with her, then he cast her aside and then…but that's a whole other story. In any case, Rosaline Redfeather was the most successful doll Dad's company ever made. Nearly every little girl had at least one."

"I remember those! I think my aunty gave me one for my birthday." Freya neglects to mention that she had subsequently employed the doll in a backyard BB-gun ballistics game.

"Oh, how lovely! So, you know it then. Such beautiful skin, such bright blue eyes! Well, when I was born, Mum and Dad gave me a horrid, boring name. I always hated it. I never felt like it suited me, like wearing big clunky shoes as a child that your parents insist you will grow into but by the time you do they're all worn out anyway. And then…this, you know, this thing happened and my family changed. Yes, I suppose changed is the right word, isn't it? I decided that I didn't want my old name anymore. I didn't want to be that *person* anymore. I didn't like her failures, her shortcomings, her, her...um...trials and tribulations...and so I changed my name to Rosaline."

"Your parents didn't mind you choosing a new name?"

"Well, they were, you know, at that time, they um...they were worried about other things. So I focused on becoming what I'd always wanted to be: glamorous, refined, pretty. All those things. It helped keep my mind away from...everything else. And now I've got nearly everything I'd ever hoped for! I live in a great house, with a family that looks after me, and new friends!"

Freya accepts Rosaline's hug in the same manner a death row prisoner accepts their fate. When Rosaline has finished enveloping Freya in a storm of pink-drenched saccharine affection, she pulls back and continues, "And, of course, I've got my Prince Charming! And soon children, starting a family of my own, what more could a girl want, right?"

What more could a girl have wanted in 1853, perhaps.

"Just like the family I should've had as a child, before everything got...messy. That's why I still keep all the dolls I had as a kid, why I need a whole room for them. I have every type of Rosaline Redfeather, from Summer Fun Outfit to What's Cookin'? to my favourite, Magic Wedding Dress Rosaline. And one day I'll wear a dress and it will be just like hers. Perfect."

Freya tries and fails to think of something appropriate to say, so she elects to squeeze Rosaline's hand in sympathy.

Rosaline beams at her. "Oh, dear. Look at me blathering away with my whole life story! You seem a little down, is there something you wanted to talk about?"

"It's nothing. One of the guests rubbed me the wrong way, that's all. Yvette Rothwart or something. That bitch really puts the 'super' in 'superficial'."

Rosaline bites her lip, hard. Freya sees a tremor run through her, like a road beneath the weight of a passing truck, and then very quickly Rosaline is shaking so hard that she has to put her glass down before she drops it. Her face is flushed violent red and her eyes look as though they are about to pop right out of her skull.

"She is a complete *cunt*!" The word blurts out of her like a grenade and smacks Freya so hard she nearly stumbles. Rosaline sags with the effort. "Oh! Oh! My goodness! Forgive me! I shouldn't! I mustn't...I have to go!" She runs down the hall as if every ruler-toting nun on Earth is chasing after her, demanding her penance.

Excerpt from *The Sins of Adonis*

I think what surprised me was the complete lack of regret. The act itself was almost irritatingly simple to complete. A bribe here and there, a few phone calls to the right people. I even bought a special black sporting outfit especially for the occasion. I'm starting to think about wearing the shirt, still stained with his blood, to the funeral. Underneath a jacket, of course.

The most revolting part was the gargling sound he made when I slipped the knife through him. God, it lasted for an aeon and change. Thank goodness the lonely bastard lived by himself. It was over quickly. A little too quickly, perhaps. Next time, I think I might try something a little slower, give myself time to savour the moment. The Chinese are good at that sort of thing, aren't they? Might need to do some research before I pick my next quarry. I wonder where one can purchase chloroform nowadays?

14

Aristocrackheads

Freya looks back over at the crowd beneath her, thinking that this would be the perfect place to start picking people off with a sniper rifle, if one were so inclined. In the distance she spies headlights cutting through the darkness and makes her way down the stairs to greet her fashionably-late-as-per-fucking-usual best friend.

As she weaves through the crowd, she feels a hand placed gently but decisively on her shoulder.

"Freya?"

"Hi, Harland."

"Enjoying yourself, I trust?"

"Yes! Of course! You Vincettis throw a mean shindig."

He smiles and drains his glass. There's a sway in his step and it's barely after eight. "Thank you. The band will be starting soon. I trust I can rely on you to join me for a dance?" He looks at her and through her at the same time.

"Sure, why not? Listen, I have to go meet my friend. I'll find you later."

She runs towards Callum's car without waiting to see the reaction she's provoked. Hopefully Harland's too busy getting drunk and chasing the several dozen other young women on his dance card to be troubled by her hurried departure.

Callum passes his car keys to the valet and waves at her.

"Well, look who finally gets around to showing their offensively good-looking face."

"What? It's barely after eight! I would have thought it rude to show up any earlier than an hour after suggested arrival."

Freya grabs him by the hand and pulls him towards the house.

"Cal, it's like I told you eleven and a half million times already, rich middle-aged people have a whole different set of party etiquette to us plebs. Arrive at seven *means* arrive at seven."

"I wasn't aware that we were so beholden to other people's social standards."

"Cal, I fucking live here. I could hardly show up late with a reasonable excuse, now could I? Which means I've spent an hour in the company of a bunch of self-important aristocrackheads talking about their vineyards and Fabergé egg collections and holidays on islands where they won't even stamp your passport unless you own a Picasso."

"I didn't realise."

"That's alright, you can make it up to me by pretending you're my carbon-trading boyfriend and you've just gotten off a conference call to Tokyo."

"What? When?"

"Here. Now."

"So! This must be the lucky man!" Yvette appears as quickly and unexpectedly as a warning light on a cockpit dashboard.

"Callum, this is Yvette Rothwell."

"How was your conference call? Successful, I trust?"

"Very. We've acquired a great deal of carbon. And…sold a lot, too. Which is good, obviously, to be both selling and acquiring. Much better than just selling. Or just acquiring. Better to do both."

"So, the time difference doesn't bother your business too much, then?"

"Well, no, the global age and all that. What with the Internet and, er, Bluetooth and the synergising of global interfaces and so forth."

"Yes, I see. Although, it's odd that you would conduct business with Tokyo at this time of night, given they are only an hour behind."

Freya nearly buckles. *Should have fucking thought of that*, she swears internally, hoping the fallout of the collapsing lie won't entomb both her and Callum before the diamond-clad black widow is done.

"Anyhow, thirsty work. I need a drink. Freya?"

"Moscow Mule please, make it a double. Bar's over that way."

Callum nods, acknowledging that he knows this means she wants a triple.

Yvette's eyes settle back on Freya as though she is sizing her up for a body bag. "Soooo, Freya. He's quite a catch."

"I'm a lucky girl," she replies, while searching for the closest implement she could conceivably use to perform a covert Cluedo-style murder.

"So, are you and Elijah getting along well then?"

"Yes. Of course."

"It must be a very...special bond, the rapport between carer and patient."

"It is, yes."

"I'm not sure if you know this, but Elijah and I used to be...very close." The tiny pause between her words sufficiently explains exactly how, at the mere mention of Yvette's name, Rosaline transformed from "sweet and coy" into "burn and destroy."

"Such a tragedy, that accident. And poor, dear Rosaline when she found out about what he'd done."

Freya inhales sharply as she waits for the explanation, but finds her attention abruptly captured by a burst of fireworks. She watches them shower and flare and fade. This is the one time when everyone else sees the world the same way she does:

filled with light and colour and energy rippling in streams and exploding through the air. Usually she is glad to have her little Kandinskys, her private way of viewing the world in constant coloured cacophony, but sometimes, just sometimes, she wishes everyone else could see life the way she does. Of course, the world happens to think the same thing about her.

Callum returns and hands her a triple-strength Moscow Mule and they clink glasses. For a moment Freya forgets Yvette and Evelyn and Harland and all the trials, tribulations, and temptations that fill her life and just enjoys watching the cascade of colours with her best friend, drink in hand. Minutes later the last green flash cuts a luminous swathe across the sky and the final "oohs" and "aahs" fade out like the finale of an old Motown song. Freya is about to attempt to pry a few tantalising hints about Elijah's accident from Yvette's forked tongue when the string quintet launches into a series of ecstatic and swirling crescendos. Freya's vision is swarmed by green and purple, and she staggers to regain her balance.

Yvette's perfectly manicured claws descend gently on her as she sways. "Oh, darling, are you alright? Perhaps that cocktail was a little too rich for your palate?"

Freya is about to wrench the diamond from Yvette's neck and beat her over the head with it when she hears Harland's voice booming out of the speakers behind them. He's on the second-floor balcony, waving, with Evelyn standing beside him as though he were a monarch addressing his subjects.

"Ladies and gentlemen! Thank you once again for gracing us with your presence. It's been too long since I've seen most of you, and not long enough since I've seen others."

Begrudging, scattered laughter. Harland coughs and continues.

"Well, it's been a little more than four months since our favourite son had his tragic accident..."

From anyone else's mouth, naming a favourite of two sons in front of a crowd of hundreds would be offensive. For Harland, it is no more unusual than reciting a shopping list.

"You all know our boy's long list of achievements, his work with AIDS victims in Rwanda, a two-time silver medallist at the Olympic Games, his support of Amnesty International, his work for Médecins Sans Frontières, his inspiring compositions. For one so young, he achieved more than any of us could hope to equal in several lifetimes. Elijah, the heir of the Vincetti family empire and legacy that has been a proud cornerstone of this city for one hundred and sixty-five years, struck down by the cruel hand of fate—"

"He really needs to hire a better speechwriter. He sounds like a drunk B-grade celebrity making a speech at a charity gala," whispers Freya.

Callum spurts both vodka and laughter, drawing glares from the aristocrankies around him.

"When Elijah had his accident, I thought none of us would ever recover from the shock. Luckily, that wasn't the case. We've worked together as a family, and slowly he's been healing, as have we. I have every confidence that, maybe even sooner than any of us had dared to hope, he'll be back to full strength. And now, without further ado, it's time to bring out the guest of honour!"

The doors of the main atrium spring open and Rosaline appears with her trademark real estate agent smile. She waves with a nervous giggle and then runs back inside, before reappearing with Elijah, looking comfortably numb from the safety of his luxury mobile bed, which is lined with plush velvet and adorned with sterling silver trim.

Silence descends on the crowd; a sort of awkward ectoplasm that smothers and shifts across the assembly. Finally, two hands meet in a timid collision, and within moments the clap spreads until the whole crowd is applauding.

From the balcony Harland begins to sing, "Haaaaaa…" and that first telltale syllable leads the whole crowd into singing.

"Happy birthday to you…"

Freya and Callum stare at each other as though they are bearing witness to a human sacrifice.

"Am I the only one who thinks that every one of these people is crazy?" whispers Callum.

"No, I think they know how barking mad this whole thing is. I think it's just an Emperor's New Clothes type of thing. Everyone looks so awkward," Freya replies.

"How much did you say they were paying you?"

"Not enough, I'm starting to think."

As the crowd begins to launch into "For He's a Jolly Good Fellow," Freya hisses, "Are you kidding me? How long is this going to go on for?"

Madonna's voice blares from Callum's pocket. "Seriously, Cal, even your phone has bad taste in music."

"Screw you. Hello? Yep. What? Hang on a second, I can't hear you." Callum ducks behind one of the trees to talk in private. Freya watches the farcical fanfare unravel in front of her as the last voices die down and the string quintet takes over. The crowd is noticeably relieved when they are allowed to return to mingling. Freya sneaks away and sits on the garden swing chair outside the kitchen doors.

"Fancy seeing you here."

"Jack! How nice of you to show up. Some party you've got going on here. There's so much eye candy I think I'm getting ocular diabetes."

He throws her an impish grin. She has to admit he can be quite charming when he's not being a strange, nervous introvert. Although, she thinks, he does look a little off-colour. "Are you okay, you look a little pale and sweaty?"

"Oh, no, it's ah…it's nothing. Just, you know, allergies. I get like this when I go outside sometimes. Just trying to reinforce that reclusive writer stereotype, you know." He's not a good liar, but Freya doesn't feel like pushing. "Haven't you missed your flight?"

"What?"

"It's 10:23. Wasn't your flight to Timor due to leave a few minutes ago?"

"Yes, it was."

"Guess you're stuck here with me, then," he says with a grin.

"Could be worse."

They glance back up at Harland waving from the balcony like a jovial dictator.

"You didn't feel like making an appearance on the podium before all of Harland's loyal subjects?" asks Freya.

"God, no. I hate public speaking. Actually, I hate the public in general. Plus, I wouldn't want to detract from any of Eli's attention; it is his oh-so-special day, after all." His sarcasm almost masks the traces of bitter contempt.

"I guess not."

"Who's the boy?"

"That's my best friend, Callum. But if Yvette asks, he's my carbon-trading boyfriend."

Jack twitches slightly, then nods.

"But we're not…you know…He's actually gay. I just wanted to mess with her. I can't really explain why."

"She tends to bring out the worst in people. Personally, I wouldn't let that vile vixen within spitting distance unless, of course, it was for the express purpose of spitting on her."

Freya laughs. "You bitter, jaded man."

"Like I said, it goes with the trade."

"Jack, you'll have to forgive me for being blunt…"

"I'd be disappointed if you were anything else."

"Well, good. Don't you think all this is a bit fucking weird? Don't your parents think that maybe Elijah isn't really getting all that much out of the festivities held in his honour?"

Jack smiles. Nods. Sighs. "I have, numerous times in the past months, attempted to broach the subject with Lord and Lady Vincetti. The result was like shaking a sleepwalker carrying an armful of knives. Eventually, giving up on talking sense seemed like the only sensible option. Besides, they don't have a lot of time to focus on the lesser child when the golden boy is in such a delicate state. The Lord and Lady are perfectly comfortable as monarchs of their own private kingdom of delusion."

"Delusion can be a powerful thing. Have you ever seen Marilyn Monroe? We spotted her the other night, in the city."

Freya elects to leave out the part where her car became intimately acquainted with a pole while she was escaping from a pair of enraged delinquents.

"What do you mean, Marilyn Monroe? 'Happy Birthday, Mr President' and all that?"

"Yes. You've never seen her?"

"I don't get out much these days. The world outside has too many street marketers and discount food outlets for my liking. I prefer the world inside my head."

"Okay, point taken. In any case, she's been around a long time. She dresses like the real Marilyn, and I don't just mean the odd feather boa and set of killer high heels. I mean she cakes on the makeup, the beauty spot, the accessories. Even the way she walks, it's uncanny. Every time I see her she's in a different knockout get-up. The sad thing is, though, the real Marilyn died so young that in a way she immortalised her beauty. She never grew old and gained weight or wrinkles or grey hair. For this Marilyn, the years haven't been so kind. She's getting older and wider, there's this incredible sadness that lurks beneath the thick coats of makeup, like every day the reality is slowly overtaking the fantasy."

"It's like the old cliché: tell a lie for long enough and you will start to believe it. Sometimes people can focus so intently on constructing the walls of their fantasies that the real world starts to matter less and less, until it becomes nothing but a backdrop. Given time, they just mix and match the parts of reality that fit the fantasy."

"So, what about you then, what's your dream?"

Jack's eyes dart towards the cluster of party guests bustling around Elijah and Rosaline. He grimaces. "My whole life is a dream. I'm a writer. I deal in fantasy and delusion. It's the real world that terrifies me."

Laughter erupts from the group of revellers gathered around Elijah's bed. Rosaline throws her arms up in the air and shrieks with joy.

"Some party your family throws, and quite a crowd. I bet every yacht club and Masonic centre in town is empty tonight."

"They aren't my kind of people."

"And who exactly are your kind of people, Jack?"

"When I find out, I'll let you know. But in the meantime, I wouldn't mind getting to know you a little better..."

"Why Jack, are you—?"

Freya is interrupted by Callum's return. He slips his phone into his pocket as he swigs champagne. "Sorry, Frey. Sam was having a relationship crisis. Again."

"That's okay. Callum, this is Jack Vincetti."

"How lovely to meet you. This is a fabulous home you have. I was wondering, Jack, what with you being filthy rich and all, how is it that we don't see more of you in the media?"

"I prefer to keep to myself. I've never been fond of bright lights and red carpets."

"And what exactly are you fond of?"

"Cal-lum. Could you please behave yourself for a few hundred seconds? Gentlemen, if you'll excuse me for a moment I have to go powder my nose, or whatever euphemism women are supposed to employ for needing to piss these days. Be good, both of you."

She pushes through the crowd of Armani- and Versace-clad revellers. The guests have relaxed a little now; champagne has loosened ties and tongues. Eyelashes are batted, lips are licked, and boasts are being made. The air is thick with arrogance and innuendo.

We're all just teenage boys and girls trying to get laid. The bicycle tricks get replaced with luxury cars, and the bragging of girls making out with girls gets replaced with plunging designer necklines. But it's all the same game, played with different equipment.

She closes the door behind her and admires her surroundings. It's quiet in here. Calm. Still. She sits down and "powders her nose." The quiet trickling echoes around the marble and red interior of the room. Freya flushes and checks her reflection in the mirror. It confirms the beauty people keep telling her she possesses. Her hair is strikingly red under the bright fluorescent light.

She unlocks the door and is about to open it when it bursts towards her, sending her sprawling back onto the bathroom floor. A hand reaches down to her.

"My apologies, Freya. I shouldn't have been so clumsy." Harland's voice is slurred but confident.

She takes his hand and he pulls her up. His grip is firm and strong. "No problem, Harland. Great party."

She pushes to get past him as quickly as politeness will allow but he grabs her shoulder and says, "You want to share a little party powder with me? It's good stuff, imported directly by an Argentinean colleague."

"Thanks, but I don't think I should."

"I won't tell Evelyn, I promise. She'd go ballistic if she found out I had any myself, you know."

"No, Harland. I'm not interested."

Harland looks at her with unwavering eyes that are very much accustomed to acquiring whatever they desire. They travel down the contours of her chest and thighs and then back up again in a markedly unhurried fashion. Harland's lips curl upwards. "You sure about that?"

Freya reaches for the door and wrenches it open, then hurls herself outside. She straightens her dress, scratches at the itchy red patch of skin on her wrist and makes her way towards the bar.

15

The Danger Room

Freya resists the urge to charge straight back to the only two people in this collection of walking stock portfolios who she feels she can even remotely trust. She nearly collapses with relief when she finds Jack nursing a drink by the main entrance. He looks nervous and ill at ease, his head darting around like a meerkat looking out for predators.

"You took your time," he says.

"Don't even start. Where's Callum?"

"Phone call again. You okay?"

"Not even slightly. Can we get out of here?"

"Sure. Roof?"

"God, yes."

Jack takes her hand and leads her back through the crowd. She snatches a beer from a drinks tray as they move around the back of the house in what feels like a series of Escher-inspired tableaux before reaching the ladder that takes them onto the roof. Jack goes up first, and she is equal parts annoyed and impressed when he offers his hand down to her for a second time. She obliges and he pulls her up. They survey the inebriated battlefield below.

"Do you think they'll see us up here?" asks Freya.

"I think they're all too blinded by narcissism and their eye-fucking of each other's wives to be bothered by us."

They listen to the distant laughter and watch the crowd orbiting among a constellation of candles below.

"Jack, if you hate it here so much, why don't you leave?"

He doesn't answer for a while. For so long in fact that she wonders if he has even heard her. She is considering whether or not to repeat herself when he says, "I could ask you the same thing."

"You could, but I asked you first."

Jack shrugs and replies, "Where else would I go?"

"What do you mean? It's not like you're strapped for cash. You could go anywhere."

"Frey, I don't like the thought of faraway places. I spend too much time inside my own head to worry about what might be going on anywhere else. It's safe here. Comfortable. And besides, who would I go away with? I don't know anyone."

"You could meet new people?"

"No, thanks. A stranger is just a jerk you haven't met yet. I find it hard to get to know people. Vice versa, I guess."

"I'd go away with you, if it was somewhere fun. And you know me."

"That's true. But you don't know me."

"Oh, please, don't play that stupid introspective-melancholic-artist card with me. I'm a painter, remember? I've spent far too much time around boys who cry into their red wine to get girls to open their hearts...and legs."

Jack laughs. "You've met my family, right? We've each got more than our fair share of neuroses and psychoses; I'm just a little better at concealing mine. Take my father, for example."

"I'd rather not," she snaps.

"What do you mean?"

Freya plays with the label of her beer. Peels it off. Rolls it into a ball. Flicks it. "He made a suggestion to me." The words creep tentatively out of her mouth.

"He said something to you?"

"Well, not explicitly."

"But…?"

"He was hitting on me."

Jack rises slowly to his feet, surveys the crowd and then smashes his beer bottle against the roof tiles. "I'm going to slam his fucking face into a brick wall."

Freya grabs his arm. "Jack! It's very chivalrous of you to get all knight-in-shining-armour on me but I can handle myself, okay? He made the offer, I turned it down, end of story. It was gross and if it happens again I'll quit or sue or write a memoir about it and promote it on daytime talk shows or whatever, but you don't need to go spoiling your brother's party just so you can get vindication."

"Frey, are you serious? It's disgusting! The fact that he would try that on, with Evelyn a few hundred metres away—"

"Hey, point taken, okay? But it's like I said, he put the offer out, I turned it down. He didn't try and force anything. It was disgusting, but I've been propositioned by plenty of silver foxes before, although they're usually wearing hospital dressing-gowns and hopped up on morphine, not clad in Armani and blasting coke. He was being a prick, but he was clearly higher than a hippie in a dirigible. I really just wanted to vent about it, so can you please be my shoulder to cry on without trying to be my knight on a white horse?"

He frowns and looks out across the festivities below. Ripples of laughter travel towards them. His teeth grind. His fists clench and unclench. Freya suddenly feels scared and uneasy seeing him like this. "If he touches you again, I'll kill him." He states these words not as a threat, but as a simple fact, like a scientist explaining a chemical reaction.

"Okay, okay I get it. You're angry. Will you please just sit with me for a minute?"

Reluctantly, he resumes his place beside her. "I get a little carried away sometimes."

"It's okay. Happens to the best of us, and to the rest of us."

"Would you really come away with me?"

"Maybe. Would you want me to?"

"Yes."

Freya slides off her gloves, slowly and carefully. She places her scarred hand within his. It feels good to do this. Comfortable. Safe. Welcoming. Her hand finds refuge in his.

"There's a lot we haven't told you," he says. "I haven't told you. About Elijah. His accident. What happened before the accident. Some of it's because I can't, some of it's because I wasn't sure if I could trust you, and some of it's because I honestly don't know."

"What wouldn't you know about your own brother?"

"You mean apart from everything? Think about it; he was twenty-seven, and he was a Winter Olympian, a doctor, a composer, a humanitarian. Does nothing about that strike you as strange?"

"Yes. But I think I've been too preoccupied with all the other kinds of strange in this house to be able to fully process it yet."

"We need to get into that room."

"Now?"

"Now. The security records are about to go offline and all the guests are distracted. Look." Jack removes a wallet from his pocket and flips it open. A photo of Harland's sombre face pops out at her.

"You stole your dad's wallet? What are you, a fifteen-year-old delinquent in a movie of the week?"

"I'd like to think I'd rate at least straight to video release. But this is what I'm after." He removes a slim black keycard with similar dimensions to the white one Freya keeps in her pocket.

"Will that get us in?"

"That, and the PIN, and the retinal scan of a family member."

Freya downs the last of her drink and smashes it on the roof, its debris joining Jack's.

"Well, Mr Vincetti, I can't think of anyone else I'd rather accompany me while committing a minor felony. Shall we?"

He grins and scrambles down the ladder. "You'll need to keep watch."

"Why do I have to be watchman? Or girl?" She follows him and then scrambles along the hallway and down the stairs as he says, "I have to open the lock with the retinal scan."

"How come they don't give you permission to open this thing yourself anyway?"

"Anytime you feel like asking Lord or Lady Vincetti that question, you go right ahead."

"Alright, fine. I'll be lookout while you scout around, but then we swap, okay?"

"Sure. Pass me the keycard."

Blip.

Jack places his eye against the scanner and a red laser light trawls over it. Freya bounces nervously on her feet, listening to the sounds of revelry outside, praying that no one approaches and trying not to think about what would happen if they got caught.

SCAN COMPLETE

ACCESS GRANTED: ELIJAH VINCETTI

"What? 'Elijah'? Why would—?"

"I don't know. Must be some kind of computer error, probably something to do with the system update. Keep watch, I'll be right out." The door eases open with a series of hissing and clicking sounds that pop like a Fruit Loops commercial in front of Freya's eyes.

"Hurry up!" she whispers urgently after him. Adrenaline slams through her system, her pulse and breath quicken.

"What the fuck?" says Jack.

"What is it?"

"I think it's down here!" a voice calls from along the hall.

"Shit! Jack, someone's coming!"

"Stall them! I just need a minute!"

Freya's head is dizzy with dissimulations. She starts forward, feigning a limp. As she rounds the corner she bumps into a giggling grey-suited man and a woman who, at first, appears as if she is being consumed by some gigantic animal but is simply wearing an oversized fur coat. The two are leaning into each other, whispering and laughing like a pair of high-school lovers.

The woman notices her and says, "Hi there, sweetie, we're looking for the bathr—"

"Argh!" Freya yelps, clutching at her ankle.

"Are you okay?" asks the man.

"Ahh…I think so. I was looking for the bathroom, too, and I opened a door hoping to find it, and there was my boyfriend, Callum, with some bitch wearing a diamond the size of a baby's head. She had him pinned against the wall and he was pushing her away and she just grabbed at his crotch! Callum pushed her off him, then she saw me and came running past and shoved me to the floor. I think I may have twisted my ankle. Callum's gone to fetch me some ice…but I can't bear the thought of that succubus out there leeching on some other woman's man. Do you know the one?"

The couple look at each other with a knowing gaze and the man answers, "Any man with a stock portfolio and a pulse has found himself colliding with Yvette Rothwell at some point. Don't worry, dear, she's a well-known trollop. I'm sure your man's not the least to blame. Can we help you?"

"If you could find my Callum and bring him here? This place is like a maze and he has no sense of direction. I'm quite sure he's got lost."

"Our pleasure, darling. Do look after yourself," the woman says, wrapping her fur around herself and steering the man back towards the garden.

When they are safely distant Freya runs back to the door of the Danger Room and calls out, "For fuck's sake, Jack, let's go!" She reaches the door just as he is escaping out of it and, in the second before it slams shut, she glimpses inside.

The room is dark.

"Okay, well, that wasn't as enlightening as I had hoped," Jack murmurs, fumbling to remove his hand from his pocket.

"What did you find?"

"Nothing really. It was dark, couldn't find the light switch. Staggered around for a little bit, bumped into a chair. It felt like it might be an old storeroom. There're half a dozen other rooms in this house exactly like it."

"That doesn't make any sense. Why would they keep a storeroom locked up like that?"

"I'm guessing there must be a safe or something hidden in there. We'll have to come back and try another time."

"Why don't we just look now? I didn't even see—"

"Did you hear that? I think—"

"Freya!" calls Callum. "Where in the four-letter word have you been? I've been looking for you for an hour. Some woman wearing a Chewbacca costume told me not to worry about Yvette and that you'd hurt your leg but you'd be okay?"

"Cal! There you are," Freya sighs.

"Yes, but where the fuck have you been?"

"I should leave you two," Jack mumbles as he scurries away. "I'll chat to you later," he says over his shoulder.

"No! Jack! Wait, I don't...well. That was rude."

Freya looks up at Callum and smiles. "You know, when you're really upset you get this little wrinkle right in the centre of your forehead that is completely adorable."

"Is that your attempt at an apology? I got stuck talking to some guy about European handball, the world's dumbest sport, for half an hour. I now have knowledge swilling about in my brain I need to supplant with alcohol and trashy TV at the earliest opportunity."

"I know, Cal. Tonight has been twelve kinds of horrible. I promise I'll explain once my head stops spinning."

They embrace and she relaxes in the comfort of his arms. For a few seconds she blocks out all three hundred sixteen thoughts of fear, concern, and anxiety currently bombarding her.

"Drinks?" he suggests.

"And how! Let's go onto the r—. Oh hi, Evelyn. Great party."

Evelyn is framed by the flicker of candlelight behind her, making her features sharp and accented by shadow. "What was Jack frowning about? He looked appallingly morose. More so than usual."

"Uh…I think he lost his keys," Freya says, the lie shuffling feebly out of her lips.

"That boy. Always frowning and moping, you'd think he was eternally fifteen. Would it be too much for him to fake a smile for the few hours of his brother's birthday party?" She appears to notice Callum for the first time. "And you would be?"

"I would be Callum. Lovely to meet you, Mrs Vincetti. You have a magnificent home."

She eyes him like she is sizing up prey.

"Indeed. Callum, would you be so kind as to excuse us for a moment? We need to have a talk, girl to girl. Someone like you should know what that means."

Callum keeps his expression resolutely blank as he nods, then offers a curt smile and backs away. When Evelyn turns her back to him he mimes to Freya over the woman's shoulder, "I don't like her!" and draws a finger angrily across his neck. He disappears around the corner.

Evelyn asks, "Enjoying yourself?"

"Very much so. You Vincettis really know how to throw a pa—"

"Yvette told me she saw you coming out of the bathroom. Followed closely by Harland. Is that true?" she says, each word an icicle.

"Look, Evelyn, I'm sure I'm not too far out of line if I say that Yvette is about as trustworthy as a mob witness—"

"Is. It. True? I can always tell a lie."

Freya stares into her vicious green eyes, experiencing a hateful glare she's certain is familiar to dozens of Evelyn's prior targets.

"Nothing happened. I promise."

The wrenching of her head backwards is as disorienting as it is painful. Clutched between Evelyn's fingernails, Freya's hair looks like a fistful of fire.

"I *know* Harland. If I found out you touched him, or let him touch you, then the consequences will be far more dire than a mere loss of employment. I am a very powerful and influential woman, Freya. I have friends in both high and low places, and I always, always get what I want. Are we clear?"

"We are."

Evelyn's hand slips from Freya's hair and slides back to her side. "Good. That will be all. Rosaline will be caring for Elijah for the rest of the night. Enjoy your evening."

A fresh anger is blossoming in Freya's chest. She looks back at the locked door. *Evelyn isn't the only one who always gets what she wants.*

16

We Have to Save the Penguins!

It's quiet in the room, the air imbued with an eerie stillness. Not the stillness of funerals, but of hospital waiting rooms at three a.m. A quiet, sickly absence of motion. This is his kingdom, as it were.

In this bustling, outré house, this room is the most calm. There is one clock but it has long since stopped working and no one has ever seen the point in mending or replacing it. The only sound comes from his so-called "beepers." Constant. Rhythmic. The sounds of his heart amplified for all to hear.

Beep.

Beep.

Beep.

Outside the door, footsteps approach.

A hand presses against the door and opens it. The owner of the hand enters with a quiet purpose, glances furtively around the room, closes the door and pushes a chair under the door handle. He's been doing this far longer than Freya. He crosses himself in a mock religious gesture and says, "Forgive me brother, it's been twenty-nine years since my last confession." He stands next to the sleeping figure and strokes his hair. "You got all the good looks, you know that? You pull that perfect jaw and chiselled features card and what do I get from the genetic wheel of fortune? This... condition that I can't explain or endure or even fucking..."

He stops his sentence and calms himself. A breath. A pause. He rubs at the bruises on his arms that incessantly migrate from one part of his fragile form to another. "Some party last night, huh? Fireworks, champagne, string ensemble. Like something out of a Baz Luhrmann film. For my last birthday, our revered progenitors gave me a blender. Three weeks late, but still. Partial credit to them for eventually remembering, I suppose, though demerits for forgetting they gave me the same blender the year before, so I guess that's a wash.

"Yvette was there, of course. She had quite a run-in with Freya; you should have seen it. She's a lot more impressive than that French girl we had tending your wounds. I certainly wouldn't say no if she offered to sponge-bath me as well, just quietly."

"*Haaarrrland*!" Evelyn's unmistakable shriek reverberates through the house.

"That sounds like trouble, doesn't it?" He crouches next to the bed and examines the web of wires and machines. "I wonder how many African kids could access clean drinking water if their village had the money they're dropping daily here to keep your shiny wax husk looking crisp and clean?"

Beep.

Beep.

Beep.

"I've thought about bringing an end to those bloody beeps before, you know. More than once. Taking that custom-made pillow and pressing it over your sickeningly handsome face. Sometimes, I wonder if you'd convulse, or gasp, or just be the same as always? I'm not really sure how these things work. I'd never actually go through with it, of course. I'm a writer, I'm supposed to fantasise, never actualise." A quiet pause. "God, I hate it here sometimes."

He stands up, looking at nothing.

"I finally made it into the Danger Room. Not quite what I anticipated. But then again, I was half-expecting a ritually sacrificed goat in the centre of a pentagram and a couple of suitcases of heroin, so that's probably a bonus. I found a little souvenir, though. I think Freya caught me. Hopefully that won't get me into too much trouble.

"Remember after your sixth birthday party how we went into the Darrell Lea store and stole a few pocketfuls of caramel snow bars? It felt almost the same. That same rush…equal parts excitement and fear. By the time we got those things home, I barely cared about them, I was just happy we got away with it. You were different, though. You hoarded them like trophies. Like a serial killer keeping their victims' nail clippings. You were weird even then."

Beep.

Beep.

Beep.

"I don't hate you, you know. Even though I want to. We're still brothers, right?" He runs his hand along Elijah's cheek. "Then again, so were Cain and Abel."

His hands clench and unclench by the side of the bed. There is a whole day of anxiety and uncertainty ahead of him, and he hasn't the slightest inkling of how to deal with that prospect. "Well, I expect you've got a lot of beeping to get on with so I won't keep you. I should get back to not writing, not cleaning, and not exercising anyway."

He moves towards the door. He pauses, looks back.

"I think I'm probably going to tell her. About what happened. Not just yet, but soon." He pulls the chair away from the door and quickly exits.

Elijah is alone.

◇◇◇

Freya's hangover is almost comforting. That banging, ringing feeling in her head usually reminds her of a brilliant night of revelry, or at least that she drank herself half to death trying to have a good time. She groans and reaches for the glass next to her bed and drinks it quickly, then spurts it out just as rapidly when she realises it is riesling, not water.

"Fuck!" she shrieks. At least white wine won't stain the sheets.

She checks the space in the bed next to her out of habit, finding it thankfully unoccupied. This much, at least, is a relief. And then, in sharp and jarring jolts, last night's memories assail her.

Freya clutches her face with her hands. She isn't due to tend to Elijah for several hours. The decision to bury herself beneath the blankets and read Anaïs Nin is as immediate as it is satisfying.

She glances at her phone on her bedside table and picks it up, spying a torrent of texts laden with Where are you?s and Why haven't you called me?s. She chooses to ignore these, but can't go past a message from Jane: OMG did you hear about those poor penguins?

She flips open her laptop and looks at the morning's headlines: *"Celebrity debutante arrested at airport with 2kg of cocaine," "Scientists unlock the secret to happiness: are you eating enough asparagus?," "Politician caught in scandal with colleague's underage daughter,"* and finally, *"Worst oil spill since 2010 puts thousands of penguins in danger."*

> A massive oil spill on the coast of Patagonia early this morning has left thousands of penguins covered in oil. Environmental groups fear that as many as 30,000 Magellanic penguins may freeze to death if they are not attended to immediately.

How can a penguin freeze to death? Freya thinks, just before a scream stabs into her ears.

"*Haaaaarrrrlllaaaand*!" This is followed by frenzied yells exchanged between Evelyn, Maria, Harland, and Rosaline. Freya can't quite make out what they are saying, but there is no doubt she won't be spending much time with serenity today.

Tap, tap, tap, tap.

"Freya! Freya! Are you awake?" barks Evelyn.

"Well, actually—"

"There's been an emergency! Come quickly."

"Evelyn, I—"

"*Quickly!*" Freya's frustration is mildly abated by thoughts of the glorious revenge she will eventually exact on the manic matriarch. She watches Evelyn's frantic figure scamper away and quickly pulls on underwear, jeans, T-shirt, and armband, then splashes her face with water in an attempt to banish her hangover.

Rosaline greets her at her bedroom door, locking her in an embrace. "Oh Frey, it's so horrible, isn't it?"

Freya is nearly choked by Rosaline's perfectly smooth, tanned arms. "Well, that's hard to say, given I don't know what 'it' is?"

Rosaline releases her and stares at her with a rabbit-in-the-headlights expression. "No one told you? The penguins! We have to save the penguins!" She takes Freya's hand in hers and drags her downstairs at breakneck speed.

Freya's brain, already lumbering with alcohol-induced dehydration, takes some time to join the dots. When the connection sparks, she feels her stomach lurch in disgust, although this might also be the hangover.

"John, Paul, George, and motherfucking Ringo," she curses to herself.

Freya struggles to ensure her uncoordinated feet manage to make contact with each of the stairs. When she looks up, she sees Harland and Evelyn at the bottom of the staircase, both barking into their mobile phones.

Harland speaks quickly and with composure, "Get Ron onto it. If he's still in Panama, get Lisa, but by all that's holy, don't let Jason anywhere near this, the man's a walking disaster. Yes, it must be today!"

Evelyn's tone is like a warrior queen instructing her troops: "Ship them through Exeltonia. Yes. Yes. I've got some of my people coming to help with the rest this afternoon. The press release should read: 'Heroic intervention by the Halcyon Corporation, who stated that care for the environment was foremost on the company's agenda,' etc. Excellent. Keep me updated."

Freya's face burns with a quiet rage that requires all her powers to restrain. She fortifies her feigned sunny exterior and quietly requests her hangover to fuck off. *They did this. They caused a fucking oil spill!*

Harland and Evelyn slide their phones back into their pockets with identical smooth and practised actions, like gunslingers re-holstering their six-shooters. Evelyn addresses Freya and Rosaline. "Ladies, thanks for helping us. Your assistance is greatly appreciated. We've just received news of a tragic oil spill off the coast of Patagonia. The extent of the damage won't be known for a few days, but right now there are tens of thousands of penguins freezing to death."

"Did you say freezing? Don't penguins like the cold?" Freya darts her eyes around at the various Vincettis, who regard her as though she's successfully auditioning for the role of village idiot.

"A penguin's insulation system relies on its feathers. When they get slicked with oil they can't lock the heat into their bodies and they'll quickly die. Until they're able to recover, they'll need human assistance, which is why we are here." Harland turns and strides down the main corridor. "Follow me."

Freya follows, bewildered, as they walk past nursery number one (girl's version), nursery number two (boy's version), the ski gear storage facility, the lower floor gym, billiard room number three, and a host of other as yet unexplored rooms before they arrive at their destination.

Ahead of them, at the end of the hall, is Jack's room. Freya lands her gaze at its white wooden door for a moment, and then a moment more. But it is the adjacent door that grabs her attention. Its large steel lock is the equivalent of fifteen teenage boys yelling, "*Double dare*!" on a cliff over a lagoon. Freya wants to jump. More than anything else in the world.

Blip!

Harland unlocks the door, flicks on the light and illuminates boxes upon boxes of the tiny woollen mystery objects.

Penguin jumpers! Tiny penguin jumpers.

Harland hands her a large box that's not so much heavy as cumbersome. "Take this out to the front. Maria's bringing the car around."

"Sure thing," says Freya, her manic grin concealed behind the cardboard. Her hands clutch at the box. She feels like a teenager with the keys to her first car.

Penguin jumpers. I am carrying a box of penguin jumpers.

Outside, Maria folds the seats down in the car to make room for the woolly cargo. "*Buenos dias, chiquita.*"

"*Hola, Señora bonita. ¿Que tal?*" says Freya, her tongue fumbling slightly over the Spanish sounds.

"*¡Ay!* I'm okay, but my knee is hurting a bit. It gets like that sometimes. I'm not so young anymore. I hear Mr Harland is give you some trouble? And that awful lady, Yvette, as well?"

"I see you've had your eyes and ears to the ground as always, Maria?"

"Hey, an old lady has to entertain herself somehow. I know nearly everything that happen in this house, except for few things, like what is behind that big locked door."

Freya plonks the box into the back of the car and looks up at Maria, trying to discern if this is her way of letting Freya know that last night's escapades did not go unnoticed.

"Anyway, I no remember last time I saw these funny things." Maria takes a penguin jumper out and holds it up, giggling. "Cute, yes? Like it is for doll?"

"Yeah, pretty cute." Freya looks up at the second-floor window and glimpses Jack standing next to Elijah's bed. *Oh to be a fly on that wall...* "Maria, do you and Jack get along?"

"A lot better now that I no have to clean his room no more!" Maria laughs. "Tell you the truth, I think he is a nice boy, but very strange. He never leave the house. I mean, *never*. Young rich man like him, he should be out with his friends, a girlfriend maybe? But he just stay in his room, typing, typing, typing his stories. Or sometimes he talks to his brother. I think—"

"Freya! Freya, dear! There's lots more boxes to be loaded. Be a doll and help us, will you?"

"Sure thing, Evelyn. Be right there," Freya replies with the most contrived congeniality she can summon.

Rosaline, who is on her way out to the car as Freya heads back into the house, flashes her a pearly, exuberant grin as they pass. "Thanks, Freya! Those penguins need our help!"

Inside, Freya picks up another box of jumpers at the same time as Harland. Their eyes meet for a moment and quickly part, and Freya scurries back to the car before he can say anything. She peeks up at the window into Elijah's room, but Jack is nowhere to be seen. She loads the box into the car and hurries back inside, avoiding eye contact with Harland as he passes.

Inside, Evelyn is pacing back and forth in the foyer, bellowing into her phone. "No, we need it on primetime. I want it on CNN, Fox, and all the liberal hippie networks too. Make sure it's all over Al Jazeera in the Middle East. Tell him to get it done or clean out his desk and put in a job application at Kmart—it's his choice. Okay, keep me updated. Ciao." She stabs her finger at the phone and slips it back into her pocket, then flashes Freya a well-practised grin.

"Thank you so much, dear, I do appreciate it."

"No problem."

"Harland and I will be busy with this fiasco for the best part of the day, but when we come back this afternoon we're going to spend some family time with Elijah." She turns to walk away but then thinks better of it, instead locking Freya with a suddenly sincere gaze. "Freya, about last night. I fear I may owe you an apology. I was not myself."

I think you were yourself, which was entirely the problem.

"Please accept my apologies. You'll understand someday when you're married. Marriage is such a tender trap. I love him to death, but sometimes he can be such a bloody swine."

Freya winces at that discourteous use of "when you're married," as though marriage were as inevitable as rising sea levels. "You can have the evening off if you like. Go and do whatever it is that you do."

"Thanks. I think I will do whatever it is I do. Have fun with the oil spill."

Evelyn grimaces and seems about to retaliate but then changes her mind. Following an apology with a tirade would be undignified, after all.

Freya smiles curtly and skips up the stairs, whistling as she examines the peculiar woollen object clutched in her fingers. With each whistle, a cloud of colour dances and fades before her. The momentary distraction these clouds provide prevents her noticing Jack approaching her until she hears his voice.

"Morning."

"Hi, Jack. Did you hear about—?"

"The oil spill? Yes, I was trying to figure out the safest route from here to my room without encountering anyone who would want to drag me into the whole debacle."

"Good plan. This was officially the first and last time I've ever had to deal with an oil crisis by loading penguin jumpers into a car."

"Roof?"

"Why, Mr Vincetti aka Velles, it's as though you read my mind."

He smiles at her behind his odd blue-white eyes then leads on towards the ladder.

17

Dr Moo

"Sooner or later, you're going to have to share a few of those skeletons in your closet with me," says Freya. "You can only play the mysterious, tortured artist for so long before it gets annoying."

It's bright outside. She shields the sun from her eyes with her hand and looks out at the light bouncing off the river. Somewhere on the other side of the world, oil is dancing with water.

"Take a look at that log in your own eye before you start commenting on my twig."

"Meaning?"

He nods towards her wrists.

"Okay. Fine. I'll come clean, but only if you go first."

"I'm sorry?"

"Come on, blue eyes. There must be a story there you aren't telling me."

"Ah. I was wondering when you'd ask about my eyes. Or the bruises. Or both."

"So, what are you? Shapeshifter or a garden-variety werewolf?"

"Nothing quite so glamorous. Quite the opposite, in fact. It's a condition called Osteogenesis Imperfecta."

"OI? Brittle bone syndrome?" says Freya, conjuring up her old textbooks' images of stunted, fragile figures wrapped in elaborate casts and bandages.

"In the common tongue, yes. Type 1, to be specific, although I haven't got it as bad as some. A little spine curvature, these weird eyes, my hearing's fading prematurely, but mostly I'm just a very fragile little creature. I bruise easily and my bones are like cardboard. Ever since I was a kid I've had to avoid anything physically risky, like skateboarding, jumping castles, bicycles. You know, mostly the fun stuff. Throughout my childhood, Lord and Lady Vincetti insisted I kept to a strict regime of housebound pastimes. I had a home tutor for education and a revolving cast of nannies to clothe and feed me, although none lasted long under Evelyn's manicured iron fist. Basically I was a lonely, isolated kid who spent his spare time with his nose buried in books."

"And you grew up to be a writer, that's so—"

"Trite? Hackneyed? Clichéd?"

"I was going to say poetic, but sure, if you want to get all self-pitying on me."

"Like I keep saying, I'm not used to keeping sane company. It wasn't easy watching Elijah shove his relentless pleasure-seeking into my face all the time. His top grades, ski trips, overseas holidays. He'd come back from weeks away in Vienna or Paris or Costa Rica, toss some tasteless five-dollar souvenir in my lap to twist the knife and then run off to whatever new adventure awaited him. When we got a little older, he started bringing home a procession of impossibly beautiful girls. He'd knock on my door and announce, 'This is Crystal' or 'Marian' or 'Katrina,' or whatever the fuck their names were in virtually the same tone he'd use to announce purchasing a new pair of shoes. Meanwhile, I hardly got to leave the house save for the odd specialist's appointment. At one point, I developed a vitamin D deficiency and ended up looking like Gollum. Of course, my life's not so horrible; it's not as though I have some terminal degenerative disease, I've just developed a rather potent fear and distaste for the outside world."

"I treated someone with OI once. Type IV. He had it a lot worse than you, though. Crutches, back brace, the whole nine yards."

"Really? What happened to him?"

Freya frowns and looks away.

"Ah…" says Jack. "Enough about the waiting room of my youth. I believe it's your turn to share your origin story."

"Origin story?"

"Yes. The moment of truth that made you who you are today. The radioactive spider to your Peter Parker. The gamma bomb to your Bruce Banner."

"If I'd grown up reading comic books I'd be far more pro-nuclear power. They make nuclear radiation look like Popeye's spinach."

"You're stalling."

She smiles and looks at his eyes, which despite the medical explanation have an almost mystical allure for her. "I've told you about Valerie, and now I'm about to share this with you. I hope you know that means something."

"Like what?"

"I don't know. But something."

He nods and squeezes her hand. Once. Gently.

"When I was a kid, I had this doctor called Dr Moo. I'm not kidding, that was his actual name. As in, 'The cow says…' I always felt sorry for him, and not just because he had a name like a bass player in a seventies funk band. I mean, surely somewhere in those years of medical instruction they could find time to squeeze in one twenty-minute session entitled 'Your future life as a doctor: is it time for a name change?'

"Anyway, Dr Moo had the dubious pleasure of being my family doctor ever since the age I figured out that Play-Doh is a wonderful recreational substance and not a brightly coloured source of nutrition. Over the years, I witnessed his hair receding as his waistline expanded. I watched the photos on his desk slowly metamorphose from smiling portraits of himself and his big-bellied bride to a wife and proud child, to wife and child grinning with haphazard teeth, holding a small bundled-up baby sister, and finally his current photo, of him with two teenage daughters and a very noticeably absent Mrs Moo. Whether she passed away or lives on another man's desk, I can't say. I've never had the guts to ask."

"Maybe he thinks the same things about you. Wonders if that weird red-headed girl he treats has a good credit rating, a boyfriend, or a drug habit." Freya shrugs.

"I could answer all of those questions with a two-letter word. It's strange, isn't it, the way we keep people at arm's length, relegated to specific roles in our lives? As if the sole purpose of their existence is to appear as a recurring role in our narratives? I can only imagine the grief I've brought Dr Moo over the years, but at least I feel safe knowing I've helped advance his career. After all, not many doctors get first-hand exposure to a condition like mine. I was eight when he wrote his first paper on me. I remember he gave it to my family to read, and I saw it had my name on it. I figured it was some kind of weird art book. I drew a bunch of unicorns with bats' wings all over it. I had a thing for bats.

"When Mum told me those pages were very important grown-up documents I expected her to get mad, to start shouting and waving her arms around like one of those giant inflatable figures you see out the front of car yards. But she and Dad just sat at the table with their eyebrows furrowed, staring at the paper as though some evil genie was about to pop out of it. They weren't touching it, or even moving. The silence was horrible."

Freya pauses, watches Jack's hand reach for hers, then retreat. He taps his fingers against the tiles.

"The first time it happened, I was eight years old. I'd been waiting in line—it was about ten kids long—to show my homework to the teacher. I was an impatient little thing. I decided I'd water the flowers while I waited, which was one of our class jobs. I also decided I'd move them onto the windowsill so they could get some more sunlight. I was a short kid, so I was really reaching. On tiptoes and all that.

"I was trying to lift this thing that was way too heavy with my arms that were way too short, and Mr Christopher Rumples Worthington CXI—my teddy bear—was at my feet, and I was reaching, reaching and then someone in the music room next door started playing the trombone. The next part I remember vividly, almost as though it's happening right now. There were these huge splotches of bright blue that started appearing, like colourful little clouds. With each note, they materialised and then vanished again in this strange procession. I was trying to watch the little coloured clouds, trying to touch them, and I lost my balance. I fell back and screamed. Mr Stevenson came running over as the vase smashed all over the floor.

"As I lay there I was so busy watching the blue splotches do their little dance I'd barely even noticed that I'd fallen or that my leg had been cut. I thought something magical was happening, that the blue splotches were fairies or something. I didn't even notice Mr Stevenson was kneeling over me and calling my name until the trombone next door stopped playing and all the splotches faded away.

"Some of my blood got on my teddy bear. I remember I was still cleaning it off when the nurse came to collect me. I told her what happened and her face scrunched up like someone had said that her grandma had been arrested for indecent exposure. She called Dr Moo and I went to see him the next day, and told him the same story. He made some notes, asked me some questions, and two weeks later he called my parents and told them exactly what I was."

"So, shapeshifter or garden-variety werewolf?"

"Well played, sir, but no. I'm a synaesthete. Granted, it sounds like I should be in the X-Men, but all it means is I have synaesthesia, a confusion of two senses. Some people associate colours with taste, or sounds with motion. I have sound-colour synaesthesia, which means I *see* music. It's rare, around one in 100,000 people have it."

"Does it hurt?"

"Not usually, no. Though one time I was taking a driving lesson and my instructor flipped on a Cyndi Lauper tape and the explosion of yellow in front of my face nearly made me crash into a sex shop. On my fourteenth birthday I got startled by a storm of colour and cut myself with a pineapple cutter. That's how I got this."

She slowly, tentatively pulls back the cloth concealing her wrists and reveals the scar tissue.

Jack surprises her by gently smoothing his fingers over her skin. What surprises her even more is how much she enjoys it. She allows his fingers to move across her flesh, trying to remember the last time anyone has wanted to touch rather than avoid that part of her. His hands retract and she pulls the gloves back into place.

"It might seem strange to keep it covered, but I know how people think, and I couldn't stand the looks of disgust or, even worse, pity. That's why I made up the Audrey Hepburn thing. The truth is a long, complicated story."

"It usually is."

Silence hovers.

"You know Vladimir Nabokov, who wrote *Lolita*?" says Jack. "He had a similar thing, I think, seeing letters with colours."

"A few artists had it. My hero, Kandinsky, used to paint the images he saw when he heard music, which is why I've always thought of the colours in my vision as 'little Kandinskys.' The composer Messiaen and Nikola Tesla, the inventor, had it too. Some people think Marilyn Monroe might have been a synaesthete as well."

"It's genetic?"

"Neurological. It's not a disease, if that's what you mean. You're not going to catch it from touching me or anything."

Jack coughs, then laughs. "Ah, that's good to know."

"Dr Moo says it's why I have such a good memory. And it gives me ideas for paintings. One gallery owner said I had a unique view of reality, though she dropped acid like Tic Tacs so I'm not sure how credible her opinion was."

The chirping of cicadas over the river pauses the conversation. She turns to say something but finds Jack's lips on a crash course with her own and blurts a "Mrfmph!" as their mouths meet and his arms pull her towards him. She attempts a laugh through her otherwise occupied mouth, and the result is a comically awkward collision of spit, tongues, lips, and hands.

Jack pulls away and stammers, "Did I…um…I probably shouldn't have…"

"No, Jack, it's fine! You just caught me by surprise. I think you're…"

But he's on his feet and making a hurried escape even as her words trail after him. Freya sighs as the alarm on her phone beeps, a reminder that one of the other Vincettis is in need of her attention.

◇◇◇

Beep.

Beep.

Beep.

Her hands delicately remove the sticky pads from Elijah's chest, cutting the signal sending his heartbeats to the armada of sleek machines flanking his bed. With the whole weight of her body, she pushes him onto the plastic-sheeted stretcher. She finds the absence of beeping disconcerting.

"Well, Elijah Vincetti," she says, bringing herself back to her task, "I believe it's time for your sponge bath. You know the first time I told my grandmother that I had to give an old guy a sponge bath she said, 'So you're basically a prostitute who doesn't get to wear fun outfits to work?'"

Again she tries to ignore the silence, but it makes her so uncomfortable it becomes all she can think about. She flicks on the radio.

"Oh dear lord, no." Michael Bolton's schmaltzy tenor appears as the most disgusting shade of green. It looks like the time she puked after too many green beers last St Patrick's Day.

She changes stations.

"Ah, that's more like it. Nina Simone. That is a woman with class."

Freya removes his shirt, no mean feat given how heavy his dead weight is. His chiselled physique is undeniably attractive, although she's curious how his muscle tone is still in such good shape. Nina's inimitable voice dances over the piano keys.

She removes his pants and boxer shorts, folds them and places them on the bed. She soaks the sponge in water, the warmth gliding over her skin. He looks so complete, even without clothing. So calm, stoic. Like a marble Adonis. He is beautiful in his peace.

Freya squeezes the sponge and runs it over his chest, sending rivulets trickling over his chest hairs and down his sides. She listens to Nina and watches the smooth light purple fill the air and accelerate the sense of calm and rejuvenation she always feels when washing a patient. She almost forgets her hangover.

Freya lifts his right leg and washes the underside of his calf. She lifts his other leg and squeezes the sponge, about to wipe it across his skin, when she notices a tiny flick of crimson on his lower leg. She leans in close to inspect it, and discovers another, slightly larger splash of blood on the other side of his calf.

"What the fuck?" The implausibility renders this discovery hard to process. She rolls Elijah onto his side to check for other flecks, or possibly the source wound.

Although she doesn't find either, she does notice a large bruise on his hip. "Elijah, you've been keeping secrets."

Excerpt from *The Sins of Adonis*

I will admit there is a certain overbearing self-awareness that pervades these scribbles. It's difficult not to be aware of one's own greatness. Indeed, it is this awareness that distinguishes one from the common rabble. Does a lion survey a flock of sheep and think, "I am a quadruped and a mammal, and thus we are the same?" No. It sees and revels in its self-evident superiority. It hunts. Kills. Fucks. Eats.

18

Dreamers Often Lie

Rosaline smiles as the warm sounds wash over her. The music box melody she has played hundreds of times, dreaming of the day it will fall on the ears of her as-yet non-existent offspring. She loves these twin kingdoms she has created, perfect to the last detail. Every precisely placed, colour-coded teddy bear, every intricately arranged ornament, every thoroughly selected book and plaything. These two small rooms are perfect, save for one all-important detail: they lack occupants. They are museums dedicated to an era that has never existed.

She polishes. Dusts. Straightens. Wipes. Vacuums. Adjusts. Readjusts. Removes. Replaces. Everything is in its right place. She feels a quiet sense of calm wash over her with each tiny adjustment to the room. She picks up her most prized possession, Magic Wedding Dress Rosaline, and combs its golden hair with long and loving strokes.

Rosaline sighs and sits daintily on the light blue couch that she imagines she will someday occupy with a newborn baby cradled in her arms. This will happen, must happen, just as soon as Elijah returns to her.

And she has been waiting for so, so long, patiently, faithfully…

But it will happen.

It must.

She hears footsteps in the hallway. "Freya?" she inquires tentatively. The steps pause.

"Uh, yeah?"

"Come and chat with me!" A few beats pass before Freya appears in the doorway. "Hey, you. I was just cleaning. I love cleaning! It makes me feel like I'm fixing things a little, making things that tiny bit prettier, happier. Are you alright? You look a little bamboozled."

Freya sits next to Rosaline with a noticeable lack of enthusiasm and nods. She eyes the dolls and teddy bears as though they are rabid animals ready to bite.

"This isn't really your kind of thing, is it?" asks Rosaline, gently patting Freya's hand.

"Not exactly, no."

Rosaline picks up a snow globe from Canada, a perfect shade of powder blue. Its pink sibling sits on the other side of the five inches of wood and plaster that separate this room from the next. "You didn't have a room like this when you were a baby?"

"I don't really remember what my room looked like," says Freya. "We moved around a lot, until my dad got sick. Then I spent most of my time hanging out with him at the hospital, sitting there watching him sleep. Wishing I could do something to make him feel better, like Florence Nightingale. I'd sit for hours listening to my Walkman, reading, maybe watching movies. I remember when *Romeo + Juliet* came out, I watched that movie about twenty times sitting next to my dad in the hospital. He'd drift in and out of sleep, his eyes would flicker open and he'd say, 'Lord Almighty, Freya, this one again? There are other movies in the world, you know!'"

Rosaline is nodding emphatically, desperately waiting for Freya to finish before blurting out, "I love *Romeo + Juliet*!

Especially Shakespeare's description of my namesake: 'The all-seeing sun / ne'er saw her match since first the world begun.' I always thought she was so interesting and mysterious, and even though you never actually hear her speak, she's so important. And how Romeo talks about her as though he'll never find anyone else; it's so romantic!"

"Well…yeah…Until he sets eyes on Juliet and the excrement hits the ventilation system."

"Yes, exactly. With Rosaline, everything is so imagined and perfect, it never goes wrong. As soon as he meets Juliet, blood gets spilled and the world starts falling apart. The silly boy should've stuck with his first love, but because we never see Rosaline, she stays perfect and pure. Like a dream."

"*But dreamers often lie.*"

"*In bed asleep, while they do dream things true!* You really did watch that film a lot. A dream is such a perfect thing, you can shape it, change it, make it yours. That's why I wanted to become Rosaline, to make my own dream. To start again. And now I'm almost there. Almost. I just want my Elijah to wake up, more than anything else, and then my dream will be complete."

She watches the tiny fake snowflakes flutter onto the houses and their inhabitants: a miniature nuclear family with poorly painted smiles adorning their frozen faces. They are forever staring at the same roast chicken, forks poised to spear food that will never be eaten.

"When he finally does, then we'll be married and I'll have everything I've dreamt of since I was little. All those hours spent gazing at Mum and Dad's wedding album. Even after everything went…well, after things changed." She stares at the snow globe.

"Changed how?" prompts Freya, suspended on the stray thread of Rosaline's dangling narrative.

"I want my wedding day to be perfect. I mean *really* perfect. That's why it's worth waiting for. I never stopped dreaming about owning my own home, with the man I loved, and that special day when I would get to wear my own wedding dress, beautiful and white. And now I have that, at long last. I love Elijah, and I know he loves me, and he's never, ever going to leave me."

Well, you've got that part right. She takes Rosaline's hand in hers. *You poor deluded creature. You don't need a husband, you need about twenty years of intensive therapy and the most potent narcotics known to man.*

"That's why I don't care if Harland and Evelyn take control of the company; all I want is to be with Elijah."

"Take control of what company?"

"My dad's company. Firmatel. He left it to me when he died."

"*Firmatel?* The pharmaceutical company? I thought you said your dad owned a toy company?"

"It was a toy company, but after he moved to California he started expanding or merging or whatever, I don't really understand business stuff. But he bought a bunch of shares in Firmatel when they were only small and then ended up owning it. So, when Elijah and I met and started talking about marriage we decided that we should share everything, and that we'd merge all our assets. It's all just stuff anyway, right? Who cares when all you need is love!"

"So, once you and Elijah get hitched, the Vincettis are going to control Firmatel, as well as Halcyon, Happymax, and the Davies Group?"

"And they're gonna do a great job! Look at the wonderful work they did with the oil spill!"

Freya subdues her urge to scream and instead places a hand on Rosaline's shoulder as she asks, "Do you ever wonder what Elijah dreams about?"

"That's easy! Shakespeare said it all: *I dreamt my lady came and found me dead—Strange dream, that gives a dead man leave to think! And breathed such life with kisses in my lips, that I revived, and was an emperor.*"

Freya treats her to a contrived smile as she stands and says, "That's very sweet. I should probably—"

"Wait! I want to tell you about what happened before, when I was a kid. It's not an easy story to tell. Sometimes I like to pretend that it was all just a nightmare that I woke up from when I was seventeen. Would you stay? Please?”

Freya sits back down and looks at the smiling faces trapped inside the snow globe.

19

The Daughter of the Mad Bride

"My father used to bring me a new doll every week. I would unwrap it gently, tenderly, and place it next to its hundreds of sisters. I'd make up little stories for each of them; histories, hobbies, desires, and fears. While Daddy worked, I would go with my mother to the movies or the museum, and then we would come home and bake together, the smell of cinnamon and sugar pouring out from every window in the house. My mother was beautiful, like one of the dolls that I kept on my shelves. Smooth, flawless skin, pearly smile. As we walked through the city, admiring eyes would always turn to follow her.

Father would often be called away on business for a day or two, usually in neighbouring towns but occasionally interstate and once in a while across the ocean. Then one year he left to negotiate a deal in California. After a few days, he called to say that his trip was being extended. Something about negotiations taking longer than expected.

I crawled into bed that night, my stomach swimming with cinnamon, clutching a photo of my father in one arm and Magical Mermaid Rosaline in the other.

The phone rang.

I ran downstairs and picked up the receiver.

'Hello?'

'Hey sweetheart! How's my little girl?'

'It's late, Daddy. And I miss you.'

I heard a voice in the background saying something about hotel phone bills.

'I miss you too, sugarplum. I have some exciting news, I want you to listen very carefully, okay?'

'Uh-huh.'

'You know how you've always wanted to visit California, where they make all the movies? Well, guess what! Daddy and his lady friend are going to get a little place there and you can come and visit whenever you want! Doesn't that sound great?'

'Isn't California a long way away?'

'Don't be silly pet, it's barely a hop, skip, and a jump! Can you tell your mother and let her know I'll make arrangements soon?' There was more of the muffled whispering on the other end. 'Anyway, got to go. Love you!'

In the morning, I wondered if perhaps the phone call had all been a dream. I walked down the stairs in my crumpled fairy princess pyjamas and found mother baking Anzac biscuits. I rubbed my eyes and breathed in the comforting, sugary scent.

'Hey there, sleepyhead! I'm making your father's favourite for when he gets home tomorrow!'

'Mummy, what's a lady friend?'

'A what dear?'

'A lady friend. Is it like a ladybird?'

'Ah, no, it's not quite… Where did you hear that?'

'Daddy said he's getting a house in California with his lady friend. Are we going to have two houses now? Where will the lady friend sleep? Is it going to share my room?'

The mixing bowl slipped from her hands. It seemed to take an age to reach the ground, where it smashed, scattering shards and dough across the kitchen tiles. I ran over and hugged her. Her skin was cold, but felt as though it had the memory of warmth, like a cup of tea forgotten and left to sit too long.

I waited for her to move, or speak, and noticed the little red rivers at her feet. I pulled the shard from her foot and went upstairs to get a bandaid.

I made peanut butter sandwiches for dinner, they were always my favourite. Mother sat on the couch and smoked, looking like she'd aged a decade in the space of a few hours: her face ashen, her hands trembling. I sat next to her as she stared at her wedding album. It was hard to believe the woman in those photos was the same person as the one who now held them in her trembling hands.

The next few nights were the same. Mother wouldn't speak, and she barely ate. The only sounds were the drone of the television and the turning of the album pages. Cigarette smoke hung thick in the air.

Letters started to arrive, and the sound of the postman's bike outside was one of the few things that could raise Mother from the couch. The envelopes contained postcards flashing pictures of sun and palm trees and a few hastily scrawled lines, bundled with wildly varying quantities of cash. Mother would rip open the envelope and snarl at the postcard before tossing it to the floor, then shove the cash into her pockets and return to the couch.

She started spending most of the money on cigarettes and 'Mummy's special water,' which she kept high up on top of the fridge. It wasn't until one morning when she was in the shower that I managed to climb onto the kitchen bench, reach above the fridge and sip at the plastic sports bottle that I realised she had been living on a steady diet of pure vodka.

I began to race out to the letterbox at the first hint of the postman's bike spluttering in the distance. Initially I just slipped away enough notes to pay for a few essential groceries, but when it became clear that Mother didn't care about anything except having enough money to buy booze and cigarettes, I took control of our irregular income.

After a few years I got pretty good at it. I budgeted for groceries and bills and the occasional pair of shoes, and of course, cleaning products. These soon became especially important, valued almost as much as my beloved dolls. I would spend hours cleaning, polishing, dusting, scrubbing. Sometimes I wondered if making the oven door shiny enough would make my father come home again. How proud he'd be, seeing his little girl keeping everything shipshape! Mother would stop smoking and drinking and everything would be like it was before.

Once every few weeks, when my head stung from bleach fumes and my hands ached from scrubbing, I'd buy myself a new Rosaline doll. I would brush its hair, tell it stories, make it tea and biscuits and, for just a while, I'd feel like a normal little girl. But no matter how many new dolls I bought, my favourite would always be Magic Wedding Dress Rosaline. It looked exactly like Mother did in those photos she stared at day after day.

Then one morning I came downstairs to find Mother in her wedding dress. Smoking and staring. From then on it was all she wore. Sitting on the couch, smoking on the porch, walking to the shops for cigarettes. I soon became grateful that she left the house so rarely, because where once admiring eyes had followed her, now there were only cruel names and rumours. They called her 'the Mad Bride,' which of course meant that I was 'the Daughter of the Mad Bride.' Perhaps some of the whisperers thought that little girl wouldn't hear the things they said beneath their breath in the grocery store aisles, but I heard every word.

Soon the dress changed from perfect white to nicotine yellow, and then became a putrid grey. I tried to convince her to wear something else, or at the very least clean the dress so it didn't stink, but she refused. She sat in the dress, smoked her cigarettes, and stared at her wedding photos.

And finally, on a windy autumn afternoon, I came home from the supermarket, struggling with the grocery bags, and opened the door to find her suspended from the kitchen ceiling. The light behind her head shone like a halo through her golden hair. She was wearing that dress, of course. And as she swung gently back and forth, with the light radiating out behind her, she looked like a dirty, sleeping angel."

20

Delusions of Candour

The virulent yellow and steel blades of the pineapple cutter glare at Freya from the cutlery drawer. How strange that it is the same souvenir from the impossibly tacky attraction, the Big Pineapple, which her family had bought over a decade ago. Nothing like the more modern versions, sleek stainless steel, designed for safety and comfort. This is sharp, violently yellow and aggressively angular. Just seeing it makes her wrist begin to burn and itch. She selects a knife and slams the drawer closed.

Footsteps. She looks up to see Jack shuffling through the dining room. When he enters the kitchen, he picks up the salt shaker, examines it as though it's some antediluvian artefact, and then places it back on the counter.

"Something I can help you with, Mr Vincetti?"

He opens his mouth and then closes it, contorting it into a curiously shaped canyon on the landscape of his face, then finally blurts out, "About this morning, on the roof..."

"Jack. It's fine. You didn't have to run off like Cinderella five minutes before midnight. You're a nice guy, give yourself a little credit."

He smiles sheepishly. "Well. That's good. You're, you know, nice as well. Really. So…you making enough for two by any chance?"

"Possibly. What's in it for me?" she says with a smirk.

"You mean aside from karma points and good conversation?"

"Yes."

"My eternal gratitude?"

"And?"

"A promise I'll return the favour?"

"Deal. You like felafel?"

"I do now."

"Good answer. Make yourself useful, you can chop the tomatoes." She hands him the knife and he does as requested. "You spend a lot of time hiding in that room of yours. You got any other secrets you're holding out on me?"

"Plenty. What about you?"

"Of course."

Chop.

Chop.

Chop.

"I'll tell you mine if you tell me yours?" Jack says.

Freya can't tell if he's flirting with her. She tries to read his body language, but his long isolation has turned his physical communication into the corporeal equivalent of static.

"Sure. What the hell? You first."

Chop.

Chop.

Chop.

"I found something in the Danger Room last night."

Freya slams her hand on the bench and points at him with her knife. "I *knew* it! So, what the hell is it?"

"I can't tell you. Not yet. Not 'til I'm sure. And can you please not point that in my face?"

She puts the knife down and jabs at him with her finger instead. "You can't tell me half a secret!"

"It's not half. It's a whole secret. I found something there."

"That's not the same thing. It's like saying, 'I love you, usually.' Alright, you want to play it that way? When I was sponge-bathing your brother this morning..." Was that a flinch? She logs Jack's movement and files it for later analysis. "... I found something strange."

"What?"

The blood flecked across Elijah's legs flashes back into her brain, but she keeps her lips shut.

"What was it?"

She shakes her head.

"Are you seriously not going to tell me?"

Freya looks at him wryly.

"Right," he says. "Eye for an eye." A smile sprouts slowly on his face, but then slips away. For a moment he looks terrified. "It wasn't a lump or something, was it?"

"Oh, God, no! Jack!" She grabs his hand and squeezes it.

"I just...I guess I get paranoid, with him in that coma for so long. Never moving, never changing. Like a porcelain doll."

"It's not quite like that. He still has brain function, automated muscle response. There's a chance he may wake up from it. Maybe even tomorrow. Comas are hugely unpredictable."

Jack says nothing. She picks up the knife again and starts to chop the onions. Her eyes begin to water. "Fucking onions. I've always thought it was complete bullshit that a member of the plant kingdom could make me cry more than *Charlotte's Web*."

Jack tears off a piece of paper towel and dabs at her eyes. "There, there," he says facetiously.

"Very funny, you big jerk."

"So, today you got to solve the mystery of the penguin jumpers. There's at least one family secret you're now privy to."

"I suppose so. Got to admit, I didn't see that one coming."

"Yes, all part of Halcyon's proud record of appearing at the scene of disasters with supernaturally rapid response and handing out supplies plastered with their logo in front of the TV cameras. You know what's cuter than a penguin in a jumper? Nothing, that's what. It's guaranteed airtime. Halcyon gets to look like some sort of corporate guardian angel, swooping in to save the day, and in exchange they get their logo all over primetime for free. They did the same thing a few years ago after a forest fire in Indonesia, handing out shirts to adorable wide-eyed orphans so they could wrap themselves in the warm embrace of corporate-logoed clothing."

"They've done this kind of thing before? Disaster marketing stunts?"

"A few times. They're able to arrive even before Red Cross or other rapid response groups, and they have vast stocks of exactly the right supplies, no matter how unusual they may be. Penguin jumpers aren't exactly sold in twelve packs at the local grocery store."

"So how come no one's fingered them for it?"

"People have tried, but Halcyon and its various affiliates are notoriously skilled at covering their tracks. Plus they own or have influence with most of the major news outlets in the country. You see the occasional article in left-wing indie media or on some conspiracy theory website, but not often. Halcyon's not short on hush money."

"Is that why it's so hard to find any information about Elijah's accident?"

He tenses, the knife hanging frozen in hand as though he were a wax statue. Then he relaxes, puts the knife down, and regards her with weary, blue-tinted eyes. "I told you, you shouldn't ask about that." His voice is quiet, defeated. Freya takes all of this in, and elects to return to the matter at hand.

"So, why do you just sit back and let them get away with it?"

"They're still my blood. Bringing harm to your family violates one of the universal laws of fate and family. The ancient Greeks believed that spilling family blood would lead the Fates to strike you down with a mortal curse. And it's not exactly like telling your teacher that little Timmy was the one who stole the cookie.

They trade through an intentionally complex web of subcontractors so nothing can ever be directly traced back to them."

"So, what? You're going to do nothing while they burn and pillage?"

"Of course I'm going to do something. I've been documenting, recording, compiling evidence. You want to get angry, that's fine. I'd rather take action that gets results. Look at what happened to Simply Sasha. Two days ago it was one of the hottest companies around, now the stock is worth about as much as belly button lint."

"I heard about the thing with the monkeys. Whoever did that is seriously messed up."

"More messed up than the woman perpetrating animal rights abuse for the sake of profit...who encourages prepubescent girls to puke the contents of their *Dora the Explorer* lunch boxes into the toilet? She got what she deserved. I only wish it'd happened sooner." Jack's face flares with anger and disdain.

This is a side of him she has not seen before. She does not like it. "So, you're perfectly comfortable with her getting her face torn off?"

"That's nothing compared to the damage she's done to an entire generation of impressionable young women. I'm just saying that you have to look at the bigger picture."

Freya snarls in frustration. "Look, I don't want to talk about this anymore, can we just eat?"

Jack delivers a curt nod, obviously smart enough to pick his battles. "I tend to go off on rants like this. Like I said, I'm not used to having rational humans as company. I'm a little rusty."

"We don't have to agree on everything. That's not how this works."

"This what?"

"This...whatever this is."

As Freya carries their plates to the table, the domesticity of her act surprises her. Setting the table seems entirely out of place, given her discovery mere hours earlier. The sounds of china and glass making contact with the antique wood are comforting, but the image of those implausible patches of blood on Elijah's skin linger obstinately at the front of her mind.

Jack pulls a bottle of wine and a pair of crystal glasses out of the pantry, filling them both generously.

"What is this, a date?" Freya says drolly.

Jack tenses. "Ah, it's just…I thought that, you know, you made dinner, so we might as well…"

"Relax, Vincetti aka Velles. I'm messing with you. Eat up." Freya shoves the first forkful of salad into her mouth. If she hates the word "unladylike," this is due at least in part to it having been used to describe her on far too many occasions.

He gulps down a mouthful of wine and begins to eat.

"How's the new book coming along? Decided on a title yet?" she asks.

Jack shakes his head. "It's like searching for a white whale. *The Many Trespasses of Adonis…Adonis's Errors…Delusions of Candour…Last Dance in the Chamber of Innocence.* Nothing sticks. Nothing works."

"What about the book itself?"

"It's coming out a lot darker than I anticipated. I wanted to write a book about how we perceive ourselves versus how others want us to be, and the conflicts that creates: a societal analysis of the concept that we're all capable of becoming either Buddha or Hitler depending on our circumstances and the perceptions of those around us. The idea was a story about a young man who becomes the living, breathing embodiment of the desires of those closest to him and how he loses his own identity in the process. I like the concept, but it keeps coming out so dark and twisted, like I'm writing a guide to becoming a monster."

"Well, your first book wasn't exactly cupcakes and unicorns either, but it was brilliant. Why is this one emerging so differently from your original idea? It's your book, doesn't it just do what you tell it to?"

"Not exactly, no. Writing a book is like raising a child, I guess. No matter how hard you aim for a Rhodes scholar there's always a chance they'll become a crack addict. You remember that bit in *Chaos in the Kingdom* where I had Cynthia saying, 'If I ever manage to become ordinary, it will be the most extraordinary of achievements'?"

"Of course."

"Well, that's how I feel about this book. I want it to be beautiful and inspiring but also simple, capturing the poetry of everyday existence. But it won't come out that way. Everything I put down comes out twisted, contaminated. Like I'm speaking with someone else's voice."

Freya waits expectantly, sucks the tahini sauce from her finger. Jack sips at his wine, places the glass back on the table. A drop splashes onto his forearm. He doesn't seem to notice. Freya watches the tiny splash of red travel slowly down his skin.

"Do you know the poet William Butler Yeats?" Jack asks. Freya's eyes remain fixated on the red wine dripping down his arm onto the table.

"*Things fall apart; the centre cannot hold.* Yeah, I know Yeats."

"Well, he was heavily into the occult, possibly the only Nobel Laureate semi-legitimately accused of being a Satanist. He even used his wife, Georgie, as a psychic medium."

"Better than having her act as his maid, I guess."

"I suppose so. She would go into a trance state, acting as a mouthpiece for the spirit world and then he'd ask her questions. Some of Yeats' best ideas came from Georgie."

"Behind every great man is a great woman in a trance."

"That's one way of putting it. They called these spirits 'instructors.' Yeats would ask them for news of the spirit world, the answers inspiring some of his greatest poetry. The strange thing was..."

Freya raises an eyebrow and speaks with a mouth filled with food, "Stranger than getting your wife to go all trancey to dig for ideas for you?"

"Yes, stranger. Yeats was convinced evil spirits were impersonating the instructors, trying to lead him astray and use his voice as a poet to influence the world towards evil."

"So, in other words, his wife was getting pissed off at having to go spacey just to get him to pay attention to her so she started writing, 'Do the goddamn dishes or great evil will befall you'?"

"Make fun if you want. All I'm saying is that sometimes I feel that what I'm writing doesn't come from me at all. Some days, when I manage to write something I think is beautiful, I don't mind so much. But the last few months...I feed the paper into the typewriter, stare at the blank page, and then these words flood out of my fingertips. They just come. I can't stop them. Then I read them back and it's the most horrible...I can't explain. Maybe it's the same thing. Maybe I'm picking up a signal from the wrong instructors. Maybe I'm listening to the wrong voice."

Freya lets the words hang in the air for a few seconds before asking, "Where do you think the voice is coming from?"

He moves food around with his fork and hides his eyes from hers. "I don't mean to be so insufferably maudlin. What did you say about arty boys crying into their red wine?"

"Yes, well." Freya laughs. "If we're being completely honest? That has worked on me once or twice before." She fixes him with a covetous gaze.

He coughs and splutters a spray of red across the table. "Shit! Maria is going to kill me." He dabs frantically at the tablecloth with his shirt. "Fuck it." He settles back and drains his glass.

"Jack, if this *was* a date...? This would, hypothetically speaking, be where you invite me back to your room."

Afterwards he falls quickly asleep, leaving her to the chaos of his bedroom with only the gentle rhythm of his breathing to break the silence. Outside the window, the moon is bright and full. It casts gentle white light over the debris populating his room.

Her eyes scan this new territory with deliberate calm before she turns her attention to him. In this half-light, he looks a great deal like his brother. Not quite as handsome, but the basic blueprint is there, as though the two are different executions of the same design, one by a master sculptor and the other by his less accomplished apprentice. As both brothers sleep, Freya wonders if they share the same dreams, then dismisses this as a ridiculous notion.

Even in his sleep, Jack looks tense and anxious. Perhaps, she wonders, that sinister voice is talking to him even when he's not awake. She touches his bare shoulder, enjoying the warmth that greets her fingers. She casts her eyes over his landscape of bruises, tiny brown and purple islands dotting the map of his chest. It's strange, she thinks, how his condition manifests so physically, whereas hers is solely within her head.

She rests her head on the pillow, the possibility of sleep sailing sluggishly into her mind. Just before she closes her eyes, she notices something sticking out from under his pillow. She reaches her hand forward slowly, watching his closed eyes flicker behind his eyelids until her fingers meet smooth, soft plastic. She delicately slides the plastic package free and squints to examine it in the half-light. *What the fuck?*

She clutches it and moves swiftly out of bed, considers examining it in Jack's en-suite, but fears that even the quiet click of a light switch and the trace of light from underneath the door might wake him from his uneasy slumber. She finds a crumpled T-shirt on the floor and throws it over herself before exiting the room and closing the door as quietly as she can.

Freya hides the object behind her back and makes a dash for the bathroom, the cold marble floor of the dining room chilling her feet as she walks. She sees a shadow step out in front of her and freezes, her body lighting up with adrenaline. She stands motionless as she waits for her eyes to adjust to the dark.

Neither of them speak. The silhouette stands dark against the slivers of moonlight trickling in through the windows.

"*¿Estas bien, chiquita bonita*?"

"Maria, you scared the Mary, Jesus, and Joseph outta me! What're you doing still up?" She steps closer, slapping Maria playfully on the shoulder. Even in the darkness there is a discernible sadness over Maria's face.

"*No se, mi corazón.* I feel so tired, but I can't sleep. I keep having awful nightmares. Like I'm choking, like the life is slipping from my lungs."

The two stand awkwardly until Freya embraces her in a hug, careful to avoid letting the object in her fingers touch Maria's skin.

Maria's arms wrap tightly around her with a fierce and tenacious affection. "*Gracias,* my dear, you are very kind. Is so nice to have a kind person here, not so crazy like the rest, eh?" She pulls back and wipes at tears welling in her eyes and sniffs loudly. "I'm sorry to scare you, you go back to sleep. I go to my room, listen to music, maybe write letter to my sister. I'll be okay. *Buenas noches.*"

"Good night, Maria."

Maria shuffles back to her room, sniffing.

Freya continues towards the bathroom, flicks on the light and examines the object in her hands. "Fuck me…" Her whisper sounds stentorian in the late night quiet. She switches the light off before she can glimpse her reflection in the mirror and heads back down the hall towards Jack's room. It's not until she is about to pass the Danger Room that it occurs to her that returning to his bed might be a mistake.

What kind of fucking creep keeps something like that beneath their pillow? Not the kind of fetish one would list on Match.com. Freya leans against the wall, listening to the sound of nothing.

Everything is still.

Then she picks up what seems like low, quiet whistling. It is not a sound that belongs here. The sound is the first problem. The second is what she sees. After nearly two decades of coloured clouds, Freya has organised and catalogued every possible combination of chords, discords, harmonies, melodies, and rhythms into the various visions they produce. This one is something new.

With each whistle, a thick black storm cloud appears, dense and dark, almost overwhelming. They move like oil through water, filling her vision. Her hands flail at the clouds, a futile action, she knows, yet she can't resist. The darkness swallows her, the remaining light banished to the outermost periphery of her vision.

Freya knows the feeling of suffocation is psychosomatic. She can even provide a verbatim medical definition of this word and detail several case studies on the nature of this condition. But none of that does anything to lessen the feeling she is slowly going blind and choking. Rasping for air, her throat starts to itch and sting.

The melody is light and playful, but she hates it. Every cell in her body screams as each note trills. She slams her hands over her ears and stumbles away from the door of the Danger Room.

As the black clouds begin to fade Freya hurries past Jack's door, along the hall and up the stairs. Once she's inside her bedroom, she closes the door behind her and locks it, checks it is locked, then unlocks it, looks outside, closes it and locks it again. She dives beneath the covers as if she were a toddler escaping the boogieman.

She heaves great, heavy breaths, taking comfort from the familiar, natural darkness in front of her, so completely different from the vile blackness of mere moments ago. It's quiet now. She hears only her own laboured breathing.

Freya emerges from beneath the warm embrace of the covers and looks out the window at the night sky. It would be so easy to throw her things in a bag, climb out the window, and get in her car. To drive away and never look back.

But now, more than ever, she needs to know what's in that room.

EXCERPT FROM *THE SINS OF ADONIS*

Sean and I thought it was hilarious when we started literally collecting notches in our belts. Sometimes, I'd be in the middle of thrusting into some airheaded bint and all I'd be thinking about is making that next little mark on the leather.

And now that I've got this shiny new game, the only tragedy is there's no one I can share it with. Telling Sean about sexual conquests is one thing, but I'd hardly entrust him with any knowledge that could see me ending up inside a prison cell. There's Mum and Dad, of course, but I doubt they'd have the good spirit to appreciate my endeavours. It's all about business with them. And that only leaves my brother, but he'd never understand either. We're worlds apart, and sometimes I'm appalled that we even escaped the same womb. He's basically the human equivalent of a Phil Collins B-side.

Still, I have my trophies. I suppose that's something.

IV

Treatment

"Lies, intentional and unintentional, are much seldomer told in answer to precise than to leading questions."

Florence Nightingale,
Notes on Nursing: What it Is and What it Is Not

21

The Goddamn Whales

Jack dreams of his brother. Lately the dreams have been darker, denser, more vivid. He wakes up feeling ill and disoriented, as though he's downed a bottle of tequila and then crash-landed a space shuttle in the Pacific Ocean. He turns to the empty space of his bed and it is not until his head clears that he remembers. His sheets still smell like her.

He sits up slowly, rubbing his aching head, then climbs out of bed, knocking the pillows to the floor. He yawns, stretches, and is about to reach for the nearest shirt on his floor that doesn't smell like a homeless shelter when he notices there is nothing on the sheet where his pillows had been. Nothing.

"Shit. *Shit.* Fuck!" He pulls on a pair of jeans and an old Pogues T-shirt and darts along the corridor to the living room, where he finds Maria humming along to a Billie Holiday recording and sitting on the sofa, snacking on cheese and biscuits.

"*¡Buenos tardes,* Mr Jack!"

"Hi, Maria. Isn't *tardes*...isn't that for afternoon?"

"*Si*. It is nearly one."

"Ah, Christ. How did I sleep for that long?"

"Something keeping you up late? Or somebody?" Maria says, her eyes locked on the plate in front of her. Her muscles twitch with the effort of restraining a grin.

"Ah, I don't know. Listen, have you seen Freya?"

"*Si*, you just missed her. She leave about ten minutes ago."

"Right. Okay, that's, ah…Did she say where she was going?"

"No, but she was in a hurry. Jack, I must say thank you again to you and your wonderful family for my birthday present!"

"Your what?"

Maria holds a bottle of Bollinger, complete with oversized decorative ribbon, proudly aloft.

"Oh, right. I can't take credit for that, I'm afraid. I didn't know anything about it. I forgot it was your birthday. I'll pick you up something later, though. Promise. And ah, complay… complayann…"

"Feliz cumpleaños?"

"Yes. That one. Happy birthday."

"*Gracias*. I was going to save it for my birthday dinner tonight, but I'm feeling a little sneaky so I'm having a glass with my lunch." She treats him to a cheeky wink as she opens the bottle.

"Yeah, I'm sure you deserve it."

He runs to the front door and flings it open. He grunts as the sun assaults his eyes, and squints through the glare. Freya is out there somewhere, with that little packet of secret trophies, somewhere among that ocean of lost, disconnected souls. He could try and find her, he thinks, but recalls he doesn't know her number. And there are so many other things out there: shopping centres with crying children, overturned rubbish bins spewing germ-ridden debris down rusty drains, parks with dogs and snakes and spiders, lonely people with narrow, hateful eyes and sad and futile faces, car accidents, traffic lights, viruses, sirens, violence, crowds.

He slams the door and bends forward, taking a series of deep breaths to steady himself. No, it's best to wait. She'll come back.

She has to. And then he'll explain everything. But he needs to formulate a plausible explanation. Shouldn't be too hard, since he makes up lies for a living. He heads back to the comfortable chaos of his bedroom, failing to notice Maria lying limp on the floor as he passes her.

Freya and Callum stare at the whales floating above them as Callum says, "I can't believe we're doing this. Again."

"Shhh! Listen to the whales."

The sound echoes cavernously around them and Freya closes her eyes, letting the whale song envelop her. The clouds of colour drift and swirl around her head.

"You know what the whale song looks like? Bright, beautiful, soft flowing rivers of blue and gold. They float in front of my eyes, right here, where my fingers are. Right…here. It's so warm, so calm."

"I wish I could see the world like you do. The way you paint it. Too few of us have the benefit of aural-visual sensory confusion."

"And not everyone has a pathological fear of pineapple cutters either."

"Do you think whales listen to recordings of hippies moaning when they want to relax and meditate?"

"Ha! Look at them. So huge and powerful they don't give a shit about the tiny parasites living right on their chin. Imagine being that gigantic, that invincible. Nothing to fear…"

The whale song drifts over the silence between them, covering it like a veil. Freya laughs and dances her fingers through the kaleidoscope of colours that flow around the life-size humpback replicas suspended in the giant cement corridor outside the museum entrance. Visitors exiting the museum walk past them as quickly as possible. A woman whose face is amusingly similar to the dog she's walking turns her nose in disapproval.

"Gimme another one of those treats," demands Freya.

"You've already had two."

"Treats! Gimme."

Callum sighs and zips open his backpack, pulling out a Tupperware container of freshly baked hash brownies. "God, when was the last time we had these with the whales?"

"Just after Valerie died. Fuck, I was a mess."

"I remember. Better make this the last one unless you want to spend another six hours giggling at that Queen Street Mall busker who dresses like a statue."

"Boy, did he hate me! I've never seen a statue so mad before."

Freya bites into the moist brown morsel, imagining the THC working its way through her system like a meme through a social network. Callum selects a brownie and chews thoughtfully. Freya silently watches the colours, and no words are spoken between them for several minutes.

Eventually, Freya says, "I found blood on Elijah. On his legs."

"He's only human."

"Despite them worshipping him like a demigod, sure. But he's been inert for months, so how did he get blood on him?"

"Maybe someone dropped him?"

"Very funny. I couldn't see any cuts or wounds."

"What are you, a forensics expert?"

"No, but I know someone who is. And I'm going to give him this."

Freya produces a small ziplock bag containing the cotton bud with the blood sample she took from Elijah.

"Fucking hell, Freya. Who are you giving that to?"

"This guy who did first semester nursing with me but moved to forensics. He works for a DNA testing clinic now, and I'm going to give him a sample of Elijah's hair as well to see if they're a match."

"Why wouldn't they be? Frey, you think the blood is someone else's?"

"It's certainly a possibility. Also, I found this." She holds up the plastic baggie she found in Jack's room.

"What is that?"

"It looks like a collection of hair samples, eleven different specimens, maybe more from what I've counted, and a white feather. I'll get them DNA matched against the blood, too."

"Where did you find them?"

"Underneath Jack's pillow."

"You were looking under Jack's—Ohhhhh! Freya, Freya, Freya."

"Don't you give me that patronising tone! How many times have you...How much weed did you put in these treats? I feel like everything just went 3D."

"The real world *is* 3D, Freya."

"No, like IMAX 3D. Jesus. Anyway, I made a mistake. I think. But he's so...you know. Those things I like. I thought it was all going well. We hate the same things, which is always important. He seemed nice. You know how I'm a sucker for introspective arty types."

"Introspective arty types who keep multiple locks of hair under their pillows?"

"I didn't know that before I slept with him!"

"Maybe they're from each of his lovers. Do you think he has a lock of your hair?"

Freya chokes and spits brownie all over herself. "Shit! I hadn't thought of that. God, that is so creepy! Wow, Callum, I wish you could see these rivers of gold. Hey, remember that show *Cities of Gold*? How did the theme song go?"

"Freya, focus. You need to get out of there."

She bites her lip and stares up at the whales. "I can't. I can't leave. Not until I find out what's in that fucking Danger Room, with its whistling and...Argh, you should have seen that colour. It was so awful, it made my face want to divorce my eyes."

"Once again, for those of us in the back seats?"

"Last night, from the Danger Room, I heard this whistling, and the sound it made was an entirely new colour. It was like someone poured poison into my eyes. I can't leave until I find out what's in that room. And someone has to stop their precious Halcyon Corporation from spilling oil all over penguins and gaining control of more than half the world's pharmaceutical industry."

"Isn't this something I suggested in an earlier conversation?"

"Fine, you were right and I was wrong. You know what else? I'm not the only one keeping tabs on them. The housekeeper, Maria, is too. I think she's going to be able to tell me more—Look! It's her!"

"Maria?"

"No, Marilyn!"

They scamper past the museum doors and move towards Marilyn halfway between a tiptoe and a gallop, excitement battling for control of their motor functions.

"Ah, excuse me, Marilyn...um...miss?" The words tumble out of Freya's mouth like gumballs from a vending machine. Marilyn turns, her face like a geisha, plastered with layers of foundation and lipstick. Her dress is the most remarkable pink, complete with matching parasol, coupled with white gloves and a handbag that blend so perfectly it is almost impossible to tell where her fingers end and the bag begins.

"May...can we sit with you for a minute?"

Marilyn smiles and pats the empty space next to her on the bench. Freya and Callum sit and stare at her in confused awe.

"It's a beautiful day, isn't it?" says Freya eventually.

Marilyn smiles back.

"Um...Marilyn, this might sound like an odd question, but...are you...you?"

She turns to Freya, her perfect smile like a china doll's. "I've never fooled anyone. I let people fool themselves. They didn't bother to find out who and what I was. Instead they would invent a character for me. I wouldn't argue with them," she says, her voice a jar of honey mixed with gravel. She twists her parasol and looks out over the river. "Beneath the makeup and behind the smile I'm just a girl who wishes for the world." She notices Freya's gloves and reaches across to touch them.

"Yeah, I like gloves too. It's an Audrey Hepburn..." Freya trails off as she stares into Marilyn's wide blue eyes. "You know what? That's a lie. I wear them because I have these hideous scars on my wrist that I try to hide."

"If you're gonna be two-faced, at least make one of them pretty," Marilyn says with an exaggerated wink.

Freya laughs and says, "Marilyn? I think I'm living in a house filled with psychopaths or sociopaths, whatever, and they run this huge company and one of them is in a coma but somehow has blood on him and another one, his brother, had these weird locks of hair under his pillow, which I know because I slept with him because my judgement really is that bad, and I don't know what to do, and I ate some hash brownies and tried to ask the whales for advice and they showed me some gold rivers, and now my mouth keeps moving and I can't stop talking, and the whales didn't have any answers for me at all."

Marilyn laughs and places one gloved hand gently on Freya's shoulder. It feels warm and heavy. "Sometimes good things fall apart so better things can fall together."

"I think…um…I think actually that's pretty good advice."

Marilyn rises elegantly to her feet, plants a kiss on Freya's cheek and walks towards the whales. Her humming blends with their music.

"Wow. Who knew a delusional method actress could be so eloquent?" says Callum. They watch her walk away.

Freya's lips feel numb and this makes her giggle.

"Hey, hey, your pants are singing!" laughs Callum.

Freya removes her phone from her pocket and answers. "Hello? Hello? I don't understand—Oh, right, *si, hablo español. Pero, no mucho. Si, si,* ah…I can't, um *más despacio, más despacio, por favor*. Maria? Shit. Shit. Christ. *Si, claro*, ah, of course." Freya drops the phone to the grass and falls backwards onto the bench.

"Frey? What's the matter?"

Freya squints at the water. The whales' gold rivers swim in front of her eyes. She wants to lie in them and sleep forever.

"What happened?"

"Maria's in hospital."

The sound of the whale song echoes through the corridor.

22

The Ice Queen Calleth

The air here tastes different. Sterile. Torpid. Stale. No matter how hard Freya tries she can't fill her lungs, like she's stuck in a box with no airholes and the oxygen is slowly being depleted.

"There is nothing in this life I will ever hate more than sitting in hospital waiting rooms."

"Not the best quality for a nurse, is it? Like a teacher who doesn't like kids?"

"No, it's different when you're on the other side of the glass. As a nurse, you're in control. Or at least at the controls, but right now…? I'm helpless. There's a dead body in there, a 'cadaver' as they say in the biz, and a few hours ago it was a living, breathing, singing, dancing human with a penchant for eavesdropping and now it's just a lump of flesh."

The shuffling of shoes echoes down the hallway. The air is thick with the weight of nothing happening. "Being here makes me miss Valerie something awful."

Callum throws her a commiserating smile and hugs her.

"Thanks for driving us here, Cal."

"Of course." An awkward silence.

"I'm filled with angstxiety."

Callum smiles. "I'm still not sold on that one."

"Oh come on! Angst and anxiety go together like vodka and hangovers."

"Maybe." A less awkward silence. "Do you want something to eat?"

"Oh, gods, yes. I think those hash brownies have mostly worn off but I could eat a horse and all its children right now. Here." She reaches into her pocket and excavates a fistful of change. "Go to the vending machine. Get me all the things."

"Don't you want something more substantial? A sandwich?"

"Grief needs to be killed by sugar. Vast quantities of waistline-expanding sugar. I won't eat anything that doesn't come wrapped in eye-gougingly bright colours."

Callum shakes his head and disappears down the corridor, leaving Freya more alone than she would like to be. She fingers the packet of hair in her pocket and listens to the world collapsing around her. She leans back in the plastic chair and stares at the fluorescent light above her. Moment follows moment in a slow and uncomfortable shuffle.

A shower of brightly wrapped confectionary hits the seat beside her. "Callum, I love you." She rips open a Snickers bar and stuffs it into her mouth. She tears open a packet of M&M's and pours them in, too.

"Jesus, Frey, are you trying to get diabetes?"

"Chocolate makes the sad go away." She is in the process of devouring a fresh mouthful of brightly coloured candy when she looks up to see half a dozen sad brown eyes staring down at her.

"Are you Freya?"

She coughs and splutters a small explosion of caramel, biscuit and chocolate all over the speaker. "Aghthm! Ah…ah…gebruvellem, sthorry…" She chews and swallows the last of her food and tries to continue, "Yes, I am…you must be Maria's *familia*?"

"*Si.* I'm Niki, Maria's niece."

"Niki, *yo estoy muy,* um, *trist*...ah, fuck it. My Spanish disappears when I'm upset."

"It's okay."

Freya stands and reaches out her hand to shake Niki's, but finds herself enveloped in a warm hug. The rest of the family does the same, passing her round like a new puppy. A storm of Colombian kisses and commiserations enshrouds her.

"I should go," Callum says quietly in her ear when she is at last released.

"Okay. Thanks for everything, Cal. One last thing. Do you think you could get these to that friend of mine?" She presses the plastic baggies into his hands. "I'll message you his details later."

"Yeah, sure." A smile clambers onto his face but then loses confidence and slips into a frown.

Freya squeezes his hand and says goodbye, then spends the next few minutes trying to grasp snippets out of the Suarezes' wailing. Her Spanish is fairly rusty as it is, but the tears and gnashing are mauling and mangling the words so badly that their own mother can't recognise them.

A young doctor with tired eyes and a mop of tangled brown hair enters the room. His face conveys the news before his lips even open. She wonders how many times he's had to give this speech, and if it ever gets easier. Has he practised it in the bathroom mirror? Or is this just another inconvenient duty that's keeping him from his evening's television and glass of merlot?

"Hello, my name is Dr James Walton. I've been in charge of the team overseeing Mrs Suarez since she was admitted this afternoon. I'm going to do you the courtesy of being honest and direct. Mrs Suarez's breathing and heart had both stopped by the time the ambulance arrived here at the hospital. There was an attempt to resuscitate her, but this was unfortunately unsuccessful. All signs point towards a sudden onset heart attack. I hope it's of some comfort that it was quick, a few minutes at most. Someone will be with you soon to help you make arrangements. If any of you want to see her before we take her to the morgue, I'll get one of the nurses to sort it out for you. I'm very sorry for your loss."

As Niki translates for the rest of the Suarezes, the doctor frowns politely, then nods and walks away. The wave of tears and wailing resurges.

◇◇◇

Freya wakes up to drool on her face and M&M's in her hair, and a polychromatic sea of chocolate bar wrappers around her. The sight of the Suarezes chowing down on the rest of her sugary bounty stirs feelings of both amusement and confusion. She is slightly concerned that her leg seems to be trembling and is about to call for a doctor when she remembers she has set her phone to vibrate. "Hello?"

"Freya."

Ah, the ice queen calleth. "Evelyn."

"I've just heard the terrible news. Such a tragedy."

"It is."

"She will be dearly missed."

"She will."

A cold, firm silence.

"We have made arrangements for the body to be collected and the funeral service is all booked and paid for. Florists, catering, and all the rest. Please let the family know."

"That's very generous of you, Evelyn."

"It's nothing. Maria was like one of the family. I'll see you at the service tomorrow."

"Tomorrow? Don't you think you should give the family a little more time to notify everybody? What if people can't make it?"

"For heaven's sake, dear, it's a funeral. I'm sure those people will be able to clear eating enchiladas and watching telenovellas from their schedules."

Evelyn hangs up and leaves Freya silent and seething. There's no way the Vincettis could have organised a funeral so quickly.

Freya realises that the eyes of *La Familia Suarez* are watching her, waiting. "That was Evelyn Vincetti," she explains. "They've made arrangements for the funeral. They'll contact you with details."

Niki translates and the Suarezes once again collapse into a storm of wailing.

Eventually, Niki comes back to Freya and asks, "Do you mind if I ask you something, something that maybe sounds a little strange?"

"Honestly? To compete with the rest of today's events you'd have to be trying really hard to even make a dent."

"Perhaps we should sit down."

A Chokito wrapper crumples under Freya as she sits.

"My Aunty Maria. Did you get to know her well?"

"I'd only been working at the house for a week, but Maria and I talked a lot. She likes…she used to like to chat." Referring to Maria in past tense makes Freya feel like she is digging a grave with her tongue.

"If I asked you to bring me something of hers, something that she touched recently, could you do that? It doesn't have to be anything special, a toothbrush or a hairpin would do. As long as she's touched it. I know that might sound weird but…"

"Yes. Of course."

Niki hugs Freya tightly. Freya's arms squeeze weakly in a confused and feeble effort to return the affection.

"Thank you so much for meeting us here, but you know, the next few hours will have a lot of Colombian weeping. If you want to leave…"

"Yes. I should go. Give me your number."

Niki rattles it off and Freya taps it into her phone. She steps out of the room, the corridor, the building. Outside the sky is bright and glaring. Somewhere there is a radio playing an old Massive Attack song. Freya watches the colours spread like food dye dripped into a bucket of water. She feels the strength drain from her legs and sits on the pavement, her back leaning against the hospital wall for support.

Her hands touch the concrete beneath her. This is where it happened. Where Valerie's future shifted from being unknown to non-existent. Where a bright young girl with a truckload of sass and a mean Scrabble game was transformed into a mangle of flesh and formerly functioning organs.

She imagines the screeching tyres, metal dancing with metal, glass hurtling through the air. A tempest of chaos ending in the worst kind of silence and stillness.

23

Dove

He walks down the hall whistling, with his prey in his hands. He approaches his brother's door and knocks loudly. "Hey Jackie! Jackie O! Jack-in-the-box! Openupopenupopenupopenup! I've got something to show you!"

Jack opens his door. His pimply, bespectacled face and red-rimmed eyes radiate irritation and fatigue. "What the hell do you want, Elijah? I've got a physics assignment due tomorrow."

"Like Mrs thirty-year-old-virgin-squinty-face-McGee is going to fail her one and only student."

"Whatever. I don't care what your surprise is."

"Oh, I think you might!" Elijah holds it aloft, his face lit by a brilliant smile.

"Jesus fucking Christ, Elijah! What is wrong with you?"

"Shot it from forty feet away, I shit you not!" He holds the bird proudly in the air, suspended by its legs, its pure white feathers desecrated by a patch of red.

"You shot a fucking dove*? With what?"*

"How's it any different from shooting a crow, except that it's white? What are you, racist?"

"That's not funny. And you didn't answer my question. And it's bleeding all over the goddamn floor!"

Elijah shrugs. "I shot it with Dad's old Webley. Isn't that a ridiculous name for an arms manufacturer? They sound like they should make English sweets. 'Webley's Famous Suck 'n' Chews! Get 'em right here, baker's dozen for thruppence apenny!' And don't worry about the mess, Caecilla will clean it up."

"You mean Delora. Caecilla got fired last month because you told Mum that she stole the Florentine vase that you smashed, remember?"

"Right, well. Whatever illegal immigrant they got to fill her shoes."

"You're a creep, you know that?"

"You're the one with the crooked back, weird eyes, and agoraphobia."

Jack's face flares at his brother's use of that forbidden word. He tries to calm himself, remember that Elijah is just trying to get under his skin, provoke a reaction. But his brother has always had such a gift for bringing out the worst in people. He tries to restrain them, but the words charge out of his mouth.

"I do not have agoraphobia!"

"Really? When was the last time you left this house?"

"When I saw the specialist last week."

"No, the last time you left by choice?"

"I don't have time for this shit, Eli. Would you please get that fucking thing away from my door? Look! You've already got blood all over the place!"

"Boys! Boys! You aren't fighting again, are you?" Evelyn's roar rips through the mansion.

"No, Mum! Jack and I are just both really upset! Come look, come look!"

Her heels clack down the hallway towards them. Jack is silent and sullen.

"Oh my God! Eli, what are you doing touching that horrid thing? You'll get sick!"

"I had to save it! I found it by the road. I think somebody shot it! A dove would never hurt anybody. Why would anyone kill such

a beautiful creature?" Tears well in Elijah's eyes and his lip starts to tremble.

"I don't know, baby. Thank goodness for good people like you to care for poor injured creatures like this, you little saint." She kisses him on the head and hollers, "Delora! Come clean this up right now!" Her manicured talons enclose Elijah in a protective embrace. "Shh, shh, little one. Everything will be fine, I promise," she soothes.

Over her shoulder, Elijah treats Jack to a smirk.

Jack wants nothing more than to pull back his fist and ram it into his brother's nose, despite the vengeance their mother would unleash on him, and in spite of the fact that his bones would shatter like glass upon impact.

None of this logic assuages Jack's fury as Evelyn leads his brother outside to the garden to dispose of the dove. Jack is left staring at the congealed crimson pool soaking into the carpet runner and trickling onto the marble at his feet.

Jack can't sleep. Nothing out of the ordinary there. Ever since the age of twelve he has had the sunken black eyes of a middle-aged alcoholic. Lately, however, things have been a different kind of strange. Usually anxiety related to his condition is what keeps him awake; fear of a too-short life spent locked within the tiny Vincetti kingdom. But lately, things have been different.

He has been dreaming of his brother. Or, more correctly, he has been dreaming as *his brother through Elijah's eyes, and more than that, through his skin, fingers, teeth, and tongue. In these dreams he sees, feels, and tastes everything as though he were Elijah. He has just awoken from a dream where he watched as the dove's chest burst with red and the bird plummeted gracelessly to the ground. Some unholy mirth flowed through him as he ran towards it, felt its limp, lifeless body in his hands, felt its hot, wet blood run over his fingers.*

Jack sits up in bed, examines the Rorschach blot of bruises that has appeared on his chest while he slept. One of them vaguely resembles Japan, another in a long list of places he will never see.

He goes to his desk and turns on his computer. His fingers tap away at the keys and the horrors of his existence are transformed as he brings his characters to life, shapes their faces and speech and thoughts. Finally he falls asleep, his hands resting on the keyboard. In the morning he will awake to find he has written 180 pages of:

adfslkhfskkkkkkkkkkkkkkkkhjladsssssssssssssssf;
a;jjjjjjjjjjjjjjjjjjjjjjjjjaaaaaaaaaaaaaa;;;;;;;;;;;;;;;;;;;;;;;;;;
;;;;;;;;;dsssssssssssssaaaaaaaaaaaaaaaajjjjjjjkkkkkkk
kllllllaaaaadddddddddddddhu;ghhhhhhhhhhhhh
hhhakrrrrrrrrrrrrrrrrrrrrrrrrrrrrrrrrrrrrrrrrr
rrrrrrrrrrrrrrrrrrrrrrrrrrrrrrrrrrrrrrri;;;;;;;;;;;;;;;;;;;;;;f
ddddddddnsfads”””ghijr
eoooooooooooooooooooooo…

Despite her hours of scrubbing—immediately prior to her abrupt dismissal—Delora is unable to remove the last vestiges of red from the marble floor outside Jack's bedroom. The washed-out bloodstain is the first thing he sees as he exits the relatively safe confines of his room to enter the world outside. He steps over it quickly and heads to the kitchen, where he pours himself a bowl of Captain Choc's Chocolaty Chocoflakes—now with more *chocolate!—and exits onto the back verandah to watch the first ferries of the morning sway across the river.*

The crunching of the cereal reverberates inside his head, preventing cohesive thought. The ferries thrum across the river with their cargo of lawyers and teachers and waiters and builders and nurses and parking inspectors and abattoir health and safety protocol regulators; all jobs he will never have. He is happy, for a moment, to be peaceful. He is unsurprised when this does not last.

"Jaaaaaaaaccckkkkk!"

He considers his options.

1 Run. (Not possible.)

2 Hide. (Plausible, given the number of rooms in this house, but ultimately fruitless. Will have to eventually surface for food and amenities.)

3 Patricide.(…)

4 Walk proudly towards the gallows.

He stands, leaves his Chocoflakes to slowly wilt in the bowl and walks inside.

Harland is standing in the doorway of Jack's room, eyes wide with rage, nostrils flared like a belligerent bull. His father's anger does not instil quite the same fear in Jack, at the age of seventeen, as it would have a few years ago. What truly worries him is the vintage Webley service revolver Harland is clasping in his fingers.

"Jack. Explain to me. How. Did. My. Webley. Find. Its. Way. Into. Your. Drawer?"

It's the same terse, staccato manner of speech Harland uses when firing an employee. It takes a moment for Jack's eyes to disengage from the gun and register that both his mother and brother are sitting on his bed, gazing at him with sorrowful concern, genuine and otherwise, respectively.

"It was Elijah. He must have put it there while I was asleep. He was the one who found the dove because he was the one who shot it. How can you run all those companies and be too stupid to figure that out?" The words escape his mouth in a stampede. It's too late to grab them from the air and shove them back in.

"Questioning. My. Intelligence. Would be. Ill advised. At the. Best. Of times. You'd better re-examine your situation."

"Why would I bring in the dove to try and save it if I was the one who shot it?" says Elijah, brushing back a lock of his hair. "I know you're upset, but blaming me won't help anything."

"You little shit!" Jack runs at Elijah with his fist raised and his tongue coppery with bloodlust. The room blurs into the background and he can see only his brother's smug, deceitful face. He closes the distance between them, his fist rushing towards Elijah's nose. The deed is all but done save for the doing, when he catches his foot on the leg of a chair and his rage is reduced to a Chaplinesque pratfall.

He plummets to the floor, slams his shin hard against the coffee table and collapses in a fiery ball of pain and indignation. Jack's eyes close with the image of his brother looking down at him, his face radiating mock concern.

*The cast is thick and heavy, as is the doctor's tired diatribe. "Should know better"...*blah blah blah...*"Can't risk this kind of incident with your delicate condition"...*blah blah blah...*"Lucky you have such caring parents"...*blah blah blah *etc.*

Jack knows all of this, word for word, concerned shoulder pat for concerned shoulder pat. He doesn't say goodbye to the doctor when he leaves. Jack knows it won't be too long before he's back.

Elijah strides into the room just as the doctor departs.

"Sartre said, Hell is other people. *I'm beginning to see where he was coming from," says Jack, placing his book beside him as a symbol of defeat.*

"Sartre was a boring old twat who wouldn't have known a good time if it had grabbed him by the balls and stabbed him in the face with a rusty screwdriver."

"Why did you shoot that dove, Eli? You've done some pretty creepy things, but this..."

"I read an interview once where an author was asked why he wrote books. He answered, Mountaineers climb mountains because they're there. I write books for the opposite reason.*"*

"Get to the point."

"I did it because I could. Because I wanted to find out if I could get away with it. And I did, although there was some unfortunate collateral damage." Eli slaps his brother's cast with the back of his hand.

Jack refuses to give his brother the satisfaction of hearing him scream.

"My little escapades would be a lot more fun with you on board, Jack. You could be the Professor X to my Wolverine, what with that great bulging brain of yours and your adorable disability."

"Elijah, and I say this honestly, I'm worried about you. Drugs, stealing, fucking around, I can understand that. You're young, healthy, and rich—"

"Don't forget good-looking!"

"Let me finish. It makes sense to want to push the boundaries. But this…it's inhumane."

"Inhumane, as in cruel to the point of being contrary to basic human nature? I'm not sure that's a term that makes any rational sense. After all, humans are really the only animals that kill for reasons besides basic survival. I've never heard of an animal running a gulag, have you? You should worry about yourself, brother o' mine. If you aren't careful your life's going to be no fun at all. You'll end up some sort of eccentric recluse talking to your plants and spending afternoons trying to find coded extraterrestrial messages in the evening weather report. Here, I got you a present." Elijah hands him a white feather. "Think of it as a metaphorical white flag. A thank you for taking the flak. Don't worry, I cleaned it thoroughly. It's perfectly hygienic."

"Why would I want this, Eli?" Jack says, even though he takes the feather delicately in his hands.

"There, now. That wasn't so difficult, was it? They say it's better to give than to receive. Speedy recovery, Jackie boy." Elijah throws him a mock salute and departs.

Jack stares at the feather. It's beautiful.

Three weeks later, he still hasn't got the hang of the crutches. He hobbles around the house like an archaic cyborg, knocking over stools and ornaments. It takes him several minutes to get from his bedroom to the back verandah, where he finds his father attempting to enjoy a cigar.

"Harland, I need a copy of my birth certificate for my university application."

"First of all, I hate it when you address me by my given name. Second, you know I disapprove of this 'distance education' nonsense. Why study by distance when the goddamn university is a fifteen-minute drive away? And third, as I keep telling you, just give me a list of your preferences and I'll make the arrangements."

"One, sorry. Two, the distance education program is very well regarded, plus it's a lot more accommodating of my osteogenesis. And three, I want to get into university via my own merit. I've got the grades, I don't need you making deals under the table for me."

Harland looks at him hard, and the pair lock eyes for a full ten-second count, long enough for a fallen boxer to be declared defeated. "Fine. I'll get it for you." A pause. "Later." He stubs out his cigar, struts out onto the lawn and around the house before announcing his departure via the purring of his BMW's engine.

"Shit," says Jack. He walks back inside to find Elijah in the kitchen, diving into the refrigerator and surfacing with an ice-cream sandwich.

"What's the matter, Jack-in-the-box?" he chirps.

"Dad's refusing to give me my birth certificate."

Elijah grins. "Sounds like I've got a brother in need. Would this help?" He holds aloft a tiny flat piece of carved brass.

"What's that?"

"Copy of his master key. Worth its weight in gold, this thing. Ah...actually, since it only weighs a few grams, perhaps I meant worth its weight in weapons-grade plutonium."

"Get me into his office." Jack's voice is a desperate plea masquerading as a command.

"Isn't this nice? Two brothers up to mischief together? Just like a Hardy Boys novel. Hobble along then."

Elijah walks with brisk, confident strides, while his sibling's steps are clumsy, halting, movements. "You want to do the honours?" Elijah hands him the key. "Harland's been making noises about upgrading to a magnetic key system, like in hotels, so this baby might not be much use soon."

The key turns with almost disappointing ease and they enter Harland's office, which reveals itself as a dreary ode to modern efficiency. Shelves filled with books on economic theory and business philosophy, computer screens streaming information about stocks and bonds, and a desk adorned with the usual office paraphernalia.

"Alright, well say what you like about Daddy dearest, at least the man is organised. You start that end, I'll start there," Elijah

says, running to the far side of the room. "Tax reports, employee files, medical records, blah blah blah…You got anything your end?"

"Car insurance, house insurance, credit card receipts…Hmm, here's something. It's a box marked 'Family Documents'."

"Mission accomplished. Let's make our timely escape."

"It's locked."

"Wellity, wellity, well. Perhaps Daddy dearest isn't quite the dullard we thought? I wonder if we have an evil twin he's trying to keep secret. Unless…you are the evil twin!"

"Quit the vaudeville. Help me get it open."

Elijah snatches the thin metal box from Jack's hands. He grabs a couple of paperclips from the container on the desk, twists them into shape, and fiddles with the lock until it snaps open. He grins and says, "Handy, no?"

Jack looks in the box. There's a slim, lonely manila folder. "Let's see… wedding certificate, health certificate, here's your birth certificate…"

"Aaaaaaaand?"

"It's not here."

"So, you are the evil twin!"

"Stop fucking around, Eli. Why would yours be here but not mine? Wait…there are two copies of yours…"

"Hang on," says Elijah, fingering the two documents. "They're both originals. Why would they have two originals of mine and none of yours?"

"Wait," says Jack. "They're not identical. Look. The dates are different. This one is March 4th…"

"My birthday."

"And this one is a couple of years earlier, on October 23rd…"

"Why is that date familiar?" Elijah barely conceals his smirk.

The pair fall into silence.

"We have the same name," says Elijah. "And what's worse, you had it first. I'm supposed to be the trendsetter around here!"

"Is there *nothing* you take seriously? I just found out I didn't even know my real name. Doesn't that mean anything to you?"

They stare at the almost-but-not-quite-identical documents for a few seconds more before Jack slips them back into the folder and *shuts the box. He staggers out the door, falls to the ground and lies there, contemplating the ceiling.*

It's not until he's having dinner with his parents four days later that Jack summons the courage to confront them. His father has already "taken care" of his university application and Jack has been accepted, much to his parents' disapproval, into a bachelor of creative writing, with a minor in philosophy.

A dinner of turkey and Russian salad sits before them. Vivaldi is playing on the Bang & Olufsen.

"Harland..." The angry glare on Jack's father's face tells him he's off to a bad start. "Dad. I have something to tell you."

Harland stops mid-chew and lays his fork down on the table. "You haven't gotten some girl pregnant?"

"Ha! Not bloody likely," chimes Elijah.

"Eli! Don't be rude," says Evelyn.

"It's nothing like that. I have to confess something."

Harland stiffens and draws in a deep breath.

"I broke into your office to find my birth certificate."

Harland and Evelyn glance at each other. Elijah raises his glass and guzzles his juice.

"It says my name is Elijah."

"How. Dare you. Break—"

"I broke in to get something that was rightfully mine. I took nothing, changed nothing, and saw nothing that wasn't my right to see. Please, do me the simple courtesy of answering my question."

Harland purses his mouth and inhales again. He looks at Evelyn, her expression is characteristically ambiguous. Elijah's grin is so wide he resembles a Muppet.

"When your mother and I decided to have a child, the name Elijah was one of the few things we agreed on. We wanted to honour your great-great-great-grandfather, the man who made the Vincetti name something to be respected and revered a century and a half ago." He moves his mouth in what he probably imagines is a passable attempt at a smile. "We put in enrolments at the best schools,

made arrangements for language classes, piano lessons, a private tutor, and so forth. I don't think you'll ever really understand what it's like until you're an expectant father yourself, but waiting for a child to arrive is like winning the lottery and simultaneously being told you have an incurable disease. It's exciting but terrifying. We wanted the whole world for our firstborn, our precious Elijah."

Jack struggles to imagine Harland and Evelyn as starry-eyed parents-to-be. He lets his father's words seep into him.

"When you were born, I felt like nothing else in my life had mattered. None of the money I'd made or companies I'd built was close to the achievement of my son's birth." Harland pauses to drain the last of his wine.

To Jack, the seconds that pass until Harland resumes his story feel like rusty nails being scraped along his spine. But he says nothing and waits.

"It wasn't until your second week that we noticed the discolouration in your eyes. As first-time parents we thought it would clear up, some sort of early birth thing. Eventually we took you to the doctor and found out about...your condition."

Evelyn places her hand on Jack's. Her fingers are surprisingly warm. He tries to remember the last time she touched him. Her voice is uncommonly quiet, "We are proud of you, Jack, but we had so many dreams for our Elijah. It wasn't your fault, but we knew from that moment that you would never be able to fulfil them. We decided to let you be your own person, with a new name that... suited you. And then when your brother came along, well..."

Jack grabs his plate and hurls it at the wall. The smashing of the fine china is not nearly as satisfying as he had hoped.

After several hours of crying and Buzzcocks albums blaring louder than Evelyn would ever normally allow, Jack lies on his bed feeling entirely empty. Head. Heart. Stomach. All empty. He opens his laptop, stares at it as though it were a digital oracle that might produce an answer to his problems in beautiful binary.

He opens a new Word document. He stares at the blank page and watches the cursor blink.

Blink.

Blink.

Blink.

His fingers begin to move.

> I'd always wanted to pull that trigger, but I'd been waiting for the perfect moment. When I watched that pool of red spread across the dove's chest I felt like Benjamin Franklin catching electricity with a kite.

24

Home?

Jack finds Freya on the roof shovelling jersey caramels into her mouth, chewing so hard she looks like a chipmunk that's found a stash of nuts.

"Hey," he says, his voice trembling.

"Fugg orf, Jork."

"What?"

She chews and swallows. "I said, fuck off, Jack."

"I didn't—"

"Didn't what? Didn't mean to hide a creepy bag of hair and feathers under your pillow or use me to sneak into the Danger Room? Christ on stilts, Jack, that's messed up. I yearn for when life was simpler, and I just got pissed off at boyfriends for fucking my housemates on the kitchen table."

"I don't know what to say to that."

"No, neither did I. Look, I'm pissed off and I'm fucking with you. So, out with it. What have you got for me? Apology, explanation, artfully crafted deception, or all three?"

Jack sits next to her and takes the caramel she offers him. He chews ponderously. "These are pretty good." He looks at her, the blue of his eyes dulled with remorse. "I haven't been totally honest. Honesty doesn't exactly thrive around here; it's as rare as orchids on a tundra."

"Please, spare me the bourgeois writer's similes."

"Force of habit. Look, when you helped me get into that room, I fumbled in the dark and found that weird packet of hair samples. I don't know where it came from, or who it belongs to, or why it was there. I just kept it under my pillow for safekeeping. I didn't know what else to do with it."

"But it belongs to someone in your family, right? Your father, your mother, Elijah?"

"Or Rosaline."

"What?"

"I'm just saying. She may have access to that room."

"Jack, Rosaline wouldn't…couldn't hurt a fly even if it had infected her family with the black death."

"Maybe. But there's no denying she's a few volumes short of *The Complete Dr Seuss*."

"So we don't know who the hair belongs to, but what about where it comes from? And what about the white feather? And are you sure you couldn't make out anything else in the Danger Room? Or did you feel something that might give us some clues? Shrunken voodoo heads? Magic potions? Ceremonial knives?"

"No, I bumped into a chair, then just as I heard you talking to people outside, my hands felt a table and that plastic bag with the hair and the dove feather was on it. I fumbled around a bit more, and came back out."

Freya glares at him. She turns the image of the feather around in her mind, thinking of a similar object Jack had found in his desk on the day they first met.

"I never said it was a dove feather, just a *white* feather."

"Ah…but how many birds have white feathers?"

"Ibises, pigeons, seagulls, pelicans, cockatoos, cockatiels…"

"Okay, okay, but a dove's the most obvious choice, right? I'm telling you the truth. And I would have told the whole story to you this morning if you'd only asked me. Instead you run off, and I get a knock on my door from Evelyn telling me Maria is lying unconscious on the floor."

"I didn't really feel like being in a house with a new lover who keeps hair beneath his pillow. You even lied to me about your name. When you scanned your retina at the door, it said 'Elijah Vincetti'."

"It was Elijah, once. Still is, according to my birth certificate."

Freya's hand, halfway to her mouth with another jersey caramel, freezes with surprise, its payload abruptly halted in front of its final destination.

"You have the same name as your brother?"

"My parents wanted the name Elijah for their golden child, and my osteogenesis denied me the throne. Some weird-eyed glass-boned freak carrying the name would have ruined their fantasy world."

"Your family doesn't exactly have a stellar track record of honesty. Why should I believe anything you tell me?"

"I don't know. I can't make you believe me if you don't want to. Although you probably don't have a lot of other options around here."

"You saying it's the truth doesn't make it so. Jesus, Jack. You sleep with me and then I find out you're hiding weird secrets like this? Why didn't you just tell me?"

"Because I thought you'd get scared about what goes on around here, most of which I don't understand myself, and I thought you'd want to leave. I don't want you to go."

As he has been speaking, his voice has been decrescendoeing from hysterical to mournful to imploring. "I really, really don't want you to leave."

She lands the caramel in her mouth and looks at his eyes as she chews, searching for a signal as to whether or not he is lying. He stares back. His eyes, whites tinted with blue, are pleading but sincere.

"I wanted to come after you, to find you. To race out and explain."

"So, why didn't you?"

"I didn't have your number, and I suppose I could have run around town yelling your name but I'm not sure that would have been particularly effective. Also...I couldn't get...you know, outside."

"What do you mean?"

"I went to the door, and I looked outside and I wanted to go out, more than I've wanted to in years, but then I started thinking about germs and cars and knives and unregistered automatic weapons and industrial accidents and I...couldn't."

"Jack, I didn't realise you had it that bad."

"I hate it here, but I can't leave. I can't." Jack looks at her and gently places his arm around her shoulder. She leans into him. He feels frail, like papier-mâché.

"But I'm glad you came home."

"Yes, I'm glad I came home, too." The word "home" tastes like slightly burnt biscuits.

25

How to Dress for a Funeral

Freya feels disgusted with herself for googling "how to dress for a funeral," but is even more appalled when she finds a plethora of articles devoted to it, including one stipulating that "little boys should be dressed in a suit that looks like Daddy's."

1 Dress respectfully. Dark shades and colours are most fitting.

She selects a sensible black dress.

2 An excess of makeup is not considered appropriate.

Freya splashes water on her face and scrubs, but can't scrub away the black bags beneath her eyes. It feels like weeks since she's slept well.

3 Consider the temperature and dress accordingly.

She pulls on a pair of elbow-length white gloves, watching her scars slide beneath the silk.

She checks her reflection and tries to calm her battling guilt and anger, then remembers she had promised Niki she'd try to find something belonging to Maria. She pokes her head out into the hallway to scan for any lurking Vincettis, dives out the door and down the stairs. When she reaches Maria's room she slips inside the open door, trying not to think about the fact that the people who killed her sleep only a few doors away. Trying not to think about what she is going to tell Maria's family.

There. Shining on the dresser. An old, but polished, silver hairbrush amid a clutter of bobby pins and sewing needles.

She grabs it, runs back to her room and quietly presses the door closed behind her, then enjoys exactly seventeen seconds of brief and blissful calm before a sharp knocking sound interrupts it.

"Freya? Freya, are you ready?"

"Just about!"

Evelyn Vincetti translates this to mean "enter at will" and throws the door open. She is wearing a garishly red dress, potent red lipstick, and a gold necklace that wouldn't be out of place around the neck of a crunk rapper.

9 Above all, be respectful and discreet rather than ostentatious.

"Hurry up, dear! It's terribly poor taste to be late for a funeral."

They are painfully, strenuously silent. Harland tries not to look at Evelyn; Evelyn tries to glare at Freya without her noticing; Freya's gaze is fixed firmly out the window. Their chauffeur, a wiry young man with a finely trimmed beard, glances at them occasionally in the rearview mirror.

"Jack won't be able to make it. He's feeling unwell," Evelyn says for the third time. Harland snorts.

Freya decides the only way she could be more uncomfortable is if a rogue monkey escaped from the zoo, climbed in through the window and started masturbating in front of them.

"And Rosaline and Elijah are coming in the other car," Evelyn adds, also for the third time. She sighs. "Funerals are always such atrocious affairs, aren't they?"

The hairbrush in Freya's handbag feels oddly heavy. Perhaps there would be some justice in beating Lord and Lady Vincetti over the head with it. But no, revenge is a dish that must not only be served cold, but with a pleasant smile.

Several aeons later they arrive at Maria's brother's house, where most of the Suarezes are waiting outside amongst a cluster of white-clad tables. Freya steps out of the car and waves a thank you to the chauffeur as her handbag starts singing. She zips it open and takes out her phone. She's been waiting for this call.

"Hello?"

"I've got the results for you."

"Took you long enough! What kept you? *World of Warcraft*?"

"Gimme a break. I have an arsehole of a boss who keeps his desk stacked with high fee-paying paternity cases. Criminal investigations, especially freebies, get put on the backburner. You're lucky I got it done this month, what with all the seventeen-year-old girls checking if it was Joe Plumber or Jim Bartender who knocked them up."

"You really have to shelve criminal investigations for paternity cases?"

"We're a private firm. Paternity cases turn over faster and for a higher fee. It's simple economics: we make more money terrifying young men with the news they're now fathers than by relieving middle-aged men about the ultimate ends of their daughters. Murder investigations have to take a backseat."

"Glad to see the system still works."

"In any case, before I even *start* asking you about where you got this stuff…"

"Hey—"

"Before I do that, I have the results. The hair samples are from five males and six females. The blood sample matched one of the brunette women. I also ran an auto-check on the samples against our own records, something we do as a default in case there's a match with one of our past clients."

"And…?"

"It isn't good news."

"Listen, I'm at a funeral. Things can't get much worse than that."

"You're on your phone at a funeral?"

6 Talking on mobile phones is disrespectful. Avoid distractions and focus on celebrating the life of your loved one.

"I don't have time for your views on funeral etiquette right now, just tell me."

"Like I said, most of our work is paternity testing, and when I ran the scan I found something in our database from a while back, long before my time. It was eighteen years ago, a paternity case for a Hilary Green."

"I don't know anyone by that name."

"You do, actually. She married the guy…his name was James Thompson. Happy ending, right? And she'd already picked out a name for their kid: Valerie."

"Valerie Thompson? *My* Valerie Thompson?"

"DNA don't tell no lies."

"Jesus brotherfucking Christ!"

"You've got a mouth like a sailor from a bad home, you know that? And you owe me big time. I accept cash, cheque, vodka, and sexual favours."

"I'll get back to you on that. For now you'll have to make do with my undying gratitude. Bye."

Questions hurtle through her head like a litter of kittens in a tumble dryer. She walks over to the nearest table and grabs hold of it to steady herself. Her hands are trembling.

"*Señorita,* may I offer you a drink?" asks the young Latino behind the trestle table stacked with drinks. Freya appreciates the addition of a makeshift bar at a funeral and wonders why it isn't standard practice.

"Christ Almighty, can you ever. You know how to make a Moscow Mule? Um…*¿moscú mula?* No, that's okay, I'll do it." Freya grabs at the various bottles and garnishes required to make her preferred poison as the bartender looks on in bemusement. He says, "My condolences to you. I did not know Señora Maria well, but the Colombians in this city, we keep pretty close together. I met her a few times. She was a strong woman."

"I'll drink to that. To Maria!" Freya raises her glass, downs its contents in a few eager gulps and slams it back on the table.

The procession begins to make its way inside the house. Freya follows them, moving through the rows of hired fold-up chairs and choosing one as far away as she can get from the Vincettis. Rosaline and Elijah are at the back of the room, his gurney parked in a quiet corner. Elijah is dressed in a sharp-looking suit with a white carnation pinned to his lapel, causing a few guests to wonder if the funeral party has been double-booked. Maria's family regards him with a curious mix of disdain and fear. Rosaline pouts and dabs her red-rimmed eyes with a lace handkerchief.

A Colombian priest stands at the front of the assembly and begins the service in rapid-fire Spanish. Freya catches only the odd reference to God and sadness as the words flit past her. A woman in the back row collapses into hysterical sobbing. Freya gently rubs her fingers along her itchy wrists and thinks about the last funeral she attended.

Valerie had looked so beautiful in her red satin dress.

"María fue una mujer muy bonita, estaba llena de color y la luz, y ahora ella está muerta…"

"Ah, *lo siento,* I don't, ah, more slowly please! I…"

The old man's dribbled, drunken Spanish washes over her and it soon becomes clear he is not interested in conversing, so much as talking.

11 You are not a grief counsellor, but be prepared to offer a shoulder to cry on.

Freya nods at appropriate intervals and continues drinking. All around her Maria's relatives and friends are crying and laughing. Candles light the darkened living room and cast an eerie glow over the proceedings. Outside, a guitar is strumming and a group of men are wailing a song with a singularly Colombian melancholy.

Flecks of spit from the old man's mouth shower Freya's face. She tries to wipe them away unobtrusively; the *Funeral Etiquette Guide* had nothing to say about this problem. After a few minutes more of tequila spray and sobbing, she starts to back away. He does not seem to notice. She leaves him talking to a bowl of chips and a tequila bottle and walks outside.

Freya sits on the stairs to the back deck and looks out at the city below. She wishes that she smoked, if only to distract her from thinking that she is sitting on the back steps of a stranger's house celebrating the wrongly truncated life of Maria Suarez.

"Hi, Freya. I'm so sorry I haven't had a chance to speak to you."

"It's okay, Niki. I understand. You have a beautiful house. This is an amazing view."

"Thank you. It's tricky with six of us crammed in, but Colombians are used to that." She sits next to Freya and swigs from her beer. "I still half-expect to wake up tomorrow morning to the smell of her *huevos rancheros*."

A pause. Sipping of drinks. Shuffling of feet.

"Did you get that thing I asked you for?"

"Oh! Yes." Freya opens her bag and delicately removes the hairbrush.

"My grandmother gave this to her. It's beautiful, no?"

Niki unwraps the black shawl from around her neck and takes the hairbrush from Freya's fingers. "Were you wearing those same gloves when you picked this up the first time?"

"I was. Why? Are you worried about fingerprints?"

"You could say that."

Niki turns the brush over, the moonlight reflects off the silver. "Freya, you don't know me, but you were a friend to Maria and, to Colombians, a friend of my friend is my friend. *La amiga de me amiga es me amiga también*. You understand? And I think I can trust you. Would you come for a little walk with me? In the garden?"

Freya follows her through the minefield of bottles littering the grass as Niki leads her to a stone bench hidden behind an immense jacaranda tree. The perfect place, thinks Freya, for kids to hold a secret spy club, or for Satanists to murmur a few incantations.

"Sit here," Niki says, patting the stone next to her. The seat is cold and hard. The slurs of mourning and singing hover in the night air. Back at the house, a baritone is singing a hoarse but beautiful requiem. "That's my uncle Jorge singing. He has a magnificent voice. In Bogotá, he could pack out theatres."

"Those lyrics…it's about a bird?"

"Yes. *Lost dove take your last flight / strange new skies await you / you have lingered too long in earth's embrace / bright days lay ahead of you.* It sounds better in Spanish."

Niki closes her eyes to drink in her uncle's words. "My aunty, she may have mentioned this, but all the women in our family, they have something. Well, not exactly the same, but…we call it *el regalo especiale.*"

"The special gift?"

"Yes. For Maria, she would sometimes have dreams; see things that had not yet happened. I also have this kind of gift, but for me it's not the same. I can't see forwards, only backwards. If I have an object someone has touched recently, especially if they were close to me, if they are my blood, then I can sense what they were thinking and how they were feeling when they touched it. I know this sounds strange."

No more unusual than seeing music as colours.

"I'm going to do a reading, with Maria's brush. Will you stay with me? When I read an object from my family, the connection is very strong. Sometimes overwhelming. I don't want to scare you, but if anything bad starts to happen, I want you to grab the brush from my hands. You are a nurse, right? Can I trust you to look after me?"

"Caring for ESP patients isn't exactly part of the core job description, but sure. Whatever you need."

Niki smiles warmly at Freya, then straightens her back and breathes deeply, in and out, three times. She starts mumbling a mantra in Spanish, too quiet to be overheard, then lifts the brush between her hands. Her lips cease to move and her whole frame becomes as still as the stone on which they are sitting.

Niki doesn't even appear to be breathing. Shadows hang on her face like a veil. Seconds swell into minutes yet still there is only silence. Beads of sweat trail down Niki's face. The brush begins to tremble in her hands. Freya leans in close. She reaches her fingers out to Niki's cheek and lets them hover a centimetre from her skin. "Niki?" she whispers. Nothing. "Hello? Are you in there?"

Niki's head snaps back and her hands fling out as though she's been shot. A hacking, guttural wail vaults out of her throat as her eyes open and she drops the brush onto the grass.

"Niki! Are you okay?"

Niki takes a few seconds to respond. "Yes, I'm fine. More or less. Although my head feels like it's filled with razorblades and tequila." She heaves a few breaths and rubs at her forehead, her fingers trembling. Freya tries to put her arm around her, but Niki pats her hand and pushes it away politely but firmly. "You've been very good to my family."

"It's the least I—"

"But you've also been keeping secrets from us. You know it was not a heart attack that killed her."

Freya feels like Judas munching on the entrée at the Last Supper. "Niki, I don't know anything for sure. I think that maybe, just maybe the Vincettis...But I don't have any proof! Psychic readings of hairbrushes aren't admissible evidence in a courtroom."

"Fuck evidence! *Mi tía está muerta*! I saw it, Freya. I saw her drink that champagne and then fall writhing to the ground. I saw her face wretched with agony and I watched the air escape her chest. What do you expect me to do, sit here and twiddle my thumbs?"

"These are powerful people, Niki. You can't attack them without proof or they'll sue you for defamation, take your house and whatever they like. They pull a lot of important strings in this town."

Niki spits and rattles off a stream of Spanish curses. "If this happened in Colombia, things would be *very* different."

"You need evidence. *We* need evidence. I think the Vincettis did this and plenty more besides. We just need to prove it."

"How?"

Freya looks at the hairbrush reflecting the pale light of the moon. She bends to pick it up. Despite her gloves, she can feel the metal handle glowing with a gentle, pulsing heat.

V

Relapse

"I have known patients dying of sheer pain,
exhaustion, and want of sleep, from one of the
most lingering and painful diseases known,
persevere, till within a few days of death,
not only the healthy colour of the cheek,
but the mottled appearance of a robust child."

Florence Nightingale,
Notes on Nursing: What it Is and What it Is Not

Excerpt from *The Sins of Adonis*

Yvette's incessant whining has been driving me ballistic. If she didn't have the sexual repertoire of a geisha coupled with the pre-cocaine addiction body of a lingerie model, I would have stopped tolerating her long ago. Does she really expect me to cohabitate with her in some pathetic ode to mediocrity? The whole point of a woman like Yvette even existing is to stir and entice the baser instincts. The silly little tart should stick to what she's good at.

The mere thought of her greeting me at the door with a kiss on the cheek and a plate of roast beef is utterly detestable. That's what I have Rosaline for, to be my little Annie Homemaker. Still, Rosaline is something special. A perfectly deluded princess, so safe in her tiny cage of saccharine fantasies. There are days when she genuinely makes me want to be a better person, and I both adore and despise her for that.

26

Vodka and Sleeping Pills

Rosaline stumbles back from the edges of her dream and finds herself sprawled on the couch in Elijah's room. The sun streaming through the windows forms a solar stencil on her skin. Outside there is a ceaseless storm of chance meetings, awkward greetings, births, deaths, and first and final breaths. She cares for none of this right now. This tiny room and its one other occupant is her world entire.

Beep.

Beep.

Beep.

As she crawls back into consciousness, the memory of her dream hums in her mind, and a bright and gleeful grin illumates her face. She walks over to her sleeping lover and lays her head on his chest, listens to the sound of his heart.

"My heart beats in 6/8 time for you," he'd told her once, on one of those myriad sun-filled days they'd spent together. Days she had thought would never end. She feels the warmth of his skin on her cheek. Feels his warm breath on the top of her head.

"Yes. *Of course,* I will. You've made me so happy."

Beep.

Beep.

Beep.

◇◇◇

A stream of angular synthesiser notes fills the air, as if produced by a robot with an asymmetrical haircut and a faux French accent. Freya watches the watercolour wash of blues and greens accompanying the hollow sounds in her vision. Cloudland's ceiling has been rolled back for the evening to reveal an array of brilliant stars.

"Excuse me, I couldn't help but notice you dropped something?" The stranger, dressed in a black silk shirt and tight-fitting pinstripe pants flashes her what she guesses is a finely practised smile.

"Thanks. What is it?"

"My number. I'm Luke, you should call me sometime." He winks at her and passes her his card. His smile slips into an uneasy bemusement as she whips out her phone and starts dialling.

"How 'bout right now?"

"Ah…what…? Ha. Yeah, sure thing."

She holds her hand up for silence. "Shh. It's ringing."

A tinny commercial rap song, unsurprisingly.

"Why, hello there."

"Is this Luke?"

"Sure is!"

"Just letting you know I'll be scrawling your number on the wall of the men's room advertising you as a potential candidate for all-male orgies. *Ciao.*"

Luke slinks away. Freya returns to her Moscow Mule.

"Really, Frey? *That's* how you treat a guy for hitting on you?" says Callum, returning from the bathroom.

"That's how I treat that guy. His card says he works for an oil company."

"So?"

"They're a menace. They perpetrate more environmental crimes than the other Fortune 500 companies combined. Oil drilling in the Arctic, huge bucks funding anti-global warming spin."

"Who's been feeding *you* propaganda, love? Someone you slept with lately perhaps?"

Freya rolls her eyes, leans back into the lounge and stares at the clusterfuck of chiffon, velvet, gold trim, and sculpted glass that adorns the club's interior. "This place had to be designed by three different trust fund babies who never had a conversation."

"Freya, please! Do you have to criticise every place we go? Can't we ever have a quiet drink and relax?"

"I wanted to go to Black Bear Lodge and drown my sorrows to actual music played by actual humans."

Callum sighs petulantly and slumps into a chair hanging from the ceiling by a gilded chain. "I don't get to pick the places they assign me, but since *they* are paying for our drinks, even *you* can't complain about that."

"Fine. I know. I'm being a bitch. Ever since Maria…" She stops because nothing else seems worth saying. For a few moments there are no words between them, just the bleeps and tweets of electro-audio porn. "Can you get me the most expensive thing on the menu, please? I have to go to the little girl's room."

Callum nods and heads back to the bar. She can hear his product proselytising even over the sea of synth. "*I looooove the way you spin that Kahlua bottle!*"

Freya pushes open the bathroom door on a heavily bejewelled woman sobbing. Her hair hangs in a thick black veil around her face and down into the sink. Yvette peers up and shakes her hair out of her eyes, rivulets of mascara running down her cheeks.

"Yvette? What are you doing here? Are you okay?"

"Sure. I'm fucking dandy! I'm rehearsing for the lead role in a film titled *Sexy Rich Gal Who Was Dumb Enough to Fall in Love*."

"Jennifer Aniston's already made that movie five or six times."

"I'm just drunk. Don't be nice to me. It makes me feel pitiful. I've been such a perfect bitch to you."

"That's true, though I don't understand why."

Yvette rolls her eyes. "Are you serious? Couldn't you see how jealous I was?"

"Jealous? Of what?"

Yvette yanks a sheet of paper towel from the dispenser and dabs at her face.

"Wasn't it obvious? I just—"

Her sentence halts abruptly as two young girls enter, hurling verbal vomit with abundant sprays of "like," interspersed with a smattering of verbs and nouns.

"Sorry sweethearts," says Yvette, "this is a private party."

"Piss off, you old scrag!" the taller girl retorts, and the two burst into giggles as they check themselves out in the mirrors. Yvette sighs and closes the distance between them with three confident strides. She removes a gold-plated butane lighter from her bag and flicks it on. The two girls stare at the dazzling flame, the blue splashes of their eyeliner sparklingly iridescent around their hypnotised eyes.

"Gorgeous, isn't it? A sheik I had a brief romance with had this custom-made for me…as a flame that would burn as bright and strong as his love. Such a poet, that one! Pretty average in the sack, though. In any case, you are going to turn around, walk out the door, and find somewhere else to titter and giggle. If you don't, I am going to set your cheap, tarty little dresses on fire. Is that clear?"

The two girls turn and run out of the room as fast as their impractically elevated heels will allow. Yvette calls out behind them, "And I am *not old!*"

She turns back to Freya. "I'm only thirty-two, for fuck's sake. Pretty little teens like that think anyone old enough to remember the fall of the Berlin Wall is a ragged old crone."

"I'd be impressed if I wasn't scared shitless."

"Relax, I would never have set them on fire." She dabs at her face again. "Probably. Now, where was I? Ah yes…jealousy. It will make people do terrible things. Cain and Abel. David and Bathsheba. Adonis and Aphrodite. I've never claimed to be a nice person, except when it served my purposes. But you had the one thing, the one and *only* thing in the world that I ever truly loved and cared for."

"You mean Jack?"

"Oh, sweet pea, you really are as stupid as you are thick, aren't you? I'm talking about *Elijah*. I've been in love once and only once. I'd always thought all that wistful, romantic crap pop singers and the like ramble on about didn't have the slightest lick of truth to it. But there I was, gazing lovingly at photos for hours on end, my last thought before sleep, the first thought on waking, an imbecilic grin smeared across my face every moment of the day. The whole shebang." She looks at her reflection in the mirror then back at Freya.

"I assume you've figured out by now that Elijah isn't exactly the golden child everyone makes him out to be? Anyone would think he'd been raised by Mother Teresa and Mahatma Gandhi, the way the Vincettis go on about him. He slept around, for starters. Whores, diplomats, wives of best friends, high-school girls, businesswomen, whoever he could get his grubby little paws on, or inside of as the case may be. But when we met he promised me that was all going to change. He *promised* me. I was stupid enough to believe him, too. I mean, he was with Rosaline at the time, but I always knew that was just him playing one of his wicked little games. I never thought that would last."

Freya thinks of Rosaline's note, wonders if Rosaline would even be capable of conceptualising her love as anything but perpetual. It would be like asking an eight-year-old to ponder quantum mechanics.

"And then one day he tells me he's done with me. Casting me aside like I was last season's fashion. No explanation, no apology. *Nothing*. I felt smashed into tiny little pieces. The damned brat had worked his way right into my heart and I couldn't get him out. I did everything I could to forget him: exotic holidays, slept with other men, tried drugs I'd never touched before, saw a shrink. Nothing worked.

"One night, I couldn't sleep, and simply couldn't stand it anymore, so I rang his mobile at three-thirty and he picked up after the first ring. I said I wanted him to tell me to my face that it was really over, that he owed me that much. He said fine, I was right. It wouldn't be easy, but it was the right thing to do. He told me he was staying at the Hilton, to get away from his family. He gave me the room number and told me he'd leave the door unlocked.

"So, I raced over there, rehearsing my little monologue as I drove, tears streaming down my face. I felt my heart pounding in my chest as I hit the elevator button. It seemed to take an age and a day to reach the third floor. The doors slid open, and there's this young couple waiting there...you should have seen their faces when they saw me. Black rivers running down my cheeks, eyes all red. Kind of like now, I suppose." Yvette runs some more water, wets the paper towel, dabs at her face again and throws the paper on the floor. The muffled sound of bass pounds through the bathroom walls.

"I pushed past them and made my way down the hall to his room. I threw the door open and was greeted by a smorgasbord of debauchery: drug and sex paraphernalia all over the floor, used condoms strewn like wrapping paper on Christmas morning, champagne bottles everywhere, syringes, pills, baggies of coke. I'd only a second to take it all in before I saw him, staring at me, naked, leering, eyes lit with fiendish joy. God, it was horrid. Between his legs I saw a blonde head bobbing quickly up and down, his hand gripping savagely at its hair.

"He'd wanted me to see the whole thing. He'd planned it that way. What a fucking...piece of shit..." Yvette's eyes rim with red and she dabs them quickly with a paper towel. "I ran wailing from the room like some common tart. I drove home in a rage and drank vodka and popped Halcyon sleeping pills until I passed out, then spent the next two weeks doing much of the same. I turned off my phone, smashed the TV with an umbrella and tried to forget that I even existed. When I finally came round and opened a newspaper, I saw he'd been in an accident and had fallen into the coma."

"Tell me about the accident." Freya doesn't bother concealing the eagerness in her voice.

"All the Vincettis revealed to anyone was that it was a car crash. They used their usual combination of threats and chequebooks to keep the details out of the news. But I dug deeper... hired a private investigator. The whole thing was disgusting, even by Elijah's standards." She lowers her eyes, flicks her lighter open and closed a half dozen times and then lights it, watching the flame burn as she speaks.

"Elijah was driving a hooker home. He was drunk and on a mishmash of drugs and he slammed into another car. Killed both of the people in it, as well as the hooker in his car. And now the shit is in a coma and I'm *still* stupid enough to be in love with him, even after everything he's done...and she's won, after all."

"Who's won?"

"Rosaline, that marshmallow-brained twit! The Vincettis have just issued a press release and claimed that he 'couldn't wait a day longer to be married to her, that he spoke to her in a dream.' Fucking fevered delusion, more like." Yvette bursts into tears again and slams her fist against the paper towel dispenser, leaving a dent in the metal that twists her reflection like a funhouse mirror. "That crazy fucking *bitch*!" She dissolves into a heaving mass of sobbing and wailing.

Freya tentatively places her arm around her. Yvette leans into her chest and sobs for a while longer, then looks up. "Thank you for listening to me whine. You're a nice girl...the dumpy ones usually are. Can't exactly get by on your looks, can you?" She unwinds herself from Freya's arm, straightens her dress, and disappears out the door.

27

Orange Juice

Jack bounds from sleep like a lion through a ringmaster's hoop, his eyes wide, his face frantic, his body charged with electric energy. It takes him a moment to recompose himself, to verify that he is awake and no longer dreaming…of his brother, as always.

He tries to remember the last time he dreamt of anything else. Wearily, he drags himself over to his desk and swipes the clutter of notebooks and magazines to the floor. He feeds a fresh sheet of paper into his typewriter and stares at the blank page with a serene sense of oblivion.

His fingers begin to stab at keys.

Clack.

Clack.

Clack.

By the time he's aware that he has written anything at all, the words are strewn across the page like bodies on a battlefield. He reads back over them, then curses in a torrent of prolific profanity.

Where did this come from? This misogynistic, misanthropic rant peppered with God complex and haughty disdain? Jack wishes he could unplug a cord somewhere to stop these thoughts polluting his brain but every time he sits and watches his fingers move, this dross is all he can type.

He almost can't remember writing anything else.

Sounds of life, if you can call it that, he thinks bitterly, are emerging outside his room and throughout the house. He wonders if Freya is back, but decides to leave thoughts of her until after his morning routine.

He saunters into the corridor, dressed only in his pyjama pants, and then into the kitchen where his father is grumbling into the bowels of the refrigerator.

"Can't bloody find anything in here. Where the goddamn son of a bitch did that woman put the damn orange juice?"

"Maria never bought orange juice. She squeezed it for you fresh."

"Huh? Oh, Jack! Good morning. That explains it then. Right. Any idea where the juicer is?" Harland rummages through the kitchen cupboards.

Jack sighs as he grabs a spoon from the drawer. "Third drawer."

"Aha!" Harland says, pulling it open. "And the oranges?"

"Pantry."

"I don't know about you, but I am thrilled Elijah and Rosaline are tying the knot. Lord knows those two waited long enough."

"The coma might have had something to do with that."

"Ah, young people these days. They take forever to make up their minds! Always 'finding themselves' and figuring things out."

Jack pours cornflakes into a bowl but says nothing.

"How's the writing going?"

"Horrible. It's like someone else is writing through me. Like Yeats' instructors. It's all coming out so dark…and foul."

"Great! Can't wait to read it!" Harland says cheerily, having obviously not heard a word. He slices an orange into pieces, throws them into the juicer, flicks the switch and juice squirts over his jacket. "Ah, Christ! The hell with this," he says, and grabs a tea towel and rubs at it, then takes it off and hangs it over the back of a chair. He runs upstairs to find a replacement jacket.

Jack slides out of his chair, reaches into the inner pocket, finds what he needs and sits back down. Harland's footsteps thud down the stairs as he returns, buttoning up his navy blazer as he walks.

"I'll stop at Merlo's on the way to the office. Got a busy day, what with the oil spill. Publicity has been through the roof, by the way! Those penguin jumpers…a stroke of genius." He pauses in the manner he usually does when he is waiting for praise to be heaped upon him. Unfortunately for Harland, this is not the boardroom and his usual supply of yes-men are nowhere to be found. Jack pours milk into his bowl and chews his cornflakes. Harland scowls and continues.

"Terrible tragedy, of course…all those manatees or sea lions, or whatever the devil they are, dying. But you can't even eat those things, can you? Pretty sure I've never seen sea lion on a menu. So, not exactly a catastrophe. Still, all the Lefties seem pretty cut up about it."

Jack chews his cornflakes.

Harland transfers his wallet from his orange juice-afflicted jacket to his fresh one and says, "Don't forget to make yourself presentable for the party tonight. Remind me to hire a new maid as soon as this oil spill thing blows over. I won't be home until just before the party. We've hired a suit for you; it's being delivered this afternoon. Bye!" He rushes out the door.

Jack finishes his cornflakes and only looks up when the door slams. He listens to the sound of the car's engine revving up and then fading into the distance. He leaves his bowl on the table and walks to his father's study, swipes the card he has removed from Harland's wallet and enters. He surveys the room's contents before sitting at his father's desk. An intricately carved wooden box is in front of him and he opens its latch. Inside, it's lined with shaped foam with a cylindrical recess about the size of a large cigar. He closes it and slides open the top drawer.

Closes it.
    Second drawer.
Closes it.
    Third drawer.
Closes it.
    Fourth drawer.
Bingo.

28

Death of a Pineapple Cutter

Freya's smirk defies the pineapple cutter's offensive yellow veneer. She feels the cheap plastic through her gloves, places it on the wooden cutting board and then smashes it with the meat pounder. She carries the board, careful not to drop the pieces and slides them into the bin, shoving them deep in the trash to conceal them. As she does this, the cutter's blade tears at a black plastic bag half-buried under coffee grinds and fruit scraps and she glimpses a tiny glint of silver.

She rips the bag open, revealing a syringe. She removes it carefully, folds it into a tea towel and walks briskly out of the kitchen and towards the stairs. As her foot hits the first step, a quiet whistling from somewhere down the hall creates a spectral Lovecraftian fog in front of her.

The dark tendrils clamber over the walls and stairs. The tune is calm, malevolent. A serial killer's "Whistle While You Work." Her chest tightens. Her legs melt into hot, wet rubber. The floor comes rushing up to greet her face. The darkness swirls and swarms around her, slowly consuming every trace of colour and light. All that's around her is a solid, ceaseless void. And that hideous melody.

She lies there, the sound and darkness flooding her eyes, ears, and mind. She feels hands on her. Warm fingers moving over her cold, confused flesh.

And then there is only silence.

Harland and Evelyn stare at the pool. Sun beats down on their skin. A breeze ambles through the air.

Evelyn sips at her drink. "Is everything ready for the wedding, Harland?"

"Are you kidding? Rosaline has had the whole thing sewn up for months. The poor doll has been planning it since before your face was unmodified."

"You know I hate those vulgar vilifications."

"But you love me just the same."

"Yes, well, there's no accounting for taste, is there?"

Harland removes a cigar from his jacket pocket and snips the end off with his handcrafted silver cutter, a gift from the Queen of Denmark. He'd never even known Denmark had a monarchy until he'd received it as a gift from the Queen's personal assistant accompanying an invitation to a trade meeting. He lights the cigar and puffs, and feels that familiar pang of disappointment as the bitterness hits his lips. He's still waiting for the pleasure he's supposed to feel. He is a stupendously wealthy man, smoking expensive tobacco is supposed to go with the territory.

He ponders what he will do tomorrow, when he controls much of the globe's pharmaceutical industry. When billions of lives depend on him to ease their aches, pains, and maladies. From AIDS sufferers to men with erectile dysfunction, young women trying the latest get-thin-quick concoction and high-powered executives looking for a painkiller to destroy their headaches faster than their lackeys can run to get them their next mocha latte. All those people will be clutched in the palm of his not-quite-comfortable-holding-a-cigar hand.

He will wield more power than he could attain from any petty crown or government seat. Genghis Khan would have thrown down arms and taken up a business degree if he'd known that he could control nations and populations simply by acquiring brands and trademarks. Politics and warfare are fine for pastimes, but capitalism? Now there's a *man's* game.

So what will he do when he controls the game, and all its players? Cigars will be passé for a man of such stature. Perhaps he will have to indulge in the higher levels of bourgeois recreation. Romanesque orgies, that sort of thing.

"What are you thinking?" Evelyn's voice cuts through his reverie.

"Nothing."

"That's a surprise."

"I meant nothing as in, nothing I want to tell you about."

"I know what you meant."

The blue light from the pool plays across her face. Harland imagines her as a faded beauty in an underground theatre, her lips poised ahead of a soliloquy. Evelyn drains the last of her glass and says, "Do you ever feel guilty about what we've done? What we're going to do?"

"Does a lion feel guilty for devouring a zebra when it's hungry? Does it apologise for being the superior animal? For having the strength and ambition to survive?"

"I hardly think that controlling a multi-billion-dollar pharmaceutical monopoly is like an animal hunting for sustenance. No lion ever needed holiday homes in seventeen countries."

"True. Though I never did have much of a gift for metaphor. That's Jack's field. Good thing I have other, more practical talents."

Harland gives up on the cigar and stubs it into the ashtray beside him.

◇◇◇

Freya wakes to the sound of rattling computer keys. She watches his hands moving at nearly imperceptible speed, the clicking and clacking forming a musical rhythm that bounces frenetically around the room.

"Jack?"

He does not respond, merely continues stabbing the keys.

She sits up in the bed, remembering the last time she woke up here. "Jack?" Her head feels like it's been inside an industrial paint shaker. Her eyes are sore, and she can see in the mirror they are almost as red as her dishevelled hair. "How long was I out? Jack? Jack? Please don't tell me you've gone all JD Salinger on me?"

She slips off the bed and pads over to him, wraps her arms around him, not knowing or caring if this is the right thing to do. Still his hands move in their manic tap-dance across the keys. "Jack, you're starting to creep me out."

He has the glazed, empty eyes of a geriatric junkie. Freya reaches her hand out to touch his face. Her fingers brush against his skin…it's cold and clammy. She watches the words he is typing march across the page.

> had it coming, the nosy old bitch. Always sticking her beak in where it didn't belong, like anywhere outside of a bucket of cleaning materials, for instance. Strutting around as though being a busy-bodied pervert made her some sort of Latina superhero. The way she gulped down that champagne (with my added secret ingredient) you'd think she'd never seen a glass of bubbly in her pathetic little life. She made the most ghastly coughing and belching sounds as she finally shuffled off this mortal coil. Sounded like an asthmatic puppy in a blender.

Jack's hand punches the last full stop and he slumps forward as though an invisible figure has struck the back of his head.

"Mary, patron saint of motherfuckers, I thought I was supposed to be the damsel in distress here!" Freya shakes him. "Hey! Sleeping Beauty! Wake the fuck up!"

Jack emits a primal grunt and his eyes snap open. "Freya?"

"What the hell is this shit you're writing?"

His eyes squeeze tightly closed and then reopen again.

"What?"

"This! This! Fucking *this* right here!" Freya points at the page.

Jack scans his eyes over it, his lips moving as he does so. "Jesus. That's awful."

"It is! How can you be—?"

"I mean, the use of simile…it's atrocious. The pacing is all over the place…"

"Jack! It's awful because it's about Maria!"

"What?" Jack reads it again and rubs his eyes. He pulls the page out, rips it into pieces and throws them at the bin, where they cascade like tiny literary snowflakes. "There. It's gone."

He leans back and looks at her, the air pregnant with a demand for explanation. "I don't know where this stuff is coming from, Freya. And it's getting worse. I can't write anything else. Every time I sit down at the keyboard I just, I watch my hands start to move and then I…the rest of me… I disappear. When I come round again, the page is filled with stuff like that…this horrendous person talking about killing and…other things. I don't know what's happening to me."

He lapses into stillness, then with sudden and surprising speed he picks up the typewriter and hurls it across the room, where it smashes against the wall and sprays keys over the floor.

"Just like the first time we met. How sweet," Freya says sardonically. "Enough with the melodrama. We've got enough problems as it is. We should be looking for some answers, not redecorating your room."

Jack grabs a document folder from his desk and throws it on the bed. "How's that for answers? And before you start interrogating me about my little peculiarities, maybe you'd like to tell me why I found you passed out near the Danger Room holding a syringe wrapped in a tea towel?"

"I don't know. I wish I did. There was a weird whistling noise coming from the Danger Room and it scrambled my circuitry. You know how you twist and contort when someone scratches fingernails down a blackboard? It felt like that blown through three-hundred-watt speakers directly into my brain."

"The syringe?"

"I found it in the kitchen bin. I don't know what's in it or who put it there. If I could tell you any more than that, I would. Now, what the hell is in that folder?"

"A picture tells slightly more than nine hundred and ninety-nine words, which often makes me question my career choice."

Freya takes up the folder and opens it on a photograph: a grotesque smear of steel and skin, shattered glass through blond and black and brown hair, blood streaked across asphalt, fingernails scratched against seatbelts.

"Where did you get this?"

"In Daddy dearest's private study. I borrowed his keycard."

No one in the photo is identifiable. Either because their faces are twisted away from the camera or because their features have been distorted like a Picasso left out in the rain. Freya fights the urge to puke and turns the picture over.

The second shot is equally harrowing, but it's of a girl slumped forward in the front seat of a green car, the other car in the accident, she supposes. Her dress is red, although this could be because it's covered in blood. Her face is slammed against the dashboard, and her left hand is flung out the window towards the camera. From her wrist hangs a bracelet carrying a collection of silver charms.

Freya drops the folder, rushes into Jack's bathroom and expels the contents of her stomach into the sink in a fountain of reds, yellows and greens.

Jack follows her in and places his hand on her shoulder, asking uselessly, "Are you okay?"

Freya pukes again. An effective response, if a little indecorous. She runs the tap and rinses her mouth. Spits. "I am the exact fucking opposite of okay. What the fuck are those photos?"

"I thought you might know something about it. It happened outside where you used to work, and you kept asking about the accident."

"*The* accident? Your brother's? Those are photos from *his* accident?"

"Well...yes."

"Val..." Freya whispers as she buries her head in her hands, her eyes spilling hot tears. "Jack. The girl in that photo was my friend Valerie. I'd recognise her piece of shit charm bracelet a mile under water. He killed her, Jack. Your fucking brother *killed* her."

"I know." The words emerge from his mouth as if inscribed on tiny tombstones. A stream of curses runs through Freya's head but she says, "You already knew...before this, didn't you? This was the big Vincetti family secret. That their golden child killed a bunch of plebs? This is what no one would talk to me about, not even you?"

"Freya, I'm—"

"If the next word out of your mouth is 'sorry' it will be the last one you pronounce with your face intact. You knew that your brother had done this all along. The fact it was Valerie and her dad, did you know about that, too?"

"I had my suspicions. But no, I didn't know for sure until now, same as you."

"Jack, how could you hide this from me?"

"I didn't want to ruin...everything. I knew you were starting to understand that almost everything my family says about Elijah is a lie. They use him like Pygmalion's statue, casting their own desires and dreams onto him, using him as a vessel for their own private delusions. Rosaline makes him out to be a charming Renaissance man, Harland claims him to be a genius, Evelyn portrays him as some sort of unimpeachable saint. Dead men tell no lies, but sleeping men nurture and protect them. I was surprised that you didn't leave earlier, when you figured out how strange my family is...but I thought if you knew the truly horrible things that happened around here then you'd leave us. That you wouldn't want to be here. Wouldn't want to be with me."

Freya glares at him with a rancour that no one with a Y chromosome could ever hope to emulate. "How fucking *dare* you! You kept this from me because it would jeopardise your chances of getting *laid*?"

"I wanted to know the details before I said anything. How would you have felt if I'd told you my early suspicions but I'd been wrong?" Jack stands in uneasy silence, withering in the red-hot glow of Freya's fury. "Look, can we leave the imploring apologies and hopefully subsequent forgiveness 'til later? I haven't shown you everything yet. Do you think you can bottle up that tempest for a bit?"

"Do you think you could be a little more condescending?"

"I'm sorry. Again. A hundred times. A thousand. I'll pray with a rosary, say my Hail Marys, work in a soup kitchen, whatever I need to do to make penance. But first, could you please look at the rest of what's in that folder?"

"Yes. No. Maybe. I don't know. Do you understand that girl was like my sister? I gave up on *everything* after she died."

"I know. I get it. Really. But you need to see what I've found."

She nods, shoves some toothpaste on her finger and rubs it on her teeth to mute the acrid taste in her mouth. Rinses. Spits. Follows Jack back into his room.

Freya picks up the folder and sits on the bed. She turns the photos over and inspects the documents beneath them. First, there's a coroner's report for the car crash. It's been slashed and hacked with so much red marker pen it's like blood strewn across a wall in a B-grade Japanese revenge film.

> Coroner's report: 30 November '... alter paragraphs 1-4, 6-8 and 10. Reduce number of victims. Delete: John Doe, Jane Doe 1, Jane Doe 2. Omit Elijah Vincetti for transfer into alternate collision.'

"They had the coroner's report altered?"

"Yes. And you can see why: paragraph seven."

```
Victim had a BAC of 0.19, also tested posi-
tive for cocaine (22 grams on his person,
in left pants pocket) and phencyclidine.
```

"I knew about some of this. Yvette told me. Didn't realise Golden Boy was on PCP, though. Not so much touched by an angel as touched by angel dust. Falsifying documents like this...it's obviously a perversion of justice."

"We've got everything we need," says Jack. "Here. Call the cops." He throws her his phone and her fingers hover above the keypad. Through the ceiling she can hear Rosaline's soprano caterwaul a rendition of "Can't Take My Eyes Off You."

"Can't you do it?"

"They're my blood. I'm a Vincetti. I told you before, you can't raise a hand against your own kin, the Fates forbid it. Even if I've loaded the gun, I can't pull the trigger. It has to be you."

Rosaline's voice reverberates, now with an impassioned version of "Going to the Chapel." Freya puts the phone down.

"I can't, either. Not yet."

"Why? What's wrong?"

She points upwards, towards the source of the song. "That. Her. I can't bring the walls crashing down, not yet. I swear to God, Jack, if you knew her like I do, you'd understand. If we ruin this wedding, it will destroy her, and Rosaline's already had one return trip to hell. She doesn't deserve another."

"So, what do we do?"

"We wait until tomorrow night. They can have one last night of freedom before they spend the rest of their lives locked up in some minimum-security waterfront prison for rich white people. But we have to let Rosaline live out her little fantasy or it will tear her apart."

"Are you sure that's a good idea?"

"No. But I'm going with my gut. Normally it asks me to fill it with vodka and donuts, but this time I trust it."

The door flies open. Freya dives to cover up the documents, leaving her lying awkwardly across the bed, vainly attempting to look nonchalant. Rosaline's halogen grin illuminates the room. She's holding a tray of margaritas and couldn't look more like she was auditioning for a home shopping ad if she tried. "Hey, you two! What are you doing locked away in here? Let's get this party started!"

"Sure thing!" says Jack as he covers the room in a few quick strides. He places his arm around Rosaline and says with a grin to match hers, "I'll take one of those, soon-to-be-sis! Freya will be with us in a minute, I've asked her to read over a few pages of my manuscript for me. She's going to need some time alone." He guides Rosaline by the shoulders through a one-hundred-eighty-degree turn and out the door.

"Don't be too long!" Her voice trails off.

Thank you! mouths Freya as Jack closes the door behind him.

Freya can't help herself. She has to look one last time. With feeble fingers she locates the photo of Valerie, gazing once more at the red dress Val had loved so much she could have written a thesis about it. She slips the photo back into the folder and is about to close it when she spies Elijah's face peering out from one of the other shots. She pulls it out. It's taken from a distance, so it's hard to make out the car's other occupants, but it's clearly Elijah who's slumped behind the wheel. It's difficult to be certain, given the pixellation and poor focus, but she could swear that through all the blood and shattered glass, Elijah is treating her to a charming, million-dollar smile.

29

You Hit Me in the Head with a Friendship Rock?

"Gosh darn it, I can't find the pineapple cutter anywhere! Freya, do you know where it could be?"

"Haven't seen it."

"Drat! We'll have to make the punch without it."

Rosaline shoots her best the-show-must-go-on grin to the small gaggle of mannequins. She's already introduced Freya to them all, but their names entered and exited her head with unsurprising ease. Dressed in jeans and a treasured but well-worn PJ Harvey T-shirt, Freya stands out like a Banksy among a milieu of Monets.

Jack slides behind her and places his hand lightly on the small of her back. She takes a second to register his fingers, newly welcome visitors to the territory of her flesh. "So, Rosaline, who else is coming to this little shindig?"

"It'll just be a few of us: the girls from my Zumbalates class, some others from my yoga for mums and babies group, you, me, Evelyn, Harland…and Niki, of course."

"Niki's coming?"

"Oh, yes! We made such good friends at Maria's funeral. She's so lovely! She can't make it to the wedding tomorrow because she's flying back to Colombia to tie up some things with Maria's will, but she's going to drop by tonight."

The doorbell rings, Rosaline screams like a kettle and claps her hands. "I'll get it!"

"Whose hair are you wearing?" Lisa or Lucy or possibly Liesel asks Freya.

"Um…it's mine?" she answers, not sure if she's being made to look the fool or is entertaining one.

"Silly! I know that. I mean, who's it by? That colour is amazing!"

"It's the colour I popped out of the womb with."

"Oh shut *up*! I don't believe that for a second! It's simply divine!" gushes Laura or Lana or possibly Leena.

Freya smiles politely and tries to think of something to say, but fails. Silence hovers between them for slightly too long before Lauren/Lily/Leanne says, "Well, I'd best go check on the other girls…" and scampers off to her mass of mannequins.

"Apparently I'm not the only one around here who struggles with relating to the rest of the species," says Jack.

"Hey, if you want to relate with this member of the species again any time soon you'll keep those remarks to yourself."

Jack opens his mouth to respond just as Rosaline's exultant yelping bisects the room. Freya looks towards the door to see Niki arriving, clad in a chic silver and black gown. Niki's eyes meet Freya's from across the room.

"Does she really think it's smart to invite the niece of your recently murdered maid into the place she was killed?" whispers Freya.

"Rosaline's not thinking about anything that isn't borrowed, blue, old, or new at present," Jack replies, taking a strawberry and dipping it into the fondue fountain that looks as if both Louis XIV and Willy Wonka collaborated on its design. "Where did you hide the folder?"

"Under your mattress." Freya neglects to mention that she's slipped one of the photos into her handbag. Just in case, she'd told herself. But in case of what, she isn't sure. She turns to greet Niki with a smile. "Hi, how are you?"

Niki embraces her warmly and places a thick Colombian kiss on both of her cheeks as she whispers, "Any luck finding evidence?"

Rosaline interrupts them before Freya has a chance to answer. "Shall we head out to the pool for more cocktails?" She is every high-school girl on prom night compressed into an impossible mass of glee. Freya wishes she had some Valium to slip into Rosaline's drink, just to lighten the mood.

The party moves to beside the pool where the outdoor speakers are blasting a playlist that Freya decides should be titled, *Songs To Make Freya Want To Shove Her Head Into A Trash Compactor*. The mannequins clink glasses and titter at the same high pitch and Freya looks up to check if there are any bats in the immediate vicinity that might have their flight patterns disrupted.

"Don't you just love Bryan Adams?" says Rosaline.

"What I would love, Rosaline, is a Moscow Mule," Freya says, heading towards the poolside bar with belligerent knives of orange stabbing at her eyes. If she ever meets Bryan Adams, she's going to beat him with a six-string until he can no longer even remember the summer of sixty-nine.

Rosaline stands on one of the chairs and clears her throat loudly. "Everyone, thank you so much for coming! I can't believe my day is almost here! I'm nearly ready. I've got something old, that's my favourite doll, *Magic Wedding Dress Rosaline*. Something blue, that's my hairband. Something new, that's the earrings I bought yesterday. Now I need something borrowed. Does anyone have any ideas?"

Freya swishes down the Moscow Mule in a few easy gulps, her head swimming with schemes and machinations. At first Rosaline's words wash over her, until an idea thrusts itself into her mind with such potency all other thoughts seek momentary refuge. "I know!" she shouts. "What about something of Elijah's?"

"Frey! Brilliant! Do you think you can get me something?"

"Will do! Back in five."

Freya leaps out of her chair, glimpsing Jack's desperate for-the-love-of-God-don't-leave-me -alone-with-these-people glare as she runs inside. She races down the almost endless corridor of locked and unlocked doors, then takes the stairs two at a time. Freya flings open the door to Elijah's room and says, "Hey 'lijah, I…"

The sentence makes it halfway out of her mouth before it nosedives to the ground. She recoils and latches her hand onto the door to steady herself. Dozens of flickering candles light the room, casting Elijah in an unearthly, almost arcane glow. Lit by the mercurial play of light and shadow, he looks alarmingly like his brother. They could almost be twins.

"Excuse me…I didn't mean to…" Another verbal miscarriage tries to clamber out of her mouth.

"Didn't your mother tell you it's rude not to knock?" says Evelyn, who Freya now recognises as she steps out of a darkened corner, speaking in her usual blend of nonchalance and malevolence. Her gown shimmers as she moves, the light twinkling off her pearl earrings and necklace. The shadows sketch dark lines over her face, hiding her eyes and drawing sharp focus to her thin red lips. Harland too steps out of the dark, holding up a box, the shadows suggesting it's intricately carved.

"You should go, Freya. We'll be down in a moment," he says in a low and even tone. His eyes are fixed on the box.

"Sure. I thought I left something in here…but, um, I guess…" Evelyn and Harland stare at her with a shared expression that makes her feel an entirely new and unwelcome sort of discomfort.

"I should go." Freya turns and swiftly exits, deftly snatching up the razor she'd earlier left soaking in a bowl of water on the bench. She runs back down to the guests, trying to pretend she hasn't seen whatever the hell it was that she just saw.

"Got it! I brought his razor." She places it on the drinks table and notices one of Niki's eyebrows rise.

"What a curious choice. May I see that?" Niki asks as her fingers creep towards it. "Such excellent craftsmanship. Is this real silver?"

"Only the best for our Elijah!" says Rosaline.

Niki's fingers rest on the silver handle and a short, sharp pulse ripples through her body. She closes her eyes and mumbles something in Spanish, then places the razor back on the table.

"Well, that's everything! Shall we have a toast?" Rosaline smiles so wide it threatens to compromise the structural integrity of her face.

"To what?" asks Leena/Lisa/Liana. The mannequins shoot a flurry of perplexed glances at each other but come up with nothing. Words, evidently, are not their forte.

"To love against all reason!" toasts Jack and downs his drink. Freya snaps her hand over her mouth to trap the laugh.

Rosaline glares at Jack. He catches her eye but looks quickly away. Her smile slowly returns with its potency redoubled. "I need to go check on the mini-quiches!" She sails towards the kitchen and leaves a cold, clumsy silence in her wake.

"Niki, would you come with me to the ladies' room?" asks Freya.

"Gladly!"

The pair practically sprint to the bathroom and Freya slams the door behind them.

"Have you found any evidence?" asks Niki.

"I have. Enough to bury them for a few lifetimes."

Niki sighs in relief and mutters a thankful *Gracias a Dios.* "Show me."

"It's hidden in Jack's room."

"Then why have you brought me in here? In two days, I will be in Colombia and have to look into the eyes of Maria's brothers and sisters and tell them she was murdered. Before I do that, I need some scrap of hope that these people will spend the rest of their lives in prison."

"From what I've seen, you can tell them the Vincettis will rot in a rat-filled cell. But right now, I need to know what you saw when you touched the razor."

"What I saw?"

"Yes. I know there was something. Tell me."

Niki meets her gaze with furious eyes. "First you give me my evidence, then I'll tell you."

"I'm not the enemy here."

Niki studies their reflections in the mirror and fiddles with her hair. "I found a grey hair yesterday. It's like I've aged a decade in a few days. I can't sleep. She visits me when I'm dreaming. Tells me to get revenge. Tells me to bury them. Even in my dreams, she is still cleaning. Scrubbing. Dusting. Did she tell you about the bar she used to own in Bogotá? She was a legend there. Her voice, her smile. Men would throw themselves at her feet. And now she is a lowly cleaner, even in the afterlife. She talks always, pleading for penance. Begging me to bring justice. Maria, *por el amor de Dios*, let me sleep…"

Niki's head hangs low, she places her hands on the sink to steady herself, then reaches out to Freya's gloves and runs her fingers over them. "Always these gloves, what are you hiding?"

"It's an Audrey Hepburn thing."

Niki smiles at her. "You aren't such a great liar."

"Actually, I am a fantastic liar. I'm just tired. In normal circumstances, I'm quite the silver tongue."

Niki nods and drums her fingers on the marble benchtop. "Usually, with my family, with those who are my blood, the voice is strong, loud. Maria, she was so soon passed it was like screaming through a megaphone in my head. But with this Elijah, he is not my family; I have never met him. It was hard to hear. His voice was like a whisper in the heavy rain. There was so much confusion…like static on the radio, you know? Like *haruschhhhhhhhhh…*a constant buzzing. But I can tell you one thing, he is a much better liar than you are."

"What do you mean?"

"I mean, he's been—" Niki holds her sentence as Evelyn barges into the room.

"Hope I'm not interrupting? You two girls gossiping about anything important?" asks Evelyn.

"Oh, you know, planning my outfit for tomorrow. Should be quite the party!" says Freya.

Freya and Niki scramble out the door only to almost collide with Rosaline in the corridor as she carries a tray of pastry parcels.

"Mini-quiches anyone?" she asks.

"Thanks, I'll take one. Great party, Ros," says Freya, watching Niki slink away down the corridor towards the front door.

"Thanks, lovely, I'm so glad you're enjoying it. Could I ask you to help me with one little thing?" There is a slight tremor in her voice and a look in her eyes that Freya has not seen before.

"Ah, sure."

"Would you mind, if it isn't too much trouble, telling me what the *fuck* this is?" She puts the tray down on a console and slides out the photo she had been holding underneath it.

Freya frowns at the blur of metal and meat. "Where did you get that?"

"Your handbag. Lauren had a headache and I thought you might have some painkillers in there."

"Rosaline, I can—"

"*How could you do this to me?*"

Freya grabs her by the wrist and leads her through the mess of mannequins, who are looking at them as though they are already planning how to gossip about this little contretemps. Once they are clear of the spying eyes, Freya swipes her card over the nearest door and shoves Rosaline inside. She flicks on the light switch and opens her mouth, ready to explain, when she notices the boxes piled behind them.

"Christ, you have *got* to be kidding me."

"Freya Miller, what the hell are you laughing about? I tell you all about…what happened to me, I share my home with you and *this* is how you repay me? You are a *monster*!" Rosaline's eyes are brimming with tears, her lip trembling.

Freya wraps her arms around her and whispers, "Shhh. It's okay. I didn't mean to laugh. It's just, look where we are. Look. This room."

Rosaline sees the piles of boxes, their contents spilt over the floor.

"The jumper storage room."

"The *penguin* jumper storage room. One of the weirdest rooms I found when I first came here. A room with a secret, the first of many. Fucking penguin jumpers for pre-planned oil spills."

"Pre-planned!" says Rosaline. Freya notices that she's clutching something between the perfectly manicured fingers of her right hand.

"The reason I had that photo, why I've been creeping around, is because the Vincettis are corporate criminals. They caused the oil spill as an elaborate PR stunt. They want you to marry Elijah so they can control Firmatel. They killed Maria for snooping and they're going to prison, as soon as the wedding's over. I swear it's true. I have the evidence."

"*I don't care!* It's my wedding Freya, my *wedding*! The happiest day of my life, and you want to spoil it with these silly stories about conspiracies and...and...oil spills...and..."

Freya can't help but feel sorry for this fragile figure whose crystal kingdom has been suddenly shattered by the intrusion of reality. Rosaline is shaking like a freshly lit roman candle. Freya prays for movement, for more screaming, for anything but the dreadful stillness.

Rosaline raises her right hand, a smooth grey object partially visible between her fingers. In the fraction of a second before it hits her face, Freya feels almost proud of Rosaline for finally unleashing her long-suppressed anger. Then this thought and all others are knocked out of her brain as the object collides with her skull, filling her head with klaxons.

Freya clutches at the blood oozing from the wound and stumbles backwards, as Rosaline's face melts from anger into shock and then into regret. She rushes forward, crouches down and takes Freya in her arms.

"OhGodImsosorryImsosorryImsosorry. I don't know what I'm doing anymore! It was supposed to be a fairy tale, I was supposed to be a princess. I just wanted to be a princess."

The blood reaches Freya's lips. It tastes sickly sweet. She tries to remember the last time she tasted blood. The room spins with stars.

"What the fuckballs did you hit me with?" she slurs.

Rosaline is sobbing, but she reaches out, grabs the missile and hands it over to Freya. It's a smooth stone with the word "friendship" engraved in Comic Sans.

"It's a friendship rock. It was going to be a present for you. That was the real reason why I opened your handbag. I wanted to put it in there for you as a surprise."

"You hit me in the head with a friendship rock?"

"Yes."

"You are one fucked-up bitch."

Rosaline almost laughs through her sobbing, and says quietly, "I wish you wouldn't curse so much."

"I could probably make a pun here about throwing the first stone, but—"

"Are you alright? I don't know what came over me."

"I'll live. Possibly with reduced brain function but, let's face it, the alcohol would have done the same job sooner or later. Can I ask you something?"

"Yes?"

"What was your name, before it was Rosaline?"

Rosaline blushes and mumbles, "Oh, no, it's a bit embarrassing."

Freya points to the blood smeared on her forehead and says, "Kinda feel like you owe me a little something for this right here. And I've got a sense of curiosity that just won't quit. Cough it up."

"Well, I haven't told this to anyone in a long time, but my name was, um, Jezebel. Jezebel Jones."

Freya's eyes and grin expand as though her face is painted onto an inflating balloon until a giggle escapes her lips and she surrenders to roaring with laughter. "Oh God Ros, that is fucking *tragic*! Were your parents trying to raise a drug-addled stripper?"

"Hey! That's mean! They just wanted to name me after a biblical princess. But I guess…I think they just saw a list of biblical princesses and liked the sound of it—I don't think they read her history. My parents were never big readers."

"Had they never heard the term 'Jezebel' used in regards to a woman who is controlling and promiscuous?"

Rosaline shakes her head, frowning. "I don't know, I guess a hooker's client can be called a 'John,' right? I don't know what they were thinking. Growing up everyone used to call me Bel, which I liked a lot better obviously."

Freya draws herself upright, dabbing at the blood with a penguin jumper. The pain is fading from Olympic stadium to high-school gymnasium volume. "Well, Jezebel Jones—shit, it just gets funnier each time I say it—I can see why you changed it."

Rosaline pulls her face close to Freya's. "Those things you said…you're really sure? About the Vincettis?"

"Yes. They killed Maria. And I'm pretty damn sure they either attacked those corporate figureheads we've seen in the news, or hired someone to do it for them."

"But, Elijah didn't do any of that, right? He's not bad like them?"

Even through the throbbing, the naivety spilling from Rosaline's lips stings her. "Ros, he's in a coma, so that's a pretty solid alibi."

"I know he's not the angel he's supposed to be. I've seen that photo before, you know. You might find it hard to believe, but I'm not a perfect fool. You don't raise yourself with a drunk mother and an absentee father without becoming at least a little wise and resourceful. I knew about Elijah's accident. That he killed that girl and her father. That he was drunk, on drugs, and that he was with an escort. I've always known."

Rosaline wipes a tear away and draws herself up. "But I still love him. Aren't we supposed to forgive our loved ones for their sins? He made a mistake—a big one—but he's been paying for it with his *life*. Stuck in that room, trapped inside his own head. That's worse than prison, worse than anything. He's the man I love, Freya. And tomorrow, I *will* marry him. I want my wedding day. It's all I've ever wanted. After that, the whole world can go up in flames, for all I care."

Rosaline wipes her tears with her hands. Freya passes her a penguin jumper and says, "Listen, you can have your magical day, your moment in the sun. But after that, those fuckers are going to prison."

"Sure, that's the right thing to do! Just give me this one perfect day. To wear that dress. Like Mum did. After that, call the police, do whatever you need to do."

Freya nods, her head heavy with pain. She picks up the bloodied friendship rock and turns it over in her fingers. "Thanks for the rock," she laughs.

Her phone vibrates in her pocket, just barely managing to catch her attention over the thirty-one flavours of agony kicking in her skull. She pulls it out, unconcerned that she is smearing it with blood, and reads the letters on the screen. She attempts to assemble their meaning with the use of a brain that at present would much rather be spending its time processing the deluge of pain signals from her nerve endings, thank you very much. Nonetheless, moments before she slips into a short and quiet oblivion she reads:

1 new message from: Niki

Elijah is awake.

Excerpt from *The Sins of Adonis*

"Those who restrain desire, do so because theirs is weak enough to be restrained."

—William Blake

30

Our Happy Little Family

At the age of nineteen, whilst eating a bowl of Captain Choc's Chocolatey Chocoflakes, Low-Fat Variety, Thomas P. Wortz read an article claiming that people with unusual or embarrassing names were substantially more likely to have shorter life spans, drug and alcohol addictions, clinical depression, and criminal histories. Ever since then, he has considered officially changing his name 11,782 times. Unfortunately, Thomas P. Wortz is very much a man of the "better the devil you know" variety, and has always had a crippling fear of the unknown.

It is for this reason he is entirely surprised to find himself planning his life beyond his current career as a marriage celebrant. A somewhat ironic choice of vocation given that his terminal reticence and general difficulty introducing himself to women has rendered his chances of procuring a date, let alone a life partner, all but impossible.

He stands at the lectern practising his speech while doing his very best impression of not being completely confused. The ridiculously large cheque awaiting him and the equally colossal bottle of brandy he will purchase will assist his performance greatly. He wonders how long it will take before the Attorney-General's Department discovers he's married a man in a coma and revokes his licence. With a wedding so high profile, it's most likely to be in every tabloid by Monday morning. Or on a blog tonight. Or tweeted in the next thirteen seconds.

Thomas P. Wortz dabs at his sweating brow and mumbles, "Dearly beloved..."

Beep.

Beep.

Beep.

"Now, now, Elijah, don't get all sentimental on me just cos it's your wedding day." Freya pulls his crinkled pyjamas off and reaches for his pressed white dress shirt. Her hands run lightly over his chest. "Might be the last time we get to do this little dance, Eli. Looks like that slew of secrets you've kept locked in that well-toned chest of yours are finally coming out to play." She taps her finger on a tiny puncture wound she notices on the primary artery in his arm. "Like this, for example. You and I both know this wasn't my work."

She buttons him up and fastens his tie around his neck. Pulls it firm. Places his arms inside his jacket, pins a flower to his lapel. "Well, don't you look the handsome prince, ready to claim his kingdom?" She reaches for the mahogany brush from behind his bed and brushes his hair. "Have you been listening to me all this time? Letting my words flow into your head? Storing them in little imaginary boxes stacked on a vast series of teetering shelves inside the catacombs of your brain?"

Beep.

Beep.

Beep.

"Well, if you have been listening, my sleeping prince, then I want you to pay very close attention to this." She leans in, places her lips so close to his ear that they almost brush against it, and whispers, "I'm going to bring this evil empire of yours crashing down to the fucking ground." Then she places one soft kiss on his cheek.

"Everything is ready, I trust?" Evelyn asks as she pushes open the door. She is in a red-and-white dress and has elected to go heavier than usual with the makeup. She looks like the Queen of Hearts immediately prior to her loss of tarts. Harland and Jack are both behind her, their eyes locked on Freya. For the first time, she notes the subtle family resemblance. Jack's sharp, narrow cheekbones mirror those of his father. They share the same small, well-shaped nose, the same square, straight-down-to-business chin. In the right light and by an ample stretch of the imagination, Harland could very nearly be a future rendering of his elder son.

Jack looks away and the moment is gone. "Have you done something different with your hair?" he asks, inspecting her new wound-concealing fringe.

"Thought I'd go for something different. Special day and all," she replies.

The three Vincettis enter the room and stand beside Elijah's bed. "I've waited a long time for this day to come," says Harland.

Evelyn smiles and takes his hand in hers. "The roses are arriving at ten, the bar will open at five and the guests will arrive between five and five-thirty for a six o'clock start. The fireworks are set up, and the band is about to sound-check. Everything is ready."

Freya looks at the family and realises this is the first time she's ever seen all four of them in a room together. They remind her of a classic Renoir painting. She can almost see them reduced to two dimensions, framed in old carved oak and hung on a gallery wall for tourists to glance at on their way to a Rembrandt.

The silence—apart from the beeps—sits heavily between them. Freya is about to leave when Rosaline enters, wearing a resplendent white dress, her neck adorned with a cluster bomb of pearls. Her smile is so bright that Freya is concerned about the threat of permanent retinal damage.

"Well! How do I look?" she beams.

Like a doll. Exactly like a beautiful, perfect porcelain doll.

"Absolutely gorgeous, my dear!" Evelyn opens her arms and encloses Rosaline in a firm and practical hug.

"You look like a million bucks, Rosaline," says Harland, grabbing her by the shoulders and sizing her up as though she's a boxer about to enter the ring.

"Isn't it bad luck for the groom to see the bride before the wedding?" asks Freya.

"Oh, it's okay. He's sleeping, so it doesn't count. Well, here we all are, then! One happy family!" Rosaline places her arm around Freya.

"Yes. Our happy little family," says Harland.

Callum steps out of his car like a model gliding off the front cover of *GQ* magazine: handsome, dapper, composed. He should really be in black and white, thinks Freya, as she runs up and throws her arms around him.

"Hey! You sure scrub up nice! Thanks for being my date."

"I never say no to an open bar. Wow, check out all the security. It's like the Vincettis hired a black-tie militia. How is everything here?"

"The worst kinds of weird. Did you get it?"

Callum nods and passes her a leather pouch. "Jane managed to get her hands on it. She got caught by her supervisor and had to agree to do night shifts for a month to placate her. Plus she's pissed off that you haven't called her since she gave you that job advertisement card that saw you wind up in this whole mess."

"If this pays off I'll buy her drinks from now until the next time Halley's comet is in town. Thanks."

She slips the pouch into her handbag and holds out her arm for Callum to take. He smiles and links arms and they stroll towards the house.

◇◇◇

Beep.

Beep.

Beep.

◇◇◇

Jack sits on the roof, sipping a bottle of Peroni. He looks good in a suit, like a crooner in an indie rock band. Through a pair of sleek binoculars he watches the cars approaching the house.

"Thought we'd find you here," says Freya as she and Callum clamber out and sit beside him.

"Freya, Callum. You can see the enemy approaching from all angles up here. Want a beer?"

"No thanks, we've got champagne," says Callum, raising his glass.

"Suit yourself."

The sound of a string quartet drifts up from below.

"They're playing Chopin! I love this one. It's so beautiful… so blue." Freya watches the colours drift, reaching out her hands towards them and playing her fingertips between their ebb and flow. "I wish you could see this. It's like the ocean, so calm, but with the hint of magnificent power just beneath the surface."

"I wish I could see it, too." Jack watches her hands move through the air and traces his fingers gently up and down the curve of her neck.

"There's the man of the hour," says Callum. "Check out the wheels."

Elijah is rolled out in a wheelchair that more closely resembles a mobile throne than a medical aid. Freya grabs Jack's binoculars and inspects the throne's plush velvet upholstery and the oaken peak carved into a lavish medieval-style coat of arms bearing the Vincetti name. Elijah's arms are flaccid on the armrests, a fine leather strap pulls his back against the chair, his head slumped forward. He resembles a bored dignitary having a boozy snooze at some unfathomably dull charity gala. Evelyn stands behind him, greeting guests with her here-are-my-teeth-but-don't-think-that-means-I-like-you smile.

"Here comes Yvette," Jack passes Freya the binoculars again. "Dressed to kill."

"That, or maim beyond recovery," Freya mutters, disapproving of Yvette's midnight blue dress with neckline that almost plunges to her hip height leg-split. "Ugh. Did I mention I hate weddings?"

Freya listens to the chatter. Most of it is standard aristo-pragmatic gossip—marriages, divorces, best entrées and main courses, portfolios and water polo, holidays in the Bahamas and foreign exchange dramas—but among all this she detects flickers of more perceptive commentary. Behind her a portly, balding Gucci man whispers to his Versace wife, "Surely, I'm not the only one here who thinks this is crazy? The guy hasn't opened his eyes in months. Is this even legal?"

"Shut up, Chris! Do you want to sour your chances with Halcyon?" she scolds. "They could take you to the cleaners if they felt like it! Keep your mouth closed, or at least shove in some more canapés to stop your tongue from wagging!"

Freya smiles, pleased that some of the villagers are getting restless. The problem with being insane is that insisting you are not demonstrates the opposite, and, given that sanity is a matter of popular perspective, it's nice to know there are at least a few people questioning the event.

She moves from the appetiser table to the bar and procures another flute of champagne, then turns to find Yvette behind her. "Shouldn't there be a puff of smoke and the lingering scent of sulphur when you appear like that?"

"Hush, child. I'm not in the mood to cross swords. I have all my energy focused on surviving this opulent travesty." She swirls the champagne in her glass, then pours it down her throat with impressive speed. "Ugh. I'm going to need to be substantially more drunk if I have any hope of getting through this fucking mess."

There is a trace of genuine sadness in her voice, albeit masked by her familiar veil of vitriol.

Despite everything Yvette's done to her, Freya can't help but feel a tinge of sympathy. She raises her glass and proclaims, "To opulent travesties!"

Yvette returns a begrudging half-smile, shares the toast, sighs and slinks away.

"Think you'll catch the bouquet?" asks Jack.

"You'd better hope not," says Freya. "I hardly think we're ready to start building a nice little cage out of white picket fences yet."

He smiles and kisses her gently. But his skin feels damp and she senses him trembling and pulling back, beads of sweat trickling down his face.

"Phew. It's, ah…it's sure hot out here, huh?" He tugs his collar and fans his face.

"Do you think so? I feel lovely and cool. That breeze across the river is gorgeous."

Jack swigs from his drink. "What? I didn't catch that." His voice is shaky and uneven.

"You don't like it out here, do you?"

He laughs nervously. "What're you talking about? Drinks, a pretty girl on my arm? I feel like F Scott Fitzgerald."

"You don't like being outside. Not even in your own backyard. It makes you anxious."

Jack opens and closes his mouth several times, his expression alternating between confused and irate.

"That's…no, don't be so silly! It's just a little warm in this suit, is all. Look, I think the ceremony's about to begin! You'd better grab a seat, I have to go take my place."

He takes her by the hand and leads her towards a chair. She can feel his palms are sweaty even through her gloves.

As she sits, she overhears two men speaking in hushed, urgent whispers: "Am I the only one who thinks that this whole wedding is batshit crazy?"

"People are thinking it, they just aren't saying it. If you really want the whole of Halcyon to blacklist you, go ahead. I look forward to visiting your new headquarters in Guatemala."

Freya takes her seat next to Callum, who is holding a tray of eight full champagne glasses. "I always stock up before the event," he passes her a glass.

Evelyn is standing under the garden pagoda, which is decorated in white lilies and ribbons. In front of her sits Elijah, implausibly upright in his throne-on-wheels, regal and ridiculous. Elijah and Evelyn are flanked by two dark-suited security guards and a triumvirate of Rosaline's mannequin companions. They are mirrored by Jack and one of Harland's business associates, who has promised himself that if he doesn't get a fucking raise after this malarkey then he is going to work for someone more reasonable, like the next Bernie Madoff.

Thomas P. Wortz dabs the sweat on his face with a monogrammed handkerchief. He stares out at the crowd, watching the collection of CEOs, CFOs, PhDs, MDs, QCs, and OBGYNs take their seats and stare back at him, each pretending not to be appalled by the events he is about to officiate over.

He drains the glass of water in front of him and clears his throat as the string quartet strikes up Bach's *Arioso*. The crowd murmurs its doubts, its concerns, its compliments on dresses, its inane comments about the weather. The strings hum through the cool early-autumn air.

And then Rosaline arrives and the quartet stops playing. A hush falls on the crowd, crushing all speech as effectively as the morbidly obese woman sitting next to Freya had crushed her designer sunglasses.

Standing there, bouquet in hand, glowing virginal smile, her father-in-law-to-be at her side, she truly has transformed into Rosaline, her beloved childhood doll; as if freshly unwrapped from her packaging with the scent of plastic lingering on her alabaster skin. All eyes are on her. This is the moment she has been dreaming, planning, anticipating her entire life.

She closes her eyes, counts to three and, as she takes her first step forward, the string quartet launches into "Here Comes the Bride." She breathes in the moment, feels the grass passing beneath her, the languor of the clouds, the music in the air. She drinks it all in, recording every minute detail in her head.

At a deeper level, her consciousness is nagging her with the fact that tomorrow this gossamer castle of fantasy will disintegrate into ruins. But right now, reason's whisper is unable to compete with delusion's roar.

She is almost there. At the altar, her comatose, dreaming lover awaits, strapped to his wheelchair. Harland's arm is tucked tightly into hers. Perhaps a little too tightly. She turns to face the crowd and nods, then sits in the chair extravagantly decorated in white lace and laden with lilies that sits beside Elijah's throne. She takes her betrothed's limp hand in hers.

Thomas P. Wortz clears his throat and, for the 242nd and final time, recites the regulation atheist/agnostic vow: "Dearly beloved, We are gathered…If any person can show just cause why they may not be joined together, let them speak now or forever hold their peace."

The crowd remains deathly silent. A woman sneezes and several people around her jolt as if it were gunfire. Yvette, a few rows ahead of Freya and Callum, snaps a lighter on her first in a series of cigarettes.

"We won't need the next bit," Evelyn hisses quietly to the celebrant. Thomas, not the most courageous of men, is so terrified of her he would probably strip naked and do a one-man rendition of *A Streetcar Named Desire* if she asked.

"No…no…of course not. Shall we…?"

In the third row, an elderly, rotund man bulging out of his white suit begins to stand. Evelyn's eyes immediately lock on to him.

"I have a…weak bladder…the…bathroom," he mumbles, his head turning this way and that as if to gather support. But he slumps back into his seat, defeated. Evelyn's eyes return to amber alert.

"The groom will now say his vows." Even as the words tumble out of his mouth, Thomas regrets them.

"You bloody fool! Skip to the next bit!" Evelyn barks.

"Y-yes, yes, certainly! The bride will now say her vows, which she has composed herself for this special occasion."

In fact, Rosaline had scribbled her first set of wedding vows at the age of twelve, with a marker on the back of a pamphlet for Hair 'n' There Hairdressing. Since then, she has worked on them like a sculptor on a treasured stone, refining them, editing them, perfecting them, and practising them aloud. She beams as the well-rehearsed words spill out of her mouth.

"I, Rosaline Grace, take you, my darling Elijah Vincetti, to be my husband, my loving partner, and my lifelong companion. I pledge that my love will be as steadfast as mountains yet swift as the swallows in spring, as strong as tidal waves yet as soft as raindrops, as endless as the vast blue sky and as constant as my beating heart. I will stay by your side, your hand in mine, through good times and bad, through ups and downs, fair weather or foul. Nothing shall tear us apart...not...not even lady friends, or California."

At this the assembly raises its collective eyebrow. Freya nearly chokes on her second glass of champagne.

"I pledge to you that together we will build a life that is based on foundations of purest love—you my prince, and I your princess. I swear that I will always be true, faithful, and honest, and never go to the grocery store in my nicotine-stained wedding dress."

Freya can see that Rosaline is trembling, her eyes are wet with tears, not quite hidden behind her veil.

Evelyn leans towards Rosaline's ear, places her hand on her shoulder and whispers, "Dear, let's skip the poppycock and get to the meat and bones of it, shall we?"

"No!" yells Rosaline, slapping Evelyn away. The crowd gasps as if it is a live TV studio audience. "Don't tell me what to do! This is *my* moment!"

Evelyn's eyes flicker with rage but she nods curtly.

"Elijah, my love, for months I have dreamed of you as you have dreamed of me. I have waited, prayed, and hoped for this moment. I've forgiven you for what came before…the lies, the cheating and…well, the accident, of course…"

At this, Harland grabs her wrist and yanks her behind one of the decorative potted trees, causing the crowd to gasp again.

"The hell with this," moans an impertinent voice somewhere to Freya's left. The speaker, his plump cheeks cherry-red with indignation, pulls his wife to her feet. "Come on, Dianne. This is beyond a joke." He moves towards the aisle, but his passage is blocked by a gorilla-sized guard who shakes his shiny, buzz-cut head and simply points back to the couple's vacated seats. The man nods sheepishly and he and his wife sit back down.

Harland and Rosaline return to their positions, too, each holding a ring box.

"Get on with it!" barks Harland at the celebrant, who is already in the process of planning how he will retell today's events to his therapist.

"Is…is there a ring for the bride?"

As if there isn't, thinks Freya.

Harland passes the ring to Rosaline.

"Do you, Rosaline Grace, take Elijah Vincetti to be your wedded husband, to love him, comfort him, honour, and keep him as long as you both shall live?"

She nods repeatedly, "I do…I do!" and slips on the ring.

"And do you, Elijah Vin—"

"Of course he does, you insipid dolt!" Harland rebukes him.

Rosaline slips the ring on Elijah's inert finger.

"You may now kiss the bride," announces Thomas, counting down the moments until his getaway.

Rosaline removes her veil, leans down towards Elijah and raises his chin with her fingers. Their lips converge.

"Ladies and gentlemen, I present to you, Elijah and Rosaline Vincetti!" announces Thomas, his impending exit closer to his heart than the Vincettis' union.

The applause begins as a patter of two uncertain hands, stops, starts again and then spreads like a pandemic until the entire crowd is clapping, cheering, whistling.

The celebrant leads Rosaline to a white marble table to sign the marriage certificate. Harland and Evelyn drill their eyes into her as she scratches the pen across the paper. As soon as she places the pen down, Harland snatches the certificate, rolls it up, passes it to one of the security guards and points back towards the house. The guard nods and walks away, clutching the sheet to his chest.

As Beethoven's "Ode to Joy" floats over the crowd, Rosaline wheels Elijah along the aisle. The guests rise, a significant contingent of them anxious to get to the bar. Jack nods at Freya and she grabs Callum's free hand and leads him quickly towards the house.

"That was one of the most tasteful travesties I've seen in years. Right up there with the birth of the royal baby," he says, downing the last of his champagne and throwing the glass across the lawn.

"We have to be quick. Jack said he's going to keep an eye on Lord and Lady Vincetti while we distract the guard, get inside the Danger Room, figure out what the fuck is in there and hopefully find some more evidence then make like a tree before absconding. Hopefully, Lord and Lady Vincetti will be distracted by the festivities and we'll be able to make a clean… um…Hello, there."

A gigantic guard who appears to be missing a neck blocks the door with his 150 kilos of steroid-infused muscle mass. "Good evening, ma'am, sir," he says from behind his aviator sunglasses. "Access to the house is unavailable for the time being. The party is outside."

"But we aren't guests. I live here. Callum's with me."

"No exceptions, ma'am."

"But I—"

"No. Exceptions."

"For fuck's sake! What are they paying you? Twenty bucks an hour? Here's…here's three hundred-forty-five dollars," Callum says, holding the bills up to the guard's emotionless face. "Go buy yourself a nice protein shake or something."

The guard shakes his head.

"Please step away from the entrance or I will be forced to use force."

"'Forced to use force?' Sheesh. There's no point talking to this guy," Freya mutters as she inserts a syringe into his neck, causing the giant to plummet to the ground like she'd cut his beanstalk.

"What the hell did you inject him with?"

"Quazepam."

"What's that?"

"A high-potency sedative. Same stuff the Vincettis have been injecting Elijah with."

They step inside the house, which is eerily quiet compared to the chaos outside. Freya looks back to see Jack is not far behind them. "Callum, shhh. I'll explain later, but don't mention the sedative to Jack, okay? Hey, handsome," she says as Jack catches up to them. "Did you manage to get Harland's keycard?"

"Yes. Got it when he left it in his jacket in the kitchen. Strange time for that guard back there to take a nap."

"You know what these steroid junkies are like, always messing with their system. Screws up their circadian rhythm," Freya replies.

"Right, I guess it's probably easier if I pretend I believe that," says Jack. "We'd better be quick if we want to get in there." He nods towards the Danger Room.

"Is this place going to be booby-trapped or anything? Or filled with mutant crocodiles or cyborg ninjas or stuff like that?" asks Callum as they approach the door.

"Only one way to find out," says Freya. "Jack, will you do the honours?"

He nods and scans the keycard, then presses his eye up near the retinal scanner.

SCAN COMPLETE

ACCESS GRANTED: ELIJAH VINCETTI

"Elijah?" whispers Callum.

Freya shakes her head and whispers back, "Don't get me started. One enigmagnetic crisis at a time, okay?"

Jack swings the door open. "This time I am going to find the goddamn light switch. Freya, will you keep watch?"

"No way, I seem to recall that ended in disaster last time. I'm coming in."

"Callum, how 'bout you?"

"Screw that. Safety in numbers. I'm coming in, too."

The three look at each other, then at the darkness awaiting them. "Fine," says Jack. "We'll all go in together." They step inside and Jack pulls the door closed behind them.

"The light switch?" says Jack.

Callum pops up the light on his phone, and the others do the same. Three weak circles of light flicker around the walls.

"Ah, here we go. Weird place for a light switch, halfway across the room," says Callum as he flicks it on. Four halogen lights spark into life, though they start blinking, creating a disorienting strobe effect before settling and filling the room with light. The walls are a cold and sterile white. This, paired with the pale marble of the floor, gives the room an eerily institutional feel. Sound echoes easily around the open space. Piles of books are pushed flush against every available wall space, stacked between three and four feet high.

The room's sole furnishing is an ornately carved wooden desk and chair. Freya approaches the desk, upon which is resting an old-fashioned brass bank lamp, a white feather quill resting in an inkpot and a tattered leather notebook.

Freya picks up the notebook in front of her—the leather has a thick and heady scent—and flips through its pages. She furrows her brow, confused by the melee of images, and skims through them until she reaches one that gives her pause. She begins to shake, her head filled with a tribal pounding. Callum sees her lips trembling and before he can offer to hold her, she utters one word and collapses to the floor: "Valerie."

31

A Collection

Yvette feigns interest in Harry Leeson, heir to the Morotech empire, as he babbles on about his achievements. Her eyes, however, are locked on Rosaline and Elijah. Rosaline's hand clutches Elijah's as she chats with guests and periodically convulses with laughter and playfully slaps their shoulders.

"Harry darling," Yvette purrs, all the while seething that Rosaline is so happy, "would you mind grabbing me another drink?"

"Of course! Champagne?"

She nods but rolls her eyes as Harry scurries off, as eager as the private-school boy she imagines he once was, running out the wrought-iron gates at the three o'clock bell.

So, this is it, Yvette thinks. This is how it ends. Not with a bang but a simper. Despite her beauty, charm, and cunning she sees she has been defeated by this little maniac. Yvette walks down to the river, away from the noise and the crowd. She senses Harry approaching and sighs but, with consummate skill, transforms her remorse into coquettish charm. "Hello there, handsome. You sure don't like to keep a girl waiting, do you?"

"Of course not! Especially not a girl like you! Cigarette?"

"Good Lord, I thought you'd never ask!"

He hands her the pack. With her beloved gold lighter she lights her cigarette, and then his, as she stares past him at the sprawling facade of the Vincetti mansion. When Harry's mouth begins to spew a dreary account of his latest Italian holiday, Yvette fixes her mouth in a smile and her eyes on the house.

She flicks her lighter open.

Closed.

Open.

Closed.

Open.

Closed.

Open.

◇◇◇

Freya runs her fingers over Valerie's picture. She looks so happy, frozen in a perfect two-dimensional wonderland where she is eternally young, smiling and pretty. "Why is her high school yearbook photo here? Why is any of this here?" Freya flips through the notebook; Valerie is not the only one pasted in its pages. Subsequent pages feature Valerie's father, followed by a host of vaguely familiar faces all smiling, laughing, posing.

Most are not home photos or holiday snaps, but cut from magazines and newspapers. Together, they crowd in a jumbled collage of frozen felicity. As Freya looks closer, she notices that marked above each head is a roman numeral. Valerie, it seems, is number VII.

"Is that Sasha Fairlane?" asks Callum, pointing. Sasha is seated in a sultry pose, on a white throne, applying a stick of Crimson Infidelity to her lips. She is saturated with light and colour. XI is scrawled above her head.

Callum takes the book from her hands and flips through it. "Look at this, it's an article on Wilson Davies, with the number

IX. And this photo from *Time* magazine, Kyle Engels. He's number X."

"The toy company guy?" asks Freya.

Callum nods. "I don't recognise these other people, but they look important. These photos are all clippings from the financial pages…they have the numbers I through V. Why is there a photo of a dead dove here?"

"Callum, Jack, look! Is that Maria?"

It's an old photo. Faded. Crumpled. The face doesn't yet tell the stories that Maria's wrinkles did and this figure is slim. She looks different but the smile is unmistakable, as is the trademark twinkle in her eyes. Around her people are laughing and they are all posing under a sign, *Corazón Del Sol.*

"It's a trophy collection…"

◇◇◇

Harland has always loved the smell of money. From an early age he trained himself to distinguish between national currencies by their scent alone. Very handy in the dark. He particularly enjoys the scent of American greenbacks, printed on their flimsy paper, passed from the palms of lawyers to drug dealers to doctors to hot-dog vendors to waitresses to bank clerks to strippers to bus drivers. For Harland, American money retains the smell of these stories in a way Australia's more sterile plastic currency can't.

His mind is performing a series of complex calculations weighing up the pros and cons of alternative currencies as the home for the fortune his gormless daughter-in-law is about to bestow on him. Finland currently looks like a viable option, though he's a little worried about the notes carrying the odour of herrings.

Numbers twist and turn and pirouette through his head as his mouth runs on autopilot with various "Mmm"s, "Yes, quite"s and "Oh, how funny"s. What eventually distracts him from his mental monetary masturbation is Rosaline. She approaches him at the head of her entourage of bridesmaids, exchanging laughs, hugs and kisses on cheeks. She is filled with the glow that various romantic poets he has never bothered to read are always blathering on about. She's completely deranged, he doesn't doubt that, but she looks so obscenely *happy*. Harland can only recall feeling so joyful once, but the origin of that moment of true happiness is currently in a vegetative state.

He looks square on at the pallid cretin he has been pretending to converse with and decides the charade is not worth the effort. "Listen, James, I'd rather lick a dog's balls than hear the rest of your sentence, whatever it was."

Harland waves James' astonished face away and heads to Rosaline, who ensnares him in one of her freely given hugs. "Harland! Or should I say Dad?"

He extracts himself from her grasp, reaches into his jacket pocket for a cigar and a cutter, snips the end off and lights it. He takes the first puff and tries to avoid grimacing at the foul taste. "Rosaline? How do you do it?"

"Do what, Harland?"

"Be so goddamn *happy* all the time?" His voice sounds angrier than he means it to. It's become his default setting these days.

Rosaline beams and takes him by the arm, leading him down to the banks of the river. She points to the other side where kids are playing frisbee. "See those little kids? Do they have more knowledge than you, or less?"

"Less, of course." Harland puffs at his eighty-dollar cigar and resists the urge to gag.

"Do they have more money than you, or less?"

"Less, obviously!"

"And happiness? Do you think they have more or less happiness than you?"

Harland puffs but says nothing.

"I've got to get back to the guests. Would you keep an eye on Elijah for me?" She leaves him at the riverbank, staring at the small children throwing a plastic disc back and forth. He feels deflated and angry.

Harland walks over to Elijah, still seated in his extravagant wheelchair, and smiles. The only source of happiness he's ever had. He places a hand on his son's shoulder, and wonders what Rosaline would say if she knew the truth about her new husband.

He notices a small pool of red running down his son's shirt-front. Harland grabs desperately at Elijah in search of explanation. "Eli! Eli, what's happened?!"

It takes him a moment to notice the guests closest to him are silent. None of them is panicking, calling ambulances or moving any part of their body except their eyes. All of them are focused not on Harland, nor Elijah, but on Harland's head chief accountant, Ramsey. In Ramsey's shaking hand is a freshly emptied wineglass, streaks of red creeping slowly down its edges.

"I...er...tripped and...I spilt my glass on...I can pay for the dry cleaning?"

The pathetic apology is ended by the sudden meeting of Harland's fist with Ramsey's chin, eliciting a fray of yelps and screams from the crowd.

Ramsey hits the ground and stares up at Harland. He raises his hands in an awkward flailing motion; not in any serious attempt at defence so much as because he believes this is the done thing in such a scenario. In the midst of the storm of pain that clouds his skull, he is for some reason keenly aware of the unusual hairiness of Harland's knuckles as they slam repeatedly into his increasingly bloody face.

32

Grendel's Mother

The wheels of Elijah's throne spin like twin steel suns as Rosaline pushes him towards the house in search of temporary respite from the gaggle of guests. When she sees the guard on the floor inside the doors, she calls out, "Hello? Is anyone there?"

Freya pokes her head out of the Danger Room and motions Rosaline to join her.

"Freya? What are you doing in there? I thought this room was locked? And that guard…what happ—?"

"Shhh! Quick, get in here before someone sees you!"

Rosaline pushes her freshly minted husband through the doorway and Freya quickly closes the door behind them.

"I've always wondered what's in here! What is that book you're looking at, Jack?"

Freya removes a syringe from her handbag, rolls back Elijah's sleeve, and taps at his arm to find the vein.

"What are you doing? What's that you're giving him?"

"Flumazenil. It's a benzodiazepine antagonist, kind of like an anti-sedative. Basically like injecting half a dozen cans of Red Bull straight into your veins."

Rosaline's lip quivers like the tremor preceding an earthquake. "You mean you're trying to wake him up?"

"Yes. My guess is he'll be with us in a few minutes."

Rosaline's face builds into a grin then collapses into a frown.

"My Elijah is coming back to me?"

"He'll be awake again, Rosaline, but you have to understand the Vincettis have been keeping a lot of secrets from you. There are some things about him that you might not want to—"

"If he wakes up, he'll be all mine again…"

"Well, yes, but…" Freya tries to continue, her voice edged with frustration.

"My sleeping prince—"

"*Rosaline!*" Freya grabs her by the shoulders and snaps her fingers repeatedly in front of her face. "Focus. We can deal with your dozing Adonis…oh, shit…I didn't mean to…"

Rosaline's body shudders with sobs. It's a short, convulsive rhythm, like an old car sputtering to life.

"Rosaline! I know you're upset but you need to be quiet or someone will hear us! He—"

"I don't want him to wake up!"

"What?"

"I don't want him to wake up! Not ever! Not after the horrible things I found out about! If he wakes up, my dream will be dead! Please don't let him wake up! Haven't you ever had a dream you didn't want to end? Oh God, I'm going to wind up just like Mummy…I'm never taking this wedding dress off…"

"Freya—"

"Not now, Jack!"

"Freya, I can hear someone coming! I th—"

SCAN COMPLETE

ACCESS GRANTED: EVELYN VINCETTI

Yvette downs her eighth champagne and feels the sky start to spin. She feels weightless and free, as though she could be borne away to some magical foreign land on a warm summer breeze. Soon this crowd will be all wailing and gnashing of teeth but, for now, she is content to revel in the sweet, dizzy bliss.

She floats over to the mob gathered around Ramsey, whose suit is drenched with lakes of crimson. "Somebody call an ambulance!" a woman yells.

"No no no, I'm fine. Just a bit…uh…I feel quite faint…No! I'll be fine. More embarrassed than anything. But could, ah, could someone take me home?"

Yvette eyes his Cartier watch, Ferragamo shoes, Yves Saint Laurent belt. "I could take you. I was about to leave, anyway. I may have left my iron on at home."

Ramsey eyes the woman leaning over him, her curtain of dark hair hanging against the elegant curves of her ivory cheeks, her jewels glimmering in the light, her resplendent smile. Behind her shimmers an ethereal orange glow. His head spins and he mumbles, "Are you an angel?"

She laughs. "Not even close, my dear." She bends down, throws his arm over her shoulder and helps him stagger to his feet. When she gets him to her car, Yvette heaves him into the passenger seat and then, as she walks round to the driver's door, points and shouts out to the watching crowd, "Oh my, is that a fire?"

Laughing, she leaps into the car, turns on the ignition and screeches the tyres as she takes off. Hundreds of guests run towards their cars—none faster than Thomas P. Wortz—and tear off into the night as vicious red tongues of fire consume the Vincetti mansion.

The Danger Room door swings open and Evelyn fixes each of them with a fierce, calculating stare, like a warrior queen surveying her enemy on the battlefield. Her eyes linger for a moment on Elijah, whose right hand is moving with a barely discernible twitch. "Hmph," she pronounces, before kneeling next to Rosaline, huddled wretchedly on the floor, and patting her gently on the back.

"There, there dear. It'll be alright. I promise."

Jack, Callum, Freya, and Evelyn hold their positions and listen as Rosaline's sobbing fills the room.

Elijah convulses and groans.

Evelyn jumps to her feet. "Will someone explain what the hell is happening?"

Jack passes her the notebook. "Evelyn—"

She shoots him an apoplectic glare.

"Mum, you're not going to like what you see here…"

"I don't like what I'm seeing already, so it can't get too much worse." She drums her fingers on the book cover without opening it, then looks at Freya. "You remind me of myself as a girl, you know? Brash, selfish, curious, charming."

Freya wraps her arms around Rosaline.

"When," says Evelyn, "did you figure out we'd been sedating him?"

"Not as goddamn quickly as I should have. I found someone else's blood on him a few days ago. And then I found a syringe of quazepam in the kitchen bin."

Evelyn nods curtly. "I should've been more careful. Emptying the damn bins, that was always Maria's job…"

"Why the hell would you keep Elijah sedated?"

"Do you really have to ask, Jack? After that car crash, when he killed that poor girl and her father, not to mention that prostitute, Harland and I figured a coma was the only way to keep him out of prison. This way we could give him a day off now and then…better to live a day as a lion than a thousand as a lamb, and all that. We made him promise to keep his… activities quiet. Now, pray tell, what's in this little black book?"

"It's a scrapbook. Of Elijah's victims," says Freya. "A trophy collection. All the people he's killed and harmed on his 'days off,' including Maria."

"Don't be so hysterically hyperbolic, girl. It's true Elijah said he was going to take care of Maria when she started sticking her nose where it didn't belong, and I assumed he was simply going to get her deported, but instead she had that heart attack..."

"Do you really believe that?"

"Yes," says Evelyn, her voice devoid of its usual conviction.

"You managed to organise Maria's funeral rather quickly."

"I have two personal assistants, and a secretary. Does mere efficiency qualify as evidence of some ridiculous conspiracy?"

"Look in the book, Evelyn. See the truth about your son."

Evelyn bites her lip, scratches lightly at the book cover then throws it at the wall. "No. Burn it. Burn it now."

"Evelyn, your son has been *killing* people, and you've been providing him with a perfect alibi," growls Freya.

"It's not true!"

"It is!"

"Fine! It is true, but *I don't want to fucking believe it*!" Evelyn screeches.

Rosaline looks up with fearful, teary eyes.

Everyone stares at Evelyn, her face red, her steely composure vanquished. "I'm not a perfect fool. But I'm his *mother*. I can't believe he would ever do anything so completely awful. Not my perfect little boy. I don't care what evidence you show me. I won't believe it. I won't I won't I won't I *won't*!"

Evelyn expels a frenzied, spluttering sob and wipes at her eyes.

Rosaline stands and places her arms around Evelyn, who buries her face in the white puffs of Rosaline's shoulder pads.

Elijah shuffles and emits a low, grumbling moan as the door opens.

"Does anyone smell smoke?" asks Callum, sniffing at the air.

"That's my cigar." Harland enters, puffing a large Cuban. "Someone want to tell me what's going on here?"

"Grrrumuphlgh," mumbles Elijah.

"Well, that can't be good," says Harland.

Jack picks up the notebook and hands it to his father.

Harland flips through it, grunts indignantly, then presses his cigar to the pages until they start to blacken and smoke. "Elijah, you damned fool, just when everything was going so nicely..."

"No!" yelps Rosaline, smacking the book out of his hand and stomping on it.

"My. Elijah. Is. *Not* going. To go. To *prison*! His actions. Are. A *family* matter!" roars Harland.

"I am your family now, you lecherous, grey-haired swine!"

Everyone stares at Rosaline, stunned into silence. Her fury is as fearsome as it is unexpected.

She inhales.

Exhales.

Inhales.

Exhales.

Inhales.

Exhales.

She holds up a manicured finger and shoves it under Harland's nose. "He's waking up, and it's too late to stop. He's waking up and he *is* going to prison. He will atone…make penance."

"*You. Think. So. Do you, my little princess? We'll just see. What. My lawyers. Have to say. About that!*" spits Harland.

Evelyn nods. "I can assure you, Elijah will be dealt with in the Vincetti manner. In *our* manner."

"Which means," says Jack, "you'll sweep it all under the carpet, like always."

"Elijah is a killer…a monster," says Freya. "You've shaped him into some idealised Renaissance man, something from myth and legend, but the mythic figure he most closely resembles is Grendel in *Beowulf*. He hunts and kills for sheer pleasure, simply because he can. And the only thing worse than Grendel in that story," she starts, but sees Evelyn's blank look. "Doesn't anybody *read* anymore? Help me out here, Jack."

Jack looks at his mother and says, "Grendel's mother. The only creature more terrible than Grendel was his mother."

Harland grabs Jack by his lapel and pulls his face close. "You'd. Best. *Watch*. Your. Tongue." Then he drops his cigar to the floor, and crushes it with his heel. "Bah. I'm done with cigars." His teeth scrape some of the residue off his tongue and he spits it out. "They taste like charred possum droppings."

"I really do smell smoke," says Callum.

"As I said, it's…ah…" As Harland opens the door and pokes his head out, a thick cloud of smoke and a wave of heat invade the room. "Shit! The house is on fire! The whole fucking place!"

Evelyn and Harland converge on Elijah, who is beginning to drool and shake.

Freya yells, "*Run!*"

Jack and Callum dash out the door, but Rosaline stays rooted, her eyes darting frantically between Elijah and Freya.

"*Now!*" Freya grabs Rosaline by the hand and pulls her out the door, with the Vincettis trailing close behind. They run through the smoke, coughing, their eyes burning and skin stinging with heat. Outside is a maelstrom of screeching voices and tyres as the wedding guests escape. Rosaline trips over a rug and her hand slips from Freya's, who turns to glimpse the Vincettis through the smoke behind her. She sees Elijah's eyes fluttering open. Even through the obfuscating haze, they are a spectacular blue.

A veil of flame licks feverishly at a wall hanging ahead of the Vincettis and they disappear in the orange and blue flash.

"*Run!*" Freya shouts, pulling Rosaline to her feet. "Come on! Fucking *run*!"

Rosaline shrieks as the fire flares in front of her, then scrambles after Freya. Up ahead, Callum shoves the front door open on a starry night sky and runs to his car.

Jack reaches the door and pauses, looking back inside.

"What are you doing? *Fucking get outside!*" Freya screams as she catches up to him and then staggers out into the night air, her lungs racked with smoke. Rosaline tears past her and tumbles onto the grass, no longer caring about her frills and pearls.

Freya sees Jack standing frozen in the doorway, looking back as the flames hungrily caress walls and curtains, sending out heat in thick, heady waves.

"I have to go back for Elijah!"

"You can't! You'll fucking die. Come out here now!" Freya screams.

"I...I don't want to," he stammers. "I can't leave my family, my home."

"Jack, your home is about to become ash and rubble and your brother is a deranged sociopath!"

"But...out there. I can't go out there! There's...all the, you know...I can't. I can't leave my family. Go without me."

"Jack, we need to leave *now*! Come with me, okay? I'm obviously in love with you, you stupid jerk!"

Callum screeches his Mazda to a halt in front of the house. He jumps out, grabs Rosaline by the arms and drags her into the backseat. Freya helps him lift her feet in, then turns back to see Jack still staring at her from the doorway.

"I can't...I'm sorry," shouts Jack above the cracking of the flames and the falling debris.

"Not as sorry as you'll be if you don't get in the fucking car!"

Jack's face is a war of fear and confusion; he shakes his head and walks back into the house, fading into the smoke. Freya runs after him, reaching the door just in time to see him disappear underneath a falling chandelier, the flames flickering kaleidoscopically in its myriad facets. She screams and pulls at him, trying to free him from the mess of glass and steel.

Callum rushes in beside her and helps her drag Jack out from underneath the chandelier. The pair of them lift him up and throw his arms around their shoulders and carry him out to the car. Callum climbs into the driver's seat and Freya sits beside him, with Rosaline and Jack slumped in the back like a pair of mob victims.

As the house recedes into the distance, a flash in the rearview mirror catches Freya's eye. She can barely make out three figures clustered together on the roof. She squints at the three of them, silhouetted against the violent orange wall of flame. Then the roof collapses beneath them, and they are devoured by the inferno.

VI

Recovery

"It seems a commonly received idea among men and even among women themselves that it requires nothing but a disappointment in love, the want of an object, a general disgust, or incapacity for other things, to turn a woman into a good nurse."

Florence Nightingale,
Notes on Nursing: What it Is and What it Is Not

33

Karma Coma

It's a dream. She knows it the moment she enters the Danger Room and runs her hand along its cold, concrete walls. They are defiant and tangible despite existing solely within her imagination. She picks up the notebook and slowly tears out the pages, one by one, leaving Valerie's until last. Stares at it. Studies the gleam of her smile and her eyes, their shine glowing with a promise that will never be fulfilled. She drops this, too, to the floor.

She walks over to his bed. He is sitting, awake but not speaking, draped in a shadow that should not exist with the lights on. But this is a dream, isn't it? It abides by the rules of physics no more than a six-year-old heeds the rules of Monopoly.

As she approaches him, it's his eyes she notices first. So blue, like the colour of Debussy's "Clair de Lune."

He reaches a hand around to the back of her neck, pulls her in towards him. Their lips meet.

Jack closes his eyes, lies back on the bed and fades out of her focus, like an old blurry movie. Freya squints, but he remains fuzzy, obscured. The sound is low at first, but steadily increases.

Beep.

Beep.

B–

◇◇◇

–eep.

Beep.

Beep.

"Freya? Freya? Wake up. The doctor's here."

Callum pushes her shoulder gently and her eyes flicker open. The beeping fills her ears.

"Freya, is it? I'm Dr Aisha Satrapi."

"Hi," she mumbles, her vision still blurry.

"Can I have a moment to talk about your husband?"

"Oh, he's not…never mind. How's he doing?"

"Well, if we're to look at the positives, much better than could have been expected. He's got a broken leg, for starters, but that blow to his head was extremely serious. He's experienced major damage to his skull. Luckily, the brain tissue, from what we can tell so far, is undamaged. Given Mr Vincetti has OI, he is very lucky to be alive. However…" She pauses, glances down at the sheet in front of her then back at Freya.

"Please, just spit it out. I don't like the sound of that 'however'."

"I'm afraid he's slipped into a coma. He's stable, blood pressure and heart rate are both low but well within the acceptable ranges. But at this stage, we can't give you an indication of when he might wake up. Comas can be very—"

"Unpredictable."

"Exactly. There's an outside possibility he may wake up tomorrow, but there's also the chance he may not come out of it for months. Or at all. Meanwhile, you may see some movement, eyelids flickering, fingers trembling, that kind of thing. They could be indications he's coming around, or just muscle spasms. Not knowing will be tough for you to deal with but, unfortunately, that's the nature of his condition."

Callum takes Freya's hand in his and pulls her close. Her tears add to the blood and ash on his shoulder.

"I'll leave you two alone. Ask the nurses to contact me if you need anything." At the door, she turns back. "I'm truly sorry," she says with a sincerity Freya imagines she has practised to a fine art.

"Goodnight, Jack. Sleep well," she whispers into Callum's shoulder. Everything smells like disinfectant.

Rosaline's eyes flutter open as though she were Sleeping Beauty. She brushes hair out of her eyes and murmurs, "Freya? Callum? Where am I?"

"Hospital. You're suffering from smoke inhalation, but you're going to be fine," says Callum.

"We made it! We escaped! Gosh, that place went up so quickly didn't it? Like it was covered in gasoline!"

"It was filled with highly flammable synthetics and electronics, basically an arsonist's wet dream," says Freya.

"I'm so glad we're all okay!" Rosaline pauses and studies their faces. "Oh…oh, dear. We're not all okay, are we?" She checks their expressions again. "It's Jack, isn't it? The poor, poor thing…Frey, are you alright?" She takes Freya's hand and gives it a squeeze.

"He's in a coma, Ros. He might never wake up," Freya says quietly, her eyes red from both the smoke and tears.

"I'm sorry to say that I know exactly how you feel. Elijah? What about—?"

"He's dead. Harland and Evelyn, too. They couldn't get out of the house in time."

Rosaline's chin slumps to her chest and her lip starts to quiver. "Oh…oh, God…"

Freya hugs her close, the first time she has dared such a manoeuvre, but Rosaline shakes herself free and yelps, "Look at my dress! My dress is *fucking ruined*!"

34

Part of the Family

Freya guides the razor over his face, carving paths in the foam. When she is finished she runs her hand slowly over his freshly shaven cheeks and dries him off. The television drones in the background; some appalling American melodrama about lawyers and their lovers. She only keeps it on so she has other human voices nearby, something to save her from the constant *beep beep beep* of Jack's monitors.

She opens the minibar and removes a bottle of vodka, which she finds even more appealing in petite packaging. She mixes it with ginger beer, throws in a couple of ice cubes and walks out to the hotel balcony. After six weeks, the view from twenty-eight storeys up still fills her with a combination of awe and nausea.

She scans the lights, the river, the horizon and, as always, she looks out towards the charred remains of the Vincetti mansion. During the day she can just make it out, a black dot among a cluster of luxury houses, as though someone has smeared a landscape painting with a careless smudge of charcoal. At night, however, it is disguised as blackness blended with blackness. She sits and sips at her drink, taking her time, watching the cars rush back and forth from somewhere to nowhere and back again.

She rises from her seat at the sound of the door opening to reveal Rosaline carrying an elongated paper bag and Callum bearing a cardboard carry tray filled with coffee cups.

"Watch the coffee," warns Callum, holding the tray out at arm's length from his body as Freya hugs him.

"I love you, Cal. Did I ever tell you that?"

"Usually when you've been drinking, yes. How's Jack?"

"You know these charming artistic types, always so elusive and taciturn. Rosaline, I know I've said this before but I can't thank you enough for organising this place for me. You know I'd be just as happy in a cheap motel."

Rosaline smiles and flicks her hand in a gesture of friendly dismissal. "Don't be silly! It's all on the company bill anyway. It's no trouble."

"Yes, how's it all going at Halcyon HQ?" asks Freya, leading them out to the balcony. They sit around the small glass table, their legs and feet warped and clouded by its surface. The city hums and buzzes beneath them.

"Good! Well, mostly good. I mean, the board is still more or less the same awful, corrupt, exploitative cretins as before—"

"You didn't manage to get any of those scumbags turfed?" asks Callum.

"Well, no. Even with the Vincettis gone and all of my shares in the company, I mean, I don't really understand all the legal stuff, but a corporation's not quite like a kingdom you know? There are always more people waiting in the ranks to keep the wheels spinning. I guess it's kind of like the Mafia, or, what was that animal in Greek mythology where you cut off its head and two new ones would grow back?"

"The Hydra," offers Freya, opening the lid of her coffee cup and pouring in a satchel of sugar.

"Right! So I guess, Halcyon has had its main heads cut off, but I'm afraid it's still pretty much business as usual, except that because of all the mess, the big merger with the Davies Group and Happymax has fallen through, so that's a good thing, right Freya?"

"Yes. It is. It means that they won't have a near monopoly on pharmaceutical production and distribution. That's a huge deal."

Callum scowls sceptically. "So, instead of one big evil company controlling the world's medicine, it's controlled by three slightly smaller evil companies?"

"Well...I guess..." concedes Rosaline.

"Business as usual then."

"Pretty much," Freya agrees as she lifts the cup to her mouth and grimaces.

"This smell weird to you? The milk off or something?"

Callum sniffs. "Nope, it's fine. So Rosaline, what about Firmatel? Freya said you had some good news to share."

She claps excitedly and grabs Freya's hands. "Yes! That's the best part! Firmatel is all mine. The lawyers managed to negotiate a complete buy-out. Daddy would have been so proud! And our charity division is all ready to go; we're going to donate thirty percent of all profits from our toys to fund hospitals and schools in developing countries. Niki is partnering with an NGO to set up the Maria Suarez Hospital in Bogotá and Freya, you're going to do such an *amazing* job overseeing the development of a brand new clinic in East Timor for the next four months!"

"Ros, you are a saint. I won't let you down, I promise. As soon as we've finished assembling Jack's medical escort I will be on a plane over there."

"Oh, shut up, you're going to be fantastic of course! And, and, and! Look, I have a prototype to show you! From our new line of dolls, we're going to start making boys too, kind of like Barbie and Ken, except ours will have realistic bodies."

Rosaline reaches into the bag and removes a slender white box. She opens it slowly, her fingers slipping under the cardboard folds and peeling them open with a sense of quiet ceremony. She slides a small humanoid figure covered in tissue paper out of the box and carefully unravels it. Freya stares at the plastic rendering of those repulsively familiar features and forces a smile. Rosaline unwraps the rest of him, revealing a green and gold ski suit, complete with two silver medals hanging around his neck and ski poles gripped between his rigid hands. "This is Winter Champion Elijah! It was...um...it was going to be Winter Olympian Elijah, but there was a copyright issue. Isn't he perfect?"

Freya smiles and takes the doll in her hands, examines its bright blue eyes and roguish smile. "He is, Rosaline. He's perfect." She hands the doll back to Rosaline and wipes her hands on her jeans.

Freya picks up the coffee cup again and sips from it. "Fuck, that is disgusting!" She slams it back on the table and runs to the sink to spit, then turns on the tap and washes out her mouth. Callum picks up the coffee cup, sips at it and frowns at Rosaline.

"What's wrong with it?" she asks.

"Nothing. It tastes fine."

Rosaline walks over to Freya and rubs her back gently. "Frey, honey, you okay?"

"Yeah, I think the milk was spoilt. Tasted like microwaved puke. Just let me sit down." Freya returns to her seat and tips her head back, groaning.

"The milk tastes fine, Freya. I got it from Brew, you usually like their coffee."

"I *love* their coffee, Callum. I love it with all of my heart and most of my liver. But I...ugh...I can't handle the smell right now, for some reason."

"Have you been unwell, Frey?" asks Callum.

"I think maybe the height is getting to me up here. I've had a little dizziness, nausea. Also I have this constant craving for peanut butter and licorice. What? Why are you making the same face you made when I told you that I was going on a date with a guy I met in a strip club?"

Freya reaches for her Moscow Mule and Callum snatches it away from her, frowning. "Freya, I think maybe that's not such a good idea."

"Why? What the fuck is going on?"

Rosaline grins like she is about to burst into song, puts her arm around Freya and murmurs sweetly, "Do you want me to design the nursery for you?"

35

Home

◇◇◇

Jane opens the hotel door to find Freya sitting in her underwear with a cigarette between her fingers. The hotel room is a catastrophic mess of half-packed suitcases and clothes strewn across every available surface. "It's okay, it's not lit. I just wanted to take a break from packing and I needed to feel the comfort of it in my hands," Freya says with a frown, before drowning the cigarette in a bottle of ginger beer.

Jane smiles and leans in to hug Freya, noticing the black bags that have formed underneath her eyes. "It's been a while. You haven't smoked in years."

"Or drunk in days. Mum would be so proud. The whole unexpected pregnancy thing might chalk up a few points against me, though. How much has Cal told you?"

Jane removes a pile of dresses from a chair and sits down. "He ran me through the highlights. I wish I'd never given you that card."

"Don't say that. It's not your fault. And it's not all bad, I finally met the perfect man. Handsome, rich, and he never opens his mouth. I'd introduce you two, but he's taking a nap right now."

Jane smiles and takes her hand. "I missed you, Frey. I never even got to see that fancy mansion you were living in!"

"Well, you can just about make out the rubble from here, if you squint. How's the apartment treating you?"

"It smells like booze and paint, but it's really nice. Kind of like its former occupant."

Freya lets go of her hand, leans back, dons sunglasses, and looks up at the sky. Jane sneaks a glance at Jack through the bedroom door.

"Should we talk about the baby elephant in the room?"

"I can't believe I have a Vincetti inside of me."

"Well, you've obviously already had—"

"Don't. You're better than that, I'm supposed to be the bitter, sardonic part of this team."

"You don't have to keep it."

Freya drums her fingers on the arm of her chair, bites her fingernail.

"Yes. Yes I do." Freya turns to look at Jane, who watches her own twin reflections in the lenses of Freya's sunglasses as she speaks.

"I've been thinking about blood a lot lately. It's something Jack likes to talk about, the laws of blood. How they're immutable, separate from the contemporary laws of the state. If I'd been knocked up by some regrettable one-night stand I'd get rid of it, no question. But this is different. I'm tied to the Vincettis now. I've spilled their blood, and they've spilled mine. And now our blood is shared. There's a certain kind of magic in that."

"Blood is science, not magic."

"Well, science is just magic in a business suit, right? In any case, it's a bond that can't be broken. We're tied together, even now that most of them are dead."

"This is all sounding very *Godfather*. You really don't have to do anything you don't want to. I mean, raising a child? Are you sure you're ready for that?"

"Everyone has to do things they don't want to and no one is ever ready to raise a child. But this isn't about motherhood or family, it's about blood and empire. I'm part of that now."

"So what, you're heir to the throne?"

"No, this is." Freya pokes at her stomach. "He. She. It, whatever. But I'm part of the bloodline. Jack was always talking about trying to make his stories come out the right way, but how they were like children that couldn't be controlled. He'd will them to be these beacons of light and they'd come out these twisted, horrid things. The Vincetti saga's had a lot of violent chapters, omissions, and alterations. Maybe I can help the next chapter of the Vincetti family saga be a good one. Or maybe this little fleshy jellybean floating inside my amniotic fluid will grow up to be a manipulating sociopath, like Elijah."

Jane furrows her brow. Frowns. Sighs. "I don't know, Freya. I don't think this is the right choice."

"It's not a choice. It's what has to be done. Cain had to kill Abel. Pandora had to open the box. Orpheus had to look back at Eurydice. Oedipus had to sleep with his mother."

"I don't know how many times I've told you not to explain things with mythological or literary references."

"Sometimes the old stories are the best ones. And the truest."

Jane sighs, "Well, if there's anything that history has taught us, it's that arguing with you is a complete waste of time. I think you're more fun when you're drunk and belligerent than all high-minded and philosophical."

Freya grins and replies, "It's funny because it's true."

Jane inspects the pile of books on the coffee table and picks up a tattered paperback.

"*Chaos in the Kingdom of Cynthia Green*. Isn't that the one that sleeping beauty over there wrote?"

"Yes, it's one that I like to come back to a lot, especially lately. You should read it."

Jane flicks it over to read the blurb and then places it into her handbag.

"You know I never have time to read, but maybe I can make an effort just this once."

"You'll have plenty of time when you come over to Timor. I'll let you set your own hours."

"What?"

"Come and run the clinic with me. We'll have adventures every day and all the time, and you have to say yes or I'll cry forever and that'll probably hurt the baby. Do you really want to be responsible for that?"

"I can't believe you're using your unborn child as a tool of highly implausible emotional blackmail."

"I can't believe you haven't said yes already."

Jane rolls her eyes, gently bites her lip as she inhales.

"You're doing your serious thinking face. You're going to say yes, aren't you?"

"It's not a choice, it's what has to be done."

Beep.

Beep.

Beep.

The radio is on, but mostly just to fill the air with voices. Night has descended while Freya has been absorbed with attempting to learn basic phrases in Tetum. She hasn't moved from her seat to turn on the lights, thus the only illumination in the room comes from her laptop screen and the city outside. Freya rubs at her eyes, closes the window of Tetum phrases and runs a final check on Jack's medical escort.

"You know, for a guy who lies around all day doing nothing you sure are a pain to move *par avion*, you know that? Good thing you've got the cash for a charter plane and plenty of doctors.

Beep.

Beep.

Beep.

"You sound just like your brother." Freya closes her laptop. The room is dark. She steps over the piles of bulging suitcases and puts Chopin on the stereo, letting washes of blue cascade across her vision. Freya walks into the bedroom and watches the hypnotic scrolling of jagged green mountains on Jack's heart monitor before climbing into bed next to him. She holds his limp, warm body in her arms, brushes her fingers through his hair. "You'd better enjoy this figure while you can, Vincetti. Pretty soon I'm going to start doing a flawless impression of a woman who's swallowed a bowling ball."

Freya takes Jack's hand in hers and watches the tiny Kandinskys dance across the ceiling.

Beep.

Beep.

Beep.

Between her fingers, Jack's hand quivers, but only for a moment.

Epilogue

Excerpt from
Chaos in the Kingdom of Cynthia Green

I have struggled to be the ruler of my tiny kingdom for too long. I no longer want an empire, but just one small, private room. "A room of one's own," as Virginia Woolf once said. Somewhere to be myself, whoever that may be.

We are, all of us, a never-ending war of insatiable will against an insufferable world. We are the ghosts of our aspirations battling the spectres of our future failures. We are the expectations of our parents pitted against the joy of our own sweet rebellion. We are the impositions of society combating our indefatigable need for self-expression. We are the urges of our instincts against the cravings of our hearts.

We are walking dreams, fading memories, hallucinations made flesh, desires made manifest.

But for now, perhaps, that is enough.

Acknowledgments

I know a lot of authors keep this to one or two lines but I am a grateful person so this is going to take a while. Thanks to my family for being the complete opposite of the Vincettis; you guys can stop asking when the book is coming out now. The Green family and everyone at Pantera for so much hard work and luxurious Xmas hampers that made me feel like Jay-Z. Poisoned Pen Press for releasing this wild Australian creature into the Americas. The marvellous, generous, and gregarious Kelso clan. Scott Mercer, Darragh Murray, Jodi Biddle and everyone at 4zzz (the greatest radio station in the world). Busybird Publishing. Helen and everyone at Speakers Ink. All of my students past, present, and future. Everyone at Playlab.

Ruckus family and the BNE poetry posse (Fern, K-Pax, L Fox, Jo Sri, Jo Sampford et al), you are making so much magic happen in this town and we love you for it. Internet author pals and the BNE author crew (too many to name, but love you all). Michelle Lovi. Jo Vohland. Jess McGaw, Helen Stephens, Daren King, and the Anywhere Theatre Festival team. Mike 'Meeksounds' Willmett for being a magical musical wizard with amazing hair and friendship skills. Tony Gilfoyle. Sneha and Avhan. Rozi Suliman (bbff). Jo and Thom Chapman. Bron

Cottle. Paul Songhurst. Cass Ball. Alice Whittaker. Alan and Siobhan. Lachlan Kuhn (remember what you promised?). Cara 'SG' Stitzlein for everything, Australia isn't the same without you. Dave and Nicole, I love you two so much that sometimes I secretly think we should all make out together, but don't worry I won't tell anyone because that would be embarrassing.

Treehouse team (and Treehouse alumni) for constantly feeding me magical baked goods and Game of Thrones sessions. Meredith and Tiago for being the best hosts in the world and helping me fall in love with Lisbon. Erica Field for everything and everything else (again x2). Black Cat Books. Bree and Michael. Anna Cooke. Candy, Suze, and everyone at Scout Café. Laura St festival (still my all-time favourite gig). Alex Litherland (John Snow). Fraz (Dr Wright) for all of the medical advice, speaking of which I have a weird rash on my inner thigh I need you to look at…

Savage Darling clan. Tamara Dawn Johnson. Steph, Jorge and Lani. M and L Zanetti. Sarah Brischetto. Pauline Maudy. NLNL. I would like to thank the following Kates: Lindsay, Byrne, Jardine, and Cranney. Spain/Portugal road trip team: Tori, Anna, Judith, Gretchen and Jane. Sarah and Rani. Bec and Jim. Alex Adsett Publishing Services. Mutual Appreciation Society. Y and A Naghavi. Just like last time, if I forgot your name, don't worry it doesn't mean I don't love you. Grab a pen and write your name here:

J.M. Donellan is a writer, musician, slam poet, radio DJ, and teacher. He was almost devoured by a tiger in the jungles of Malaysia, nearly died of a lung collapse in the Nepalese Himalayas, fended off a pack of rabid dogs with a guitar in the mountains of India, and was sexually harassed by a half-naked man whilst standing next to Oscar Wilde's grave in Paris.

His debut novel, *A Beginner's Guide to Dying in India*, was the winner of the 2009 IP Picks best fiction award and lots of magazines gave it rave reviews, which was very nice of them.

Josh was a state finalist in the 2012 Australian Poetry Slam and was chosen as one of the top ten writers in the 2013 SOYA awards. His first play, *We Are All Ghosts*, was performed as part of the Anywhere Theatre Festival in 2014. His children's fantasy novel, *Zeb and the Great Ruckus*, was described by one child as "the best book ever, but it should have had Doctor Who in it."

To receive a free catalog of Poisoned Pen Press titles, please provide your name, address, and e-mail address in one of the following ways:

Phone: 1-800-421-3976
Facsimile: 1-480-949-1707
Email: info@poisonedpenpress.com
Website: www.poisonedpenpress.com

Poisoned Pen Press
6962 E. First Ave. Ste 103
Scottsdale, AZ 85251